STRATEGIES
AGAINST
EXTINCTION

STRATEGIES
AGAINST
EXTINCTION

Stories

Michael Nye

Queen's Ferry Press

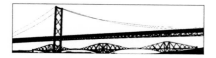

Queen's Ferry Press
8240 Preston Road
Suite 125-151
Plano, TX 75024
www.queensferrypress.com

Published 2012 by Queen's Ferry Press

Cover design by Matt Roeser

First edition October 2012

ISBN 978-1-938466-00-7

Printed in the United States of America

Praise for *Strategies Against Extinction*:

"Most first books of fiction tread uncomfortably close to the writer's life. But here's a debut collection of stories that takes us to some unexpected and remarkable places: a '50s-era sports radio broadcast, a vascular surgeon's worst moment, a bracing encounter with Vladimir Putin. Michael Nye has written his way across the divides of time and gender and place and has occupied nine diverse lives. The insights he arrives at are sharp and memorable. The writing is finely crafted. *Strategies Against Extinction* is an auspicious first book."

—John Dalton, author of *Heaven Lake* and
The Inverted Forest

"With astonishing insight and poignant precision, Michael Nye exposes the devastatingly subtle consequences of betrayal, the frangibility of our human bodies, and the quiet intensity of our desire to transcend grief and restore our families. The poet Seamus Heaney says: 'The way we are living, timorous or bold, will have been our life.' *Strategies Against Extinction* is a piercing reminder of our transient existence, a quiet cry in the night that swells to an aching song of hope, an aria of love surging beneath rage, delivering us from fear, and sustaining us through sorrow."

—Melanie Rae Thon, author of *In This Light* and
The Voice of the River

"Michael Nye has written mature stories of men and women surviving, seeking identity, their unique places in the uncontrollable, ever-changing world. Faced with their own choices, they accept, they move on, they survive. The reader struggles with them on their journeys, involved in their strategies against extinction."

—Mary L. Tabor, author of *The Woman Who Never Cooked* and
(Re)Making Love: A Memoir

"The range of characters and actions in Michael Nye's first collection is not only refreshing, but it announces he is far from a one-book writer. Nye gives us Vladimir Putin wrestling with a former Ohio governor in one story, and in another a woman who rents her ex-husband's study to a couple who need it for afternoon trysts. In *Strategies Against Extinction*, we get to know a film student who yearns to escape her hometown, a Pirates broadcaster who is not important enough to travel with the team and must re-create the action as if he were watching it, and a surgeon who trains a new doctor to be tough enough by taking her hunting. Nye's characters do not merely think and wish and yearn, but rather they act, they do, they struggle in surprising and shocking ways. This one is exciting."

—Mary Troy, author of *Beauties* and *Cookie Lily*

"In this collection of finely tuned, acutely observed stories, Michael Nye writes with eloquence about loss—of marriages, of jobs, of brothers or parents, of love and dignity—and how imagination, as a response, can sometimes yield danger but more often, salvation. *Strategies Against Extinction* is a remarkable and affecting collection by a promising new voice."

—Maureen Stanton, author of *Killer Stuff and Tons of Money*

"Precise and affecting, these stories have the slow gravitational pull of quicksand: before you know it, you're sucked into tales of men (and women) ravaged by forces beyond their control—economic, technological, cultural, political. Rich in the arcana of outmoded machinery and masculinity, these stories portray men at loose ends in peacetime, people coming to grips with ineluctable change. In one of the best of these stories, we learn about the last "re-creationist" for the Pittsburgh Pirates, a guy who in 1952 announced out-of-town games that he could not see, imagining the plays from ticker-tape summaries which he translated for his rapt radio audience, much as Nye translates for us this bygone world of men. At their best, these stories achieve what we hope great fiction will—they reveal in miniature whole worlds."

—E.J. Levy, author of *Amazons: A Love Story*

"Michael Nye's collection delivers story after story of Americans circling the twenty-first century drain—some even struggling not to go down the tubes. A subtle and striking debut from a writer to watch."

—Aaron Gwyn, author of *Dog on the Cross* and
The World Beneath

"The stories in Michael Nye's first collection unfold in straightforward, nearly transparent prose. But the magic is the life that pulses just below the surface, as fragile and relentless as the human heart. These stories remind me of Richard Ford's brilliant early stories in the way that plain-spoken people try to hold on as their lives spin, almost imperceptibly at first, out of control. The cumulative effect is uniquely moving. The emotional impact, however, is far from ordinary. Read Nye now so you can say you knew of him back before everybody else."

—Daniel Stolar, author of *The Middle of the Night*

For Edward J. Sharkey
1925–2007

But the "real"—what assaults the eye before the eye begins its work of selection—is never on the verge of dissolution, still less of appropriation. The real is raw, jarring, unexpected, sometimes trashy, sometimes luminous. Above all, the real is arbitrary. For to be a realist (in art or in life) is to acknowledge that all things might be other than they are. That there is no design, no intention, no aesthetic or moral or teleological imprimatur but, rather, the equivalent of Darwin's great vision of a blind, purposeless, ceaseless evolutionary process that yields no "products"—only temporary strategies against extinction.

—Joyce Carol Oates

Table of Contents

The Re-Creationist

17

Projection

37

A Fully Imagined World

58

Sparring Vladimir Putin

76

Exit 17 Does Not Exist

97

A Surgeon's Story

113

The Utility Room

133

Union Terminal

150

Keep

170

THE RE-CREATIONIST

Don pushed open his son's door and reached for the transistor radio buzzing softly on Timothy's nightstand. The broadcast had stopped one hour after the Pirates game ended, when the radio station, WWSW 970, signed off for the evening. Above his son's bed, hanging from thin wires, a tight formation of model P-38 Lockheeds protected a single B-24, the kind of bomber Don flew over the Pacific. Their noses were angled slightly upward as if they were climbing into the sky, and the light from the streetlamps outside dotted the cones and propellers of the planes, making each appear as if it was truly flying, the sun shimmering off the metal of its wings. Now, on the nights when Don called the Pirates game and came home late, the soft static of the radio greeted him in an otherwise still house, pulling him down the hallway as he avoided the floorboards he knew creaked, stepping into his son's room to see him for just a moment and shut off the radio before creeping to the end of the hallway, opening his bedroom door and undressing at the end of the bed, then slipping into the sheets next to his wife and falling into a fretful sleep.

The smell of bacon woke him. He reached for his wife's side of the bed knowing he would find the sheets cold. Don sat erect and swung his feet to the floor. In the bathroom he showered quickly, scrubbing last night's alcohol from his skin, brushed his teeth and drank three glasses of water, each gulp chiseling away at his whiskey-dry throat, and when he was dressed, Don entered the kitchen feeling refreshed and important.

"Hey, Dad," Timothy said. Laura looked up from the crossword.

"Good morning, everyone," Don said. His voice had a rich, sonorous cadence, a peculiar mix of his childhood Kentucky twang and odd Irish inflection, a distant part of his heritage that he emphasized in his broadcasts. When he spoke, his voice created the kind of intimacy that made people want to rest their heads against his chest and listen to him breathe. And yet, despite this timbre, he was a lean man who walked very upright and fearful, as if he expected everything he observed to suddenly disappear.

"How'd Kiner look?" Timothy asked. On the table in front of him, the box scores were folded in neat fourths. Ralph Kiner was the Pirates' best player, a powerful man who hit towering home runs, and most important to Don, he was Timothy's favorite player. Last night, Kiner had looked awful: two strikeouts and two pop-ups that didn't make it out of the infield.

"He had some good swings," Don said, pouring a cup of coffee. "He had a great at-bat in the seventh. Ten pitches. I thought he had one, but he just missed it."

"Do you think he'll hit forty again this year?"

"It's already mid-September. But he might. You never know."

Laura went to the stove and started breakfast for Don. Eggs were cracked, bacon sizzled. In bold black letters, the headline on the *Post-Gazette* stated that U.S. forces were fighting in Korea north of the 38th Parallel. Same mountains, Don thought, and same ridges they've been pissing over for two years. What was the point? When he looked up, Timothy was staring at him as if he was on the verge of a serious question.

"My teacher says I'm really good at math," Timothy said. "We take a test every Friday, and I've gotten perfect scores every week."

"You're smart. And you study. That's what it takes."

"Maybe I can get a job with the Pirates. Or I can be a

navigator like you were."

"Sure." Don sipped from his mug, the coffee's bitterness biting his throat. "You can do whatever you want." Feeling Laura's eyes on him, he turned away and looked out the window. Above, telephone poles staked this new post-war neighborhood, and in each direction was an endless stretch of new Cape Cods, every yard with two oak saplings separated by exactly twenty feet. In all directions, the Alleghenies seemed to have been pressed back into the distance by the expansion of the city. He heard a compression of air, the strain of an engine, distant but heavy. "School bus is here."

Timothy shot up and grabbed his backpack. "Gotta go. Bye, guys."

"Bye, sweetheart," Laura said. Through the window, he watched his ten-year-old son sprint to the corner, arms churning hard, racing toward the school bus now coming around the bend, his neatly combed hair shining in the sun, and Don wondered if it was possible to ever get tired of seeing this every morning.

"Did you tell him yet?" he asked.

"Sit down and eat your breakfast."

The children boarded the bus, and with a deep grind of gears, it lurched forward, exhaust smoke pluming from behind as it pulled away.

"No," she said. Her nasal Boston accent was unapparent in short sentences, which were of late the only kind she used with him. "I didn't. I just said we would be visiting Grandma at Christmas."

"I'm still trying to talk to Mr. Rickey. A contract might come any day."

"You know that has nothing to do with it."

He turned. Laura sat at the table absently tapping a pencil against her coffee mug, and in front of his seat was his breakfast plate: bacon, rye toast with a pat of butter, and scrambled eggs sprinkled with Tabasco. She wore a robe tied tight around her waist, and her blonde hair was pulled loosely into a messy ponytail.

She was pretty still, but Don could see the way the habit of their marriage had corroded the brightness in her eyes. They had only agreed last week to what Don still told himself was a temporary separation.

Don pointed at the crossword. "Need any help?"

"This is really happening, you know. It really is."

He stared at his food cooling on the table. Laura stood and said she was getting dressed for the day. She left the room, her feet pounding on the linoleum as she disappeared. He sat down in front of his breakfast, the eggs cold now, and again pictured Timothy running across the yard, trying hard not to think about how the renewal of his contract might be the only thing that could save his marriage.

The bus route took Don from Laurenceville, through Bloomfield, west into Polish Hill, then crept south into Oakland, and toward the university. He adjusted his fedora and stared out the window, listening. The bus filled as it wound through the neighborhoods, the men with hats covering their heads, and a newspaper and briefcase in hand. The women were secretaries and nurses, the ones who refused to go home when the war was over; there was a freedom in their expressions, a pleasure at not being home, and they sat with their legs crossed at the ankles, none standing, every man willing to give up his seat. These men probably were veterans of the war, the men who defeated the Japanese and the Germans, and came home as heroes. Now the war in Korea was always the headline, and Don wondered if these men gazed out at the city and its passing crowds and wished they were back overseas. Don suspected it. He suspected there were other men like him who craved the freedom of a bomber, desired the endless din of the atmosphere at thirty-five thousand feet, a place where one had to scream to be heard through their headphones, sweat pouring down their bodies despite the cold. But, the truth was he never met other men who felt this way. Here, at home, they were grateful to be alive, grateful for having a job, a roof over their heads and warm food in their bellies. The city bus was a sea of suits, of black and muted grays, of hats and glasses and briefcases, uniforms of work and responsibility. Even if this was all false, Don preferred to imagine their lives this way: purposeful and quietly noble. Out the window, Pittsburgh rolled by.

At his stop, Don stepped off the bus stairs and onto the street, and briefly into the shadows. The bus pulled away, and the warm September sun shone down on the concrete. Across the street, the brick half-archways of Forbes Field stretched as far down Morewood Avenue as he could see, its walls hugging the diamond just on the other side. Above, two tiers of concrete ramps guided fans to their seats and the intimate insides of the park. It struck him then how beautiful ballparks were, how rarely he stopped and appreciated them.

Don nodded to the security guard and took the stairs up to the third level. A little out of breath, he ducked inside the doorway and entered the crow's nest. He removed his hat, stripped off his jacket, and rolled up his sleeves; despite the open view of the field, the press box air was still and hot, and thick plumes of cigarette smoke clung to the ceiling, giving the lights the hazy appearance of the sun eclipsed by thunderstorms. The handful of sportswriters in the press box were of two types: the diligent ones looking for a scoop from a scout or ballplayer to add to their columns, and the alcoholics dazed awake by the bourbon in their blood who had stumbled to a hungover lunch, looked at their watches, and figured they might as well head to the ballpark. Both had nowhere else they really wanted to go. Typewriters clicked and whirled, and Don considered how metallic things don't sound like much except themselves.

"Afternoon, Don," Glen Sullivan said in a reedy voice scratched by too many years of cigarettes and whiskey. He had fought in Italy during the war, and came back to his hometown to cover the Pirates for the *Post-Gazette*. He was missing two fingers on his left hand.

"Giants are on a roll, huh?" Don took his seat at the front of the box and frowned down at his sheets; riding a five-game winning streak, the first-place Giants had their best starters lined up for this series against the last-place Pirates.

"They win it all when they get Mays back next year. Mark my words."

"Consider them marked. Any dirt?"

"Nothing good. We won't see any Giants on the town. With the pennant still at stake, Durocher's keeping them in the hotel every night. As for our boys, well, I can write the same 'September rookie' stories I've been writing since '48." Glen sniffed. "Hear you're talking to Rickey this month."

"How did you hear that?"

"Aren't you?"

"I don't know. He won't take my calls."

"The beat guys in Brooklyn said he was like that. Real secretive. You'd think he was trying to beat the Soviets to the moon or something. It ain't personal, Don." Glen smiled. "Dodgers might win it all this year. You know that's got to stick in Rickey's craw. For your sake, I hope he's in a good mood when you talk to him."

Don frowned. He didn't want to think about Branch Rickey. Instead, he leaned forward, stilled and concentrating hard, and when he looked into the sky he was back in the B-24 high above the Pacific, feeling the vibrations of flight, all the white noise of the press box gone. If he could hold this feeling for just a little while, the anxiety of his employment, of his marriage, would disappear. Sunlight splashed on the bright vista of Forbes Field and beyond: the brick university buildings to his left, the home developments to the north, and the green mountains to his right. He stared out beyond Forbes Field and its empty grandstands, the steady rap of line drives off hickory bats echoing from far below, and imagined soaring over it all.

On Saturday afternoon, Don hunched in front of a

microphone in the studios of WWSW, his sleeves rolled up and his tie loosened and dangling from his neck like dog tags. Sweat trickled down his ribcage and he rubbed his fingers together as if ready to grapple a man intent on killing him. He looked to his right, and waited.

By 1952, the Pittsburgh Pirates were the last club that still broadcasted "re-creations." Don didn't really know, or care, why the team wouldn't send him on road trips. Maybe one additional train ticket was more expensive than all this: a soundtrack of crowd noise that buzzed in the background, the typist and telegrapher, a small studio space in a soundproof room, and around his microphone, his notecards, a xylophone hammer, ruler, and a block of wood, all he needed to conjure a live baseball game that was really about two innings behind the live action.

Across the Western Union ticker came the information. The telegrapher handed the ticker paper to the typist, who rattled it down quickly, then yanked the sheet from his typewriter and handed it to Don. He scanned the line quickly: "Senerchia up, B1W, S1C, FLOGS, SS to 1B, Senerchia out."

Don leaned into the microphone. "Sonny Senerchia digs in. The rookie struck out in the second when Spahn got him with a fastball that tangled the youngster's arms. He did have a good rip in that at-bat. Boy, he sent a screamer into the left-field corner that just went foul in the second. The outfield has shifted just a little bit to left, knowing that Senerchia likes to pull the ball." Don pictured Braves Field, its grandstands empty, a cold Boston wind off Commonwealth Avenue barreling in from right field.

"Senerchia takes a few practice hacks and digs in. Spahn steps off the rubber and goes to the rosen. He's cruised through the first four innings, and looks to be getting stronger. Spahn gets the sign and comes set. Here's that big leg kick . . . pitch . . . curveball just missed the outside corner."

Don waited. He bobbed his index finger—Spahn liked to mix up the hitter's timing when he was in a groove—and counted two beats.

"Spahn sets and delivers. Strike one. Curveball off the plate, just nicked the black. Senerchia had a good look at it but thought it was low. He steps out and twists the bat in his hands. Steps back in, and he digs his front foot into the dirt. The rookie better be careful about guessing breaking ball here.

"The lefty's arm is dangling and he's snapping his wrist. Boy, Spahn looks really sharp today. He gets the sign and comes set now. The delivery." Don slapped the ruler on the wooden counter. "And that one is in the stands. Spahn came in high and tight and Senerchia couldn't hold back. He's in the hole, 1–2."

Don set down the ruler and picked up the xylophone hammer and block of wood.

"Here's the windup, and the pitch." He struck the wood with the hammer. "Senerchia hits a chopper to short. Logan races to the hole. Backhanded! He guns it across the infield and . . . got him! Senerchia hustled down the line, but it was a great throw by Logan. Heckuva play to go that deep. Logan was creeping toward third, but he got a good jump and made the tough throw. Pirates are down an out in the fifth: Boston Braves, 2; Pirates, 0."

The typist handed Don the new sheet: "Koshorek up, B1W, B2I, S1I, S2S, FLOGS, FLOGS, FLOGS, B3I, FLOGS, FLOGS, FLOGS, F9." Beneath the line, the typist had scrawled that there were problems, again, with the telegraph connection.

There were thunderstorms in Boston, and communication was spotty on this game, which likely finished, weather permitting, about an hour ago. Don checked his scorebook, and remembered just how he called Clem Koshorek's first at-bat, a dramatic nine-pitch battle. To Don's left were his index cards of commercials: Chesterfield cigarettes, Old German beer, and the new Chrysler Windsor. A separate set of index cards were the anecdotes and stories he collected from his interviews with players; usually, only his interviews with the star players made the pre-game show, so the rest were here as he needed them during the game. He picked one up. Six foul balls and a Western Union delay. Koshorek's at-bat was going to take a little time. What could Don throw in here?

A broken bat to be replaced. Spahn going to the rosen, but Don had already used that plenty. Charlie Grimm never has to visit the mound when Spahn pitches. Maybe Koshorek calling time? Don tugged his earlobe and leaned into the microphone.

"Koshorek digs in," he said. "Spahn comes set. Wait a minute. First base ump has his hands up. There's a dog on the field! There he goes! He's racing around the outfield now, circling around, and Jethroe and Daniels are having a good time laughing out in right-center. The dog looks pretty happy, too. He's tearing around the outfield, and the grounds crew is out now, trying to chase him down. Oh, but he's a slippery one. If I had a nickel, I'd bet on the dog! From up here it looks like a golden retriever. If he can hit, too, maybe the Pirates will sign him."

He bit his lower lip and nodded to himself. Dog on the field, that was a good one. He liked that. And why not? Why couldn't that be possible?

Late Friday afternoon, Don and Timothy were headed outside to play catch when the phone rang. Laura wasn't home. All year, on days when he was home, she managed to spend the entire day away: the library, browsing the new dress shops in Laurenceville, visiting her friends to drink tea and smoke cigarettes, anywhere but home with Don. She never hid her activities: she recited her day's events with the official detachment of a court reporter. What she didn't say, and what he didn't ask, was why she was gone all day and why they encouraged this avoidance with silence.

He pointed Timothy toward the garage and said he would be out in a moment. Reaching for the phone, Don anticipated that it was Laura's mother, and prepared an excuse to beg off a conversation about the unspoken implications of Laura's Christmas visit. Instead, a voice he didn't recognize said, "He wants to meet with you."

"Who wants to meet with me? Who is this?"

"I'm not going to tell you who this is." The voice was a New

Yorker's: curt, confident, a jumbled annunciation. "I'm not important. But he wants to see you. He'll be at the William Penn Hotel, in the coffee shop, this Saturday at 2 p.m. You should be there."

"Listen, I don't know who you think—"

But the line was dead. Don recradled the phone and put his hands on his hips. It had to be Rickey. Had to be. He nodded to himself. Rickey wanted to meet him. All right, then.

In his garage, he fished his cigarettes out of his back pocket, and took a long drag. Timothy was on the driveway, throwing the ball high into the air and then sliding under it, his steps choppy as he tried to judge each fly ball. Don picked up his glove and when Timothy noticed him, he tugged his Pirates cap down his forehead and hustled to the middle of the yard, waddling like Ralph Kiner. Always imitating, always pretending. They threw several easy tosses and talked about the game Don called that afternoon—the Pirates had lost again—and once Timothy was satisfied, his questions stopped and he began throwing harder, the sound of popping leather like absolutely nothing else.

Timothy tugged on the brim of his cap. "How come you were home Monday?"

"Travel day."

"So you didn't work?"

"No, I worked. I went down to the hotel where the Cardinals are staying and interviewed them."

"All of them?"

"Not everyone, but I tried. I know the real good players, but the bench guys and the pitchers, well, they're from everywhere. Like today, there's this guy, Bert Sandowski. I didn't know him. So I found out where he played last year, where his hometown is, if he has a family, things like that, and I write it all down on an index card. Then, during the broadcast, if I get the chance, I can tell all the listeners some interesting stories."

Timothy made a crisp throw. "Like what?"

"All kinds of stuff. When they missed a train to a ballgame.

26

A doubleheader where each game went to extra innings and it was a hundred degrees out. If they served overseas, I'll find out where they were stationed. If a player rebuilt his hitting stance, I'll ask how he did it, or what minor league team he played for, which is especially interesting to the audience if he was on a team in Pennsylvania or Ohio, even West Virginia. Things like that."

"Did you kill anybody in the war?"

Don held the ball high above his head. The sunlight, so bright and painful, heated his elbow, jutted out at a perfect ninety-degree angle. Slowly, he brought the baseball down below his waist and held it against his thigh like a weapon. Timothy stood with his arms resting straight down, as if waiting to be punished.

"Don't ask that," Don said. "Don't ever ask that. You understand me?"

His son lowered his eyes and focused on the spot between Don's shoes. Then he turned away, stomped through the garage, and Don heard the door to the kitchen slam shut. He rolled the baseball in his right hand. The cowhide was tough and dry, the seams thinning, an old baseball among many that he had in the garage to throw with his son, and he stood under the hot sun considering where this particular one came from, as if by studying it the memory would come to him, when he heard Laura's car pull into the driveway and the mechanical click of the gears when she put it in park.

She came down the driveway tentatively, holding her purse against her stomach. When she reached him, she stood with her shoulders turned away, as if ready to flee. Her eyes swept the lawn, and then she asked quietly, "What are you doing?"

"Let's get ready to go. I don't want to get to the fair too late. I'll mow the lawn tomorrow."

"Are you going to tell me what happened?"

A silence fell. For a moment, Don thought she meant the mysterious phone call from Rickey's messenger, and the idea that he might have good news for her momentarily cheered him. But when he raised his eyes and saw the accusation in the tightness of her neck and shoulders, he realized Laura was asking about Timothy. Don ran his knuckles against the baseball.

Finally, she said, "It's supposed to rain this weekend." She walked away and minutes later when Don followed her into the garage, she and Timothy were already climbing into the car. We're ready to leave, she said. Don slid behind the wheel and looked at them both: Laura's face was turned away, looking out the window at the clutter of their garage, and in the backseat, Timothy studied the stats on the back of baseball cards, frowning down at them with fierce intensity. Don put the car in gear and in silence they exited their neighborhood and headed east.

On the horizon, the Ferris wheel spun against the late-afternoon sky, the individual carriages lit up like fireflies, the dark green of the Allegheny Mountains in the distance cloaking the fairgrounds, and beneath them, families moved in great swarms, clumped together by held hands and cotton candy and soda bottles, teenagers running after one another, dodging between the adults. This Friday night was the parish's yearly fundraiser, an all-day event that brought together Catholics of Irish, Polish, and French descent from the different townships, along with the locals who didn't mind where their dollars went as long as they could play carnival games, eat hot dogs and cotton candy. Don stood with his hands in his pockets as Laura and Timothy waited in line to buy raffle tickets. With a twist of his foot, Don flipped loose straw from his shoes. He wandered toward a stage across the pathway and listened for a few minutes to an Irish folk band play a song that was vaguely familiar.

"Dad?"

He turned. Timothy held two Cokes, and extended one to Don. He took a long pull, the glass sweaty in his hand and the sugar sweet going down his throat. The band hit their crescendo and finished, and people broke into applause. Timothy was giving him a curious look.

"We needed seven to ten men in the plane," Don said. "There was the pilot, the co-pilot, gunners, engineers, and the navigator. That was me. I charted the maps, knew where we were flying, and planned the mission we got from our XO."

"XO?"

"Executive officer. We were told where to fly. An admiral will have meetings with other admirals, and they decide on a strategy, and their officers work on executing the strategy. And the pilots and the navigators did the little things, like the bombing runs."

"Why weren't you a fighter pilot?"

"When I enlisted they gave us a whole bunch of tests. The military is very careful about where they put everyone. I showed a good head for numbers and could read maps, so they made me a navigator."

"So," Timothy said, scrunching up his face. "Because you were smart?"

"That's right." Don drank his soda, the carbonation popping down his throat. Timothy seemed to be on the verge of figuring something out. Don crouched down and studied him. "Did you hear me?"

"I guess."

He raised a hand to place on his son's shoulder, but suddenly Don was afraid, and instead clutched his Coke bottle to his chest.

"Everything will be fine," Don said. "I promise. No matter what."

Timothy wore an adult expression. Don had seen this before. This was the look of men in bars, their racing forums spread in front of them, their losing bets circled, the ice in their drinks melting. It was a look of disappointment, and regret, and the expectation the world would always, no matter what, treat them this way. But before he could speak, Laura walked toward them. Her mouth was set in a tight smile, and she placed her hand on their son's head. Don stood, rising above them both. Timothy suddenly asked, "Can I stay at Jake's?"

"Of course you can," Laura said. She looked at Don. "Jake's parents are here. I already talked to them about it."

At home, dark now, Don and Laura entered their house silently and left all the lights off. He followed her to the bedroom, and they stripped off their clothes, and without speaking, made love. On his back, naked and sweaty, his pale skin nearly translucent in the moonlight, Don stared at the ceiling, the weight of his marriage pressing down on his chest. Laura wrapped her arms around him, and pressed her cheek against his shoulder. Soon, his skin felt wet, and he realized she was crying. She was a small woman, but her arms and hips were fleshy, as if there were no muscles or bones beneath her skin. He pressed his lips to her forehead. He didn't know what it was he was refusing, and for this, he was horribly sorry.

He sat silent, stroking Laura's hair until her body went limp with sleep.

Don entered the William Penn Hotel and stopped for a moment to take in the lobby's beauty. The marble floor shined. Above, the crystal chandelier was dazzling, pulling the eye upward to all the ways it refracted light. The upholstery of each chair— positioned so that important men in business suits could cross their legs and speak intimately—was taut and immaculate. The entire room could be somewhere in New York or Paris.

He crossed the lobby, taking cautious steps, peering around. Near the back of the long, orderly restaurant, cordoned off by gold banisters with neo-Victorian iron detailing, sat Branch Rickey.

Don picked up his pace. He extended his hand, and Rickey stood to shake it.

"Good afternoon, Don. How are you?"

"I'm well, Mr. Rickey. You?"

"Oh, a touch of arthritis, but nothing I can't manage." He always surprised Don with his size. Rickey had thick, meaty hands and the gait of a man in chronic pain; he had the knowing smile and neat glasses of a man used to getting his way. His jet-black hair was perfectly parted and slick with pomade, and the cut was haphazard, like a schoolboy's; his temples were gray, and his jowls heavy. He motioned for Don to sit. Rickey raised one large finger, and a waitress appeared with an extra cup of coffee. He sat silent, appraising Don with his sharp eyes, his hands folded in front of him, waiting for the waitress to leave.

"Now, Don, I'm in a bit of a hurry today." His voice rumbled, a sound like gravel churning in a mixer. Only his mouth moved: his cheeks and forehead were frozen, and Don watched the line of Rickey's mouth rise and fall, intrigued by how deep and clear the timbre of the voice was that came from such a narrow spot. "Let me get right to the point."

Rickey then proceeded to not get to the point. They spoke for over an hour and a half. Finally, after two cups of coffee, he said, "Now, I believe in being straight with people. So here it is. We won't be renewing your contract next season."

Nodding more to himself than Rickey, the tension in his shoulders strangely dissipated, and for the first time all week, Don breathed easy and full.

"We're going to be leaving WWSW," Rickey continued, "and moving back to KDKA."

"Moving back? Mr. Rickey, with all due respect, I can call the games just as well on one station as any other."

"I know it, Don. But it isn't the only thing. We're also going to stop doing re-creations, and send the broadcasters with the team for all the calls."

"Travel doesn't bother me. I've gone to Cleveland, Cincinnati, New York. Not all the road games, but plenty of them."

"It isn't a question of money. It's a question of what you are best at. What you're best at is re-creating the games, but you are not the best live broadcaster. I don't mean to be cruel, Don, but that's the fact of the matter."

"What's wrong with my broadcasts?"

"There's nothing wrong with them. They aren't, however, the standard we desire. What you're best at is making things up, being a storyteller. You aren't as good with what's literal, what's on the field in front of you."

"Mr. Rickey—"

"Don, I don't want to argue with you. This decision has been made. You have the university's basketball and baseball games, and I know several people across the country that I'm happy to put you in touch with."

"I don't need your help finding a job."

Rickey smiled cruelly. "I understand you're angry. I know you mean well. But what you do? That's a thing of the past. We're moving forward, remaking what we think the Pittsburgh Pirates need to be. Many things are going to change around here, not just your job."

"That doesn't make me feel better."

Rickey checked his wristwatch and stood up. "No, of course it doesn't. I do not mean to be flippant." He offered his hand. "We wish you the best, Don. I know you'll do a fine job during these last two weeks."

Don rose. He stood straight and rigid like he had learned to do in basic, and shook Rickey's large hand. He thanked him and before he knew it, Don was outside the hotel in the bright sunshine, pressing his hat onto his head. It wasn't until after he was halfway home that the shock wore off and it struck him that he would have to look Laura in the face and explain that come next summer, he was out of work.

When he arrived, Timothy was on the living room floor playing with toy soldiers. His face was scrunched in deep concentration. He could hear Laura banging around in the kitchen. Neither of them acknowledged his presence. He went to the bedroom and removed his shoes and tie, and waited for Laura to call him to dinner. Other than asking each other to pass the salt or a butter knife, they ate their salads and then the tuna casserole in silence. Don kept his conversation with Mr. Rickey to himself. Despite their problems, nothing was quite real, wholly formed and set, until he told Laura.

After dinner, they sat in the family room, Don in his chair

with the newspaper, and watched Red Skelton. Timothy sprawled on the floor, making various piles of baseball cards based on a criteria Don didn't understand, and Laura stretched out on the couch. Her bare feet and ankles visible, edging out from beneath a blanket, her toes reaching forward, twitching occasionally, and her heels pressed into the arm of the couch as if she was bracing herself for impact. Her jaw was clenched even with her eyes half-closed. It struck him then how unhappy she was, how long she had been unhappy, and how stubbornly he resisted acknowledging this. He knew their marriage was over.

When Timothy fell asleep, Don scooped him up and carried him to his room. Cradling his son, he sidestepped the baseball cards and newspaper box scores scattered across the floor. He set Timothy down gently in his bed and pulled the covers up to his neck. His son's forehead was sweaty and his lips chapped; he touched his forehead and knew Timothy would be sick in the morning. He flipped on the radio, and WWSW was broadcasting the news, as they usually did in-season when the Pirates weren't playing, and tucked loose hairs behind Timothy's ear, resting his hand there for a moment, feeling his son breathe. When Don returned to the family room, he found Laura had gone to bed without him. He picked up the blanket she had left on the couch, brought it to his nose, and breathed deeply. Fresh soap. Pears. He folded the blanket, placed it neatly in the center of the couch and sat down, his hands gripping his knees, his back straight as if awaiting orders, and stared vacantly at his dark, empty living room for what felt like a long time.

All during the last week of September, the entire Ohio Valley was drenched by rain and gray skies, an early autumn chill covering the region in a dense fog. On Sunday, he took a mostly empty bus to the studio, the driver riding the brake through intersections as rainwater flooded from the city sewers. When Don had left, Timothy was in bed with a fever and complaining of a stomach ache, and he absently wondered how kids could get sick so fast.

He watched the city's stillness through the downpour: storefronts closed, church crowds hidden under clusters of black umbrellas, and stepping off the bus, the patter of rain was the only sound on the sidewalks. The whole city seemed to be in mourning, as if a sacred promise had been broken.

Inside, Don sat in the studio reading *The Sporting News*, waiting for the telegraph to spring to life. It was the last game of the season, and the Pirates were in Cincinnati. They had only won twice in the last two weeks. They were a group of tired, indifferent ballplayers now, eyeing the end of the season, lining up work to last them through the winter until spring training. He decided he preferred to be here in a silent studio with a newspaper and cigarettes than witnessing the misery live. When the telegraph came to life, and he stubbed out his cigarette, the smoke hovered around him. He did the game intro, and the typist handed him the first page. As expected, the Pirates played poorly: a first-inning error; walks leading to runs for the Reds; at-bats that lasted only three or four pitches. Don, disgusted, spat out the plays, his broadcast full of simple, dry detail. If the telegrapher or typist noticed, they didn't say anything. Perhaps they too were feeling the last, dying days of the season.

But, then, slowly, the ticker began to tell a different story: Pittsburgh battled back. Down 3–0, they scored a run in the fifth, another in the eighth. They had the potential to end the season on this small high note. In the top of the ninth, the Pirates had one out, down 3–2, with a runner on first.

The typist handed him the line. A double to right, Thomas to third; Don extended the at-bat into an eleven-pitch battle before revealing the hit.

"Hughes digs in," he said. "Thomas dances off first. Here's the delivery. High and tight and—" Don slammed his ruler on the table. "Wait a minute! It's off his bat and into right field! Marshall cuts it off, and Thomas digs for third. This is going to be close. Throw a-comin'. Thomas goes headfirst aaaaand . . . safe! He's safe! He just got in there under the tag.

"That's the most peculiar thing I've seen today," he said, heart racing. "Hughes' heater got away from him and when McCullough ducked over the plate, his bat was still high in the air and the ball just ricocheted off it. That ball carried over Adcock's glove at first, but that's all the luck the Pirates needed. Boy, the Pirates are sure showing some fight in them today.

"And here comes the great Ralph Kiner. Kiner is wearing the collar, and the Pirates need his first hit of the game to keep the rally alive. Hughes steps off the mound and glances at the Reds' dugout, but manager Rogers Hornsby is going to leave him out there."

He spun around. The ticker whirled for what felt like a very long time, then spit out the line. The telegrapher handed the line to the typist, who appeared disinterested as he typed. Don waved at the telegrapher, who nodded, cupped his mouth, and yelled, "Attaboy, Ralph!" The typist handed him the sheet. Palms slick with sweat, Don read:

"Kiner up, B1W, B2W, DP, SS to 2B to 1B. End inning. End game. Reds 3, Pirates 2. End."

He laid the sheet down, and flattened it with his hands. All the air seemed to exit his body, and his shoulders curled, a steady ache running down his spine.

"Kiner digs in, and Hughes delivers. Ball one, wide."

He lit a cigarette. His tongue was dry and heavy. The dead air continued for five seconds, then ten.

"Kiner's ready. Here's the pitch. Ball two, wide."

He tapped his lighter against his palm. With one finger, he traced its rough lines, then pressed down on it hard. He imagined Timothy in bed, his forehead sweaty, leaning into his transistor radio, squirming forward on damp sheets. He imagined what Timothy imagined: Kiner, his large forearms straining on the bat handle, waiting for his pitch.

"Kiner steps out," Don said. "He's giving his bat a look. Hughes wipes his forehead. He's behind in this count, and boy, as a hitter, sitting on 2–0, you just know a fastball is coming, and

King Ralph feasts on those.

"Hughes comes set and takes a long look at Thomas, who keeps dancing off third. He eases back to third; no need to risk anything here. Not with Ralph Kiner at the plate. Hughes winds, and here's the pitch . . ."

Don clenched his fists.

"And the swing." He slammed his ruler on his desk, and heard, with perfect certainty, that it snapped in two. "It's a long drive! Deep to left! He might have gotten all of it! Abrams is back, he's racing, he's on the warning track."

He closed his eyes. "Abrams leaps . . . and it's over his glove! Kiner has done it! It's gone! A game-winning, three-run homer by the great Ralph Kiner."

He opened his eyes, aware of the eerie stillness in the room. He turned his head, keeping his mouth near the microphone, and watched as the other two men stared in disbelief. As if in shock, the sound effects for a road game home run were played, the sporadic fake cheers over the stillness of the home crowd filling the studio.

"Yes, sir," Don said. "In a year of such disappointment, the impossible has happened!"

Down the long stretch of empty desks, a phone's red light flashed. There was no ring, no noise. Who could this be? The station manager? Branch Rickey? The red light flashed and flashed, like an air raid beacon, and someone on the line would be demanding, in an enraged voice, why on earth Don McKeller just called a home run when in fact Ralph Kiner had grounded into a season-ending double play over an hour ago. Don didn't have an answer, not one he could articulate. He didn't know how he would call the rest of a ninth inning that simply would never exist. Instead, the answer was in his mind, in seeing his son pump his fist, his hair matted to his feverish forehead, Timothy cheering for slow-footed Ralph Kiner making that long, triumphant jog around the bases, slapping the third base coach five, head down, heading for home.

PROJECTION

Monica watched the reel cannibalize itself. Three large silver platters slowly rotated. From its inner ring, the top platter unspooled the film, sending it up a slender black rail and into a canted console, where the light from the projector shone stalwart; below it, the just-projected film reeled back toward the platters, first to the lowest, and then to the middle. The projector purred softly as it wound.

Monica ran all eight films by herself, working, she estimated, one actual hour out of every ten. Standing, she looked through the small window into theater four. It was the smallest theater and always showed old black-and-white films, ownership's weak attempt at nostalgia. It was also always empty. But now, one person sat in the middle of the theater, his spotless white sneakers propped on the seat in front of him. Her age, she guessed, with thick gelled hair and a fresh haircut. She looked up at the screen— a bad noir film she'd never heard of—then back down at the guy. Someone her age interested in old movies? In Ohio? Above her, the air-conditioner vent burped. Pushing her hair behind her ear, she slinked back down into the booth, flopped into her chair, and reached for a half-eaten box of Raisinettes on the desk. Chewing, cautious and curious, she again peeked into the theater. The end credits flashed; he was gone.

Sighing back into her seat, she surveyed the rotating platters, remembering her intense disappointment when she first entered the projection booth and discovered the two-reel system no longer existed. Nothing ever was what it appeared to be. She thought of the Ashland County water tower, visible from anywhere in Findlay, the county name painted in black, blocky letters. To her, the water tower was a symbol of small-town life, a deformed limb jutting from the grave of a bad horror movie. Driving home from college last week, her old summer job as a projectionist at the Findlay Omniplex 8 was waiting for her like a fat, dying watchdog. Here, mosquitoes infiltrated daily life, the town's humid stench creeping across the flatland like industrial waste, the smog from what remained of Findlay's industry leaving a thick, gray haze.

Her shift ended after midnight. Sweat formed on the back of Monica's neck the moment she exited the front doors. She palmed a cigarette in one hand and in the other slid a matchbox open and shut. To her right, she recognized the sneakers. He sat on a stone bench, smoking. Definitely her age. He stood, waved, and tossed his half-smoked cigarette onto the sidewalk.

He pointed, "No one uses matchboxes anymore."

"Thanks for the tip." She slid her hand into her pocket and clutched her keys like a weapon. Knee to the groin; jab the keys hard into the neck. "Do I know you?"

"Sort of. Not really." He scratched his clean-shaven chin with neat, manicured nails. "I'm Philip Rehezhkov. I was a couple of grades above you in school."

"The soccer player," she said slowly, remembering. "You went to Cornell."

"Still do. I'm a little slow to graduate."

Monica frowned at the math. "Aren't you twenty-five?"

"Twenty-four." He winked. "So I'm in no rush. You're old enough for a drink with an old friend, right? C'mon, I'll buy you a drink."

"We aren't friends." Single moviegoers tended to be older and pudgy, losing their hair, clothes disheveled in a way that suggested indifference. Philip was wrong: he wore expensive, pressed jeans and a T-shirt that stretched across his sinewy build.

"It's late."

"It's twelve-thirty on a Tuesday. It's summer! C'mon. New friends. What else are you going to do in Ohio?"

The fluorescent lights illuminated the cracked macadam and the faded paint of directional arrows and parking spots. One paint job overlapped the other; now, both faded, the straight parking lines angled over each other, hazy and unclear, the direction indiscernible. She listened to the distant roar of trucks racing down the interstate. It was just another common sound of Findlay, like her mother's constant tired snore or the weak wheeze of the old air-conditioner unit in Monica's bedroom window. Cornell: upstate New York, bucolic, serene, far away from here. Philip too was one of the ones who escaped and, somehow, was dragged back. She loosened her grip on the keys.

"Where we going?" Monica said.

The Anvil Bar was open until 2 a.m. Young professionals in loosened ties shot pool and staggered across the sticky floors; underaged teenage girls sat on barstools around them and chain-smoked, sipped their beers. Dusty televisions hanging in the corners showed the Indians game. Fat truckers in black T-shirts and mesh caps sat at the bar. Monica and Philip slouched at a table by the open door to the vacant back patio, the muggy outdoor air better than the bar's weak, lingering smell of sawdust and bleach. They filled their ashtray with cigarettes, and round by round pushed their empty glasses to the edge of the table.

"Michigan?" Philip repeated. "Good school."

"Good scholarship. And I didn't have to move too far from home."

"Why aren't you doing an internship or something?"

Monica shrugged, stirred her gin and tonic with a finger.

"My mom would like me to be here." She sucked her finger dry, then sipped her drink. "I miss seeing her, she misses me, but after I graduate, I won't move back here. So, last summer together and all that."

"What does she do?"

"Factory worker."

"Right." Philip drank a shot of whiskey, his fifth, and chased it with a Heineken. "You said your dad split, right?"

"When I was ten."

"I wish my dad had left."

Monica nodded. Philip lived in the wealthiest part of Findlay and drove a new Mustang. He had never eaten ketchup and cheese sandwiches for lunch, or wondered why his mother always smelled like wet copper.

"Like the theater?" he asked.

"It's okay. I get to read undisturbed, and drink all the free Diet Coke I want. It isn't hard. Lots of time to daydream."

"I like the weekly 'classic' they show. You know, like the one you caught me watching today. With all the shadows and lighting, how the actors' faces are naked."

She turned her eyes back to Philip. How had he seen her in the projection booth? He rolled his beer bottle between his palms, stared at the table.

"Have you noticed," Philip continued. "How you guys always play the angry old movies? I mean, you never show *Bringing Up Baby* or some shit. It's always one where the hero gets shot, where the world is bleak. Like the film color is the same as the movie: scary and ominous. Terminally real movies, you know?" He blinked at his beer as if it were out of focus. "What do you do up there in the booth?"

"Not much. Crosswords mostly. Clean sometimes."

"You get to watch the movies for free, right?"

"There's a switch next to the console, and it turns on a speaker, so I can listen. But, after you've seen them two or three times, it gets old. I prefer the silence."

He shook his head hard, just once. "Show me. I'd love to see that."

"Sure." She shrugged. "Later this week."

The cocktail waitress put down two more shots. Monica

swirled her drink and breathed in the bar's unmoving air. Frowning at the darkness outside, she said, "I hate the water tower. I can see it from my yard."

"Yeah, so can I. Everyone in Findlay can see it."

"Really?" She had always assumed the wealthy didn't have views of things like water towers. "It makes me feel branded. Like that tower is a scar or a deformity everyone can see when I'm walking around campus." She could picture the water tower then, as clear as if it were in the room, its faded yellowing curves, the county name like a blackhead ready to burst.

Philip reached for the shot, winked, and raised his glass.

"To the end of this town," he said.

She repeated, "To the end," and downed the shot, waiting for the burn.

She pushed her salad around the plate. "Why do you like this place, Mom?"

"We can smoke here." Her mother stubbed out her cigarette.

Monica shrugged; the Midwest did still have smoking and non-smoking sections. She wondered what she would do when she reached Los Angeles or Manhattan.

"Chain restaurants are just so lifeless," Monica said. "The cheesy décor. The uniforms. All of it."

"Can't we just have a nice meal?" Her mother tucked a strand of thick gray hair behind her ear. "What's so bad about a chain? Before your father and me were married, I waited tables at this place a couple of blocks from here. Remember Vincent's? I think it closed when you were eight or nine. Anyway, Vincent was an asshole and he ran the place like an asshole. Chain restaurants have, you know, guidelines. Things are done right."

"Soulless."

"Baby, I just want to eat. I don't want to think about what it means or who owns it. I just want to enjoy lunch with my little girl and have enough money to leave a nice tip."

Pointing at the pack, Monica asked, "Can I have one?"

41

"Help yourself." Monica snatched a cigarette and struck a match, shaking out the flame with a flick of her wrist. She breathed the smoke deep into her lungs, and exhaled. Her mother was in her early fifties and still possessed a lean, wiry figure. But decades at her factory job had turned her complexion bleached gray, and her hands and wrists ached constantly. Only stubbornness kept her mother employed, sucking down one aspirin before and after work with a glass of warm water. Massaging her hands, her mother asked how her film was going.

"Good." Monica looked at the tablecloth. "I mean, really well. I have the actors I want from the theater department. The script is good. We're going to shoot it when I get back to campus and then I have time to do some edits and rewrites before my thesis is due."

"My baby's going to be a filmmaker."

"Mom, stop."

"I wish they still had the drive-in. Remember the drive-in?"

"Sure. We saw *Raiders of the Lost Ark* there." She scratched her chin; the Findlay Drive-In had been vacant for seven years, then torpedoed to make way for a parking garage. "I miss it, too."

"Do you have one of those DVD things?"

"Everyone at school does."

"You left it there? With the colored girl?"

Monica didn't bother to be embarrassed: everyone talked this way in Findlay.

"Say 'black' or 'African-American,' okay? And I subletted my apartment to a Korean girl."

"I don't mean anything by it, baby. 'Colored' isn't a judgment. Just a word."

Monica smiled thinly. From the chair to her left, she picked up her purse and fished for her wallet.

"Sweetie," her mother said. "Let me get it."

"I've got it. I should be able to buy you lunch."

Her mother wilted. "You're so grown up."

"Just buying lunch, Ma. No big deal."

"It is to me."

Monica smiled, genuine this time.

"Are you going out with Philip after work?"

"Yeah, I think so. Have a drink or something."

"I never hear you come in anymore. I used to when you were a teenager, you know."

"Always?"

"Always." With a sly wink, her mother patted her hand and, for a moment, Monica saw her as young, when she was beautiful and laughed all the time, when her father was happy and sober, when she lifted Monica, just a little girl, high above her head and made her squeal with delight. And it vanished just as quickly, as if the image was a spliced piece of film, and her mother stood up slow and unsteady, touching her arthritic hands together.

She accompanied her mother to the car, hugged her goodbye, and walked toward the movie theater. She tapped a cigarette loose from the pack, aware only as she held it that she had taken her mother's cigarettes. Frowning, Monica watched as pedestrians scampered from the heat to the indoors. She craned her neck and stared beyond the "revival" district: three blocks up began an endless row of closed dress shops and cheap diners and local banks. Findlay was like a carcinogen aching for something to infect. Monica shook out her match. Her cigarette smoking was the only part of herself she believed to be distinctly Ohio. She had taken it up when she was fourteen, sneaking into the bathroom between classes; at Michigan, she smoked constantly and proudly her freshman year. Now, she was down to three a day.

Today she was supposed to show Philip the projection room. For three weeks, since she had first spied him, they spent the late evenings together, having drinks at a different bar each night, and not once had he tried to kiss her or even touch her fingertips. She took a hard drag on her cigarette; frowning, she flung it and the entire pack into the street. Crossing the theater parking lot she frowned, aware suddenly she would have to buy a fresh pack for her mother. Philip was always there after work, he always paid for her drinks, and he always talked with Monica late into the morning, and when she was honest, staring into the empty theaters, listening to the hum of the projectors, she knew that she had no one else.

Inside, grateful for the sudden burst of cool air, she zipped across the unvacuumed floor to the bathroom. Locking the stall, she tugged on her maroon polo shirt and black uniform pants; why she had to wear a uniform in the projection booth, she didn't know. The pants were too big and rode high on her waist, no matter how many times she yanked them down.

The theater went from eight shows at seven to four shows at ten; in between, she cleaned the projectors. The film, she had read, traveled nearly one hundred feet, from platter to projector then back again, inches from the floor, collecting dust as it moved. Trial and error taught Monica that the best device for cleaning the projector was a clean, used toothbrush, the bristles softened from use and disinfected in boiled water; the brush, with its angled head and firm plastic, was perfect for removing debris from the gears and track. Once, films only lasted three hundred reels; now, at Disney World, they could get nearly twenty thousand showings out of one reel of film before it became feeble and snapped. She cleaned the projector lovingly, running a finger over fresh spots to verify its shine.

In the booth, she waited. She told Philip which stairs to take and to be quiet, knock softly. She finished a crossword, then another. She half-watched a Michelle Pfeiffer movie, flipped the sound off. When there was finally a gentle knock on the door, low, below the handle, she believed she had been waiting so long that she had willed it to happen.

Philip entered the room carrying a leather-wrapped flask of gin and reeking of cigarettes. He stood still and stared at the projector.

"Where's the reel?" he asked.

"Platters. They don't use reels anymore."

He stared at the machine as if it spoke to him in Arabic.

"They're huge."

"Twelve-inch radius. And heavy, too. But it works better this way. The film never tears. Or rarely. Look how far it travels, how close it gets to the ground without touching."

As if snapped from a trance, Philip set his flask down on the counter and walked slowly to the nearest machine. She became conscious of the steady, whirling noise of the film and the soft, mechanical spinning of the platters. He moved his face close to the machines, looking into the projector itself and the bright xenon bulb, the corners of his mouth moving softly, as if in prayer.

"I love it," he said.

She took a step toward him, and he turned, close to her, and reached out with his fingers and cupped her cheek. Her chest tightened; until then she had forgotten how much she wanted this, to be craved, to be wanted. He kissed her hard; she licked the gin from his lips, his tongue. He pulled her tight and she backed him against the desk. Sliding her hands under his shirt, she dug her nails into his skin and traced the hair down his navel to his jeans. She yanked on his belt. The vents above them rattled and sighed out cold air. This is good enough, she thought. For one last awful summer in Findlay, this is good enough.

Soon, she was waking in his bed every morning. Sometimes he was there, sometimes he wasn't. When he was, they made love again, and then they smoked pot and went out for breakfast. When he wasn't, Monica dressed slowly, walking around his room, shaking off the cobwebs of sleep and looking at all the items around a bedroom that was the size of her room and her mother's combined. Everything was new and sleek: the computer with the extra-wide screen, the stereo system, the expensive clothes hung on cherry hangers in the custom-made closet. He had a large collection of Criterion Collection DVDs. Back in Ithaca, she was sure, Philip had duplicates of all this: the rich always owned two of everything. She left through the front door, undisturbed by his parents or a dog or a neighbor, and drove onto the highway, circling Findlay endlessly, imagining herself sitting in a dark room editing her first great film, a film premiere, her mother's praise and pride.

One morning, late in July, she woke to Philip holding out a palmful of pills and a glass of apple juice.

"What is it?" she asked.

He shrugged. She downed three pills and he crossed the room and turned on the television. A morning show came on and a weatherman was on a New York street corner predicting tornadoes in Nebraska, a yellow barricade corralling his cheering fans and their floppy paper signs. Philip tugged on a pair of jeans and started rocking back and forth, humming.

He said. "Do you know anything about boats? I want to build a boat."

Monica shook her head and looked out the bedroom window. She blinked and saw dozens of red squares shift in and out of her view; the window winked at her and a Mercedes-Benz lifted a wheel, suddenly a hind leg, and scratched its door handle. The fabric of her clothes felt thick and sticky, like peanut butter. She imagined great big boats cruising down the streets. She wanted to go sailing.

"Like Melville," Philip said. She wondered how long he had been talking. "To the garage!"

The garage floor was a clear, spotless gray, as if no one had ever changed the oil or clomped their salt-crusted boots loose of snow. Staring at the floor, she noticed she was wearing shoes but could somehow see her toes.

Philip pointed. "Grab that."

The axe, hung by two S-curve hooks that cradled the blade, rested between a hacksaw and a rake. Monica stood on the workbench, and she turned, making the wooden legs creak loudly under her weight.

"Do we need the saw, too?" she asked.

Philip ran his hands through his hair, then took his cigarette from his mouth. He nodded with vigor.

"Both. Absolutely. Hand me the axe."

Monica turned back to the tools, grasped the axe by its handle, lifted, and passed it down to Philip. She expected it to be heavy and cumbersome; instead, the contours fit her hands as if they had been molded for her grip. She liked the dark hickory handle, how masculine and solid it felt in her hands. She hopped off the workbench.

"Do we need anything else?" she said.

He lit a second cigarette with the half-smoked remains of the first.

"This is a good start. Lots to do and not sure how long it will take."

She said, "Your dad has a lot of tools." But Philip ignored her and walked out the back garage door. Monica followed, carrying the saw.

Outside, she could feel the lush, full grass through her shoes, and walking made her legs shiver with instability, like she was playing in a bin of plastic balls. In the distance, she could see the omnipresent water tower. The tower's once-white color appeared yellowed, as if suffering from jaundice.

At the end of the long, flat backyard stood an elaborate wooden jungle gym. On one side was a grid of climbing ropes that led to the top of a two-story fort, its roof a triangular beige tarp like a miniature pirate ship's sail. From the other side of the fort, one could climb out onto monkey bars and walk over the rungs, look down at three swings of equal length. Underneath the swing seats were small patches of mud where grass no longer grew.

Philip dropped the axe next to the swings. He took off his trench coat (when did he put that on?) with melodramatic flair, rolling his shoulder blades back, dropping his arms, and shrugging off his coat with a flourish. He pushed up the sleeves of his camouflage sweatshirt and picked up the axe.

"Where should we make the first cut?" he said.

"This isn't going to be enough wood. I thought we were

47

building an ark."

"We are. Definitely. Like Noah. But, see, we have to start small, and this will be a good heap of wood. For the masthead. For starters. There are trees everywhere here; we'll get plenty of wood."

The drugs coursed through her and her body produced sweat, then she sensed it pour down her arms like a river. She exhaled deeply and her breath came out in green bubbles that morphed before her eyes into swallows and flew away. Pinching the bridge of her nose, she shook her head and wondered why there were no cardinals or blue jays coming out of her mind.

"Have you ever noticed," Monica asked. "That even in the summer the streets are gray here? The salt from the winter plows never really fades away. Findlay is perpetually salted."

"Use the saw to cut the swings loose. Their rope will be good for the sails."

Monica dropped the saw and climbed to the monkey bars, batting at the rope with her feet. She craved a banana, or coconuts, something plucked from a tree. She wanted to swing through Findlay like Tarzan in the old black-and-white movies. "When's the last time you played on this?"

"Years. Ages. Another life." Philip threw away his cigarette and with the axe, climbed the ladder and stood atop the monkey bars.

Monica swung down the bars. "Let's sail. We'll go boating."

"Exactly! We'll float! We'll collect animals and when we flood the town, we'll flow into the lake, up the Erie Canal, and into the ocean, back to the homeland! Lithuania, here we come!"

"My family is Irish."

"Freedom! A theory of!"

With his feet balanced on two bars, he lifted the axe above his head, and swung it down into the thick parallel beam of the gym. The whole apparatus shook and the vibrations ran through Monica's body, reverberating through her arms like an echo in a cave.

Philip said, "After we do this, we'll nuke that goddamn thing." He pointed the axe blade directly at the tower, his arm quivering. "Down will come the tower, we'll have our flood, and off we'll go!"

Monica spun back around on the monkey bars. She kept her distance from the middle, where Philip swung the axe. She could read the word "County" on the water tower, but "Ashland" remained hidden from her view. Philip's two cigarettes fell from his mouth, past her feet and into the grass, and she imagined the tower said something more appropriate, like "Ashtray County."

"We'd need dynamite," she said.

"Drive to Michigan. They have dynamite. Michigan militia love blowing shit up." Philip swung the axe and the gym shuddered. "James Nichols lives there. That guy who helped McVeigh? He'll probably help us out. He's cool."

The gym groaned and Monica heard wood crackle like thin ice. She asked, "Should you be standing right above where you're chopping?"

Philip swung again and the monkey bars split in two. With a loud snap, the gym opened like the ground in an earthquake. He fell forward, cracking his chin into the bars. Monica lost her grip, slamming her shoulder into the ground, the monkey bars crashing against her back. All the air rushed out of her body, her ears ringing. They lay unmoving, a tangle of wood and arms and legs, and when she could breathe again, a sharp ache blossomed in her chest.

"Are you okay?" Monica asked. Blood ran from Philip's chin.

"Nothing broken. You?"

He reached out for her wrist. "I'm fine," she said, pulling away.

She stared at the ground. Next to Philip's face, in the dirt, his cigarette, half-smoked, continued to burn, and she watched the gray ash drop into a small pile. The drugs seemed to be wearing off—weak shit—and she felt sensations of real, physical pain all through her legs and back. Groggy, she sank her fingers deep into the mud.

He said in a whisper, "We're two crazy birds, ain't we?" He winked and rolled onto his back. "Below the deck, off the plank. We're going out on the Atlantic, far away. The devil and the deep blue sea."

He's insane, Monica thought, the words billowing like cumulus clouds. Turning her head, feeling the grass brush against her cheek, she could see the water tower again, and beyond it, the blue summer sky. She pressed her head back into the ground, wishing she could just sink into the dirt and vanish.

Monica said, "I need to use the bathroom."

She rose. An ache ran through her shoulders and knees, and slowly, she walked back into the house. She stood in the living room: the couches were thick and cushy, as if they were never sat on. Recessed lighting along the walls highlighted the bookcases and the colorfully bland paintings. Walking silent through the pristine room, she imagined that it cost thousands to decorate, the smell of furniture polish and filtered air tickling her nose, all for no one to ever sit in. Just a private museum to be admired.

Under the soft light of the bathroom, Monica stared at the brown marks that streaked her clothes, blending into the black fabric, noticeable only now. In the mirror, her reflection showed random spots of dirt on her face, and her mascara had smeared. She used the hand soap to scrub her hands and forearms, then her face. Brown water whirled down the drain and out of sight. Monica thought she looked so young without her makeup, girlish even. She bit her lip. How long before her face looked like her mother's? How long before she'd pull her hair back in a tight ponytail, stretching and smushing her face like those G-force rides at the carnival?

She scrubbed the film from her face, soaking the washcloth, inspecting every crevice of her skin. With wide eyes, she observed each cool rivulet of water as it ran down her cheeks and neck. She dried her face and hands, opened the bathroom door, eyes sweeping the untouchable rooms, and slipped out through the front door. On the front lawn, its color a gorgeous green, Monica imagined the road in front of her flooded with a torrent of water, trucks and telephone poles crashing down the street, cars capsized, homes sliding apart like sandcastles, all toward the lake, washing away the filth of this city, of her life. Then, Monica pierced her world, seeing unprojected through films or her wishes. And Monica saw this: a crazy boyfriend, a dying mother, and herself, still in Findlay, unmoving, and scared to be alone.

She woke at four in the morning. She reached for her blinking cell phone on the floor. A message from Philip: he was going to Chicago for a few days, see friends, he'd call when he got back. Kicking the thin sheets loose from her legs, her eyes adjusting to the dark, Monica felt the tension loosen from her shoulders and, yawning herself awake, she fully opened her eyes and listened to her window air conditioner whirl. She tugged on her jeans, her body still achy and sore, dressed, and went to the grocery store.

At home, with the sun rising, Monica tuned the radio to the news. She listened, pleased she could feel like a slice of college was with her, when the events she couldn't see and touch mattered to her and everyone else. Pancakes, sprinkled with chocolate chips, cooked in a skillet; to the right, an omelet with peppers, tomatoes, and mushrooms. She chopped slices of fresh strawberry and melon, then set two plates on the kitchen table. English muffins cooked in the toaster oven. The coffee bubbled and popped. The room warmed with the smells of food.

"What's all this?" her mother asked.

Monica turned. Her mother was in her lightweight robe; Monica could see the legs of her blue satin pajamas. Her thrifty mother had always splurged on pajamas. I love to be comfortable sleeping, she used to say.

"Breakfast. Fresh coffee, too. I didn't know what you would want, so I made a little of everything."

"Why would you waste all this food," her mother said.

Monica watched a small smile form on her face as she sat down at the table. "Are these fresh strawberries?"

"Of course. Paper's on the table, too. Pancake?"

"Well, all right, then."

Her mother sat and Monica poured her coffee. Her mother took a strawberry, and chewed it slowly. The news was soothing white noise. Outside, the grass didn't seem quite as yellow in the dawn light. A squirrel perched on the chain-link fence, then leapt into the nearest tree. Birds, what kind Monica didn't know, chirped, and the day seemed promising and cool.

"How early did you get up?"

"Early," Monica said. "Kroger is open twenty-four hours."

"You were asleep when I got home last night."

"Went to bed early."

Her mother nodded, and didn't ask about Philip. She knew, Monica was sure, in the way her mother always seemed to know. And she loved her then, achingly, and she fought an urge to cry and wrap her arms around her mother's tough, tired shoulders. Instead, she sat down, and they ate quietly and read the paper. Monica rose to get her mother more coffee, to get the muffins when the toaster sprung loud, for juice. Breakfast seemed to last a long time; then her mother looked at the clock above the doorway and patted Monica's hand. She stood and appeared, to a sitting Monica, to tower over her. Her mother kissed her on the forehead.

"Thank you," she whispered. "I loved it." And then she turned and headed for her bedroom to change and go to work. Monica sat, staring at the plates splattered with syrup and egg yolk, and saw them as projection platters spinning her life right out of this kitchen, projecting the image into the world. She wanted to cut the film, snap off the console, shut it all down.

She shifted her hips left to right, making the booth chair squeak as the wheels rocked. The crossword confused her today: too often, seven-letter answers came to her as six letters, and her inability to think of the right words irritated her.

The reel to her right sputtered, and she looked up, hoping for a tear, for the unlikely. But it was just a flutter of dust or a sprocket not aligning properly with the reel, and the film and projector continued on, not bothering to stop and ruin the afternoon matinee. Monica sucked on her teeth. She hoped for something to go wrong, for something to be destroyed.

Philip was coming home tonight. Monica tried to convince herself that she missed him. But she didn't. What she missed was having someone to observe, a person to go to the bars with, one guy who was a symbol of this small town wrapped in a tight spiral of alcohol and drugs and money. She knew now she was projecting, aiming her anger with school and her mother and herself at Philip. She stood and from the cabinets at her knees removed five clean white rags, cotton swabs, and rubbing alcohol. Bending to the sound head, she cleaned with slow, gentle turns of her wrist. She removed the dust from the sprockets until every crevice was free from filth. She cleaned for what felt like a long time. The projector shone. Leaning back on her heels, a loose strand of hair dangling down her forehead, Monica smiled. She could see herself at film school, taking notes in the theater with an illuminated pen just like the film critics use, studying color and camera angles. A good, fulfilling life far away from Findlay.

After a week without Philip, leaving Ohio seemed easy. She couldn't understand why it felt like such an oppressive burden before. Now, on her feet, the four clean projectors glimmering, Monica remembered breakfast. She could still taste the strawberries, still see her mother's smile as she eased into the kitchen chair. When he came home, Monica decided she would tell Philip she didn't want to see him anymore. In two weeks they were both returning to college anyway and she was certain he would respond with indifference.

Only when she shut off the last film did she realize it was nearly 1 a.m. and, checking her cell phone, Philip had never called. She emptied the trash, locked up the films, and walked outside clutching her keys. Her skin crawled. She was aware of his presence, but as if he was lurking, like a lion stalking an antelope. She walked slowly to her car, scanning the lot, then slowing as she spied him. His car was parked on the opposite side of hers, half-hidden from her view. She rounded the trunk. On the pavement outside the driver's door were several half-smoked, discarded cigarettes.

"What are you doing?" she said.

"Waiting for you. Hop in."

"Can we talk tomorrow? I'm really beat."

"It's important," he said, turning to face her. His face seemed refreshed, earnest. "I won't keep you out late, I promise."

"Are you fucked up?" she asked, studying his pupils.

"Sober. Tidy Bowl fresh."

She looked down at her sweatshirt. Maybe she could tell him goodbye tonight.

"Important?" she asked.

"Critical. You're gonna love it."

She crossed her arms across her chest. One talk and it'll all be over. Reluctant, she walked to the passenger side and got in. Philip turned the radio on, soft, tuned it to a classic rock station. She asked what he wanted to talk about but he answered with silence. His face, serene and calm, looked straight down the road, his driving smooth and sure, under the speed limit, the windows letting in the muggy summer air. Maybe he knew it was over, too. Tucking her hair behind her ear, the only thing that seemed peculiar about him was that he wore all black.

They drove out of the city center, toward the highway, and past Monica's house. Philip swung the car down a residential street with most of the porch lights off, then turned left down a narrow, unmarked street, and cut the engine.

"What are we doing here?" she asked.

Philip answered by popping the trunk and stepping out of the car. Monica sat, waiting. He reached into the trunk and removed two bags, then walked past the hood and through someone's backyard, heading for the tree line. Monica scrambled out of the car and called after him.

He turned. Pressing a finger to his lips, he beckoned her to follow.

They walked silently for several minutes, and then suddenly in front of them was the Ashland County water tower. Standing outside the fence, staring at the massive steel structure, its legs held in place by bolts the size of softballs, Monica was amazed at how large it was, and that she had never gone close to it in all the years she lived there.

From his pockets, Philip removed wire cutters and began to cut the fence.

"The fuck are you doing?" Monica asked.

"Don't worry, it isn't electric. It's a pretty flimsy fence. I checked it out last week. You know, I think it has the same effect as turning the lock in your door. I mean, if someone really wanted to break into your house, you have to have a deadbolt. But sometimes, just not being obvious, like a package in an open car window, keeps people away." The fence crackled under his wire cutters like snapping bones of fried chicken.

"Philip—"

"I'll show you. Here," he said, holding the fence open for her. "Walk in."

Conscious of leaving fingerprints, she jammed her hands deep into her pockets; glancing around, convinced no one was watching them, she ducked under the fence. The grass surrounding the water tower was yellow and brittle. Philip set his two bags down and put his hands on his hips.

"This is going to be a great evening," he said.

"What are you on?"

"Lied a little bit. I didn't go to Chicago. Went up into northern Michigan. Got some great stuff." He unzipped one of his black duffel bags and pulled out a tightly wrapped slab of what looked like butter.

"What's that?"

"This," he said, "is plastic explosive. I made it myself. Those Michigan militia boys thought I was a fed and wouldn't give me shit. But one of my buddies up in East Lansing is a PhD student in biochemistry, and he said, 'Dude, Phil, you can make all kinds of shit out of plain old household goods.' So we did. I fucking made plenty."

Monica laughed, weak and incredulous. This simply couldn't be real.

"It doesn't take long," he continued, "to wrap it around the legs. Do you want me to show you how, or do you just want to do the detonation?"

"I'm not detonating anything."

"This was your idea." He walked to one of the legs and bent down, sliding a long, thin wire around the steel.

Was it? She frowned at the yellow grass. Was this her idea? Had she said they should blow up a water tower? And even if she did (did she?) that was talk, the way people say they're going to kill their boss or their children. No one actually did such horrible, stupid things.

She said, "You can't blow up a water tower."

"Not trying to. We're going to explode the legs, destabilizing the tower, making it tilt and crash. No mushroom clouds here. So, yes, incorrect, but strangely true." Biting his lower lip, he contemplated her. "You sure you don't want to detonate the charge?"

She pulled her cell phone out of her pocket. Furrowing her brow, she stared at the numbers as she punched 9, then 1, and as she looked up, Philip was there, snatching the phone from her hand, reaching back and throwing it in a long, lazy arc into the woods.

"What the fuck are you doing?" she screamed.

"You'll wake the neighbors." He walked back to the tower base. "Maybe that's a good idea. Wakey, wakey, eggs and bakey!"

Monica ran. She ducked under the fence and raced through the woods, her feet hitting hard on the dirt path, and ran up to his

Mustang. She yanked the door open and reached for the ignition: no keys. She hit the horn. She hit it again, holding it down, a long, loud bleat to wake everyone. But holding down the horn, screaming now, she looked around and all the lights in all the small houses remained off. She yelled and hollered again and again, then remembering, strangely, a woman's defense class she took in college, she screamed, "Fire!" No one came. No one answered.

Exhausted, she stopped. She sucked in the humid air and looked at the houses. Listening to the stillness of the city, it was almost as if the town was already dead. As if all the residents, with their shrugs and indifference, were already gone, washed away like the debris from an upstate lake and rolled and bounced through rivers and left in the ocean to sink to the bottom. Crickets and birds, once quiet, chirped and hooted, filling the air empty of human noise with their calls.

She ran. Up the street, to the corner, where she turned left, toward the north and away from the city, slightly uphill, as far from Philip as she could. When she was out of breath, she turned back. The water tower, white and brilliant, stood against the dark sky. She wondered if her mother looked at the tower with the same disdain, if she sees it, driving to and from work, and feels trapped, pinned down. From below, almost as if from the trees themselves, there was a flash of yellow and a loud booming noise. Where was Philip? Was he in his car, racing away, or did he stay and watch? Thousands of sirens wailed around her and police cars and fire trucks zipped down the dark street and out of view. The noises curled in on the water tower, spooling themselves closer. The water tower remained stalwart; there would be no tremendous crash, no Biblical wash of water over the residents. Observing the tower, her field of view widened and in a sweeping panorama, Monica now could see the entire world, beyond Findlay, beyond Ohio.

A FULLY IMAGINED WORLD

Kyle saw her from across the far end of a large artificial glacier, its walls illuminated from behind by blue lights, a curving synthetic stretch slick and jagged just like real ice, demonstrating how the entire world had frozen over millions of years ago and stilled the land. She was folding a map, her hands searching for the glossy paper's deep grooves. He knew it was Serena. Lately, she often filled his thoughts with secret pleasure during the day: when he was folding laundry in the basement and hearing the footsteps overhead of his wife and daughter; driving home from the grocery store, the paper bags in the trunk of his station wagon rustling together as he turned through his neighborhood; sitting in front of his computer with copies of his resume and boxes of old legal correspondence covering the dining room table. Now, stepping away from the glacier and the cold air pumped through the display to mimic the freezing temperatures of an ice age, his eyes latched onto her, and a delicious tension squeezed away his breath. Kyle smoothed his shirt, one plucked from a hanger this morning rather than off the floor, pleased he was wearing something with a collar.

"Where the birds, Daddy?" Kyle reached into the stroller and ran his fingers through his daughter's curly hair. What Ellie meant was pterodactyls but at age two, everything with wings was a bird.

"Across the room, sweetie. We're going there next."

"See the birds?"

"Yes, to see the birds."

58

His daughter clapped.

All morning, Ellie had clung to Kyle, asking for juice or toys, spitting out endless questions about nothing at all, his daughter's shrill and constant chatter the only sound he could hear in the still air of his house. A headache growing acute behind his eyes, he had desperately proposed a trip to the museum to see the dinosaurs, one of Ellie's favorite things. At the ticket office, he had pulled the last twenty from his wallet, fingering the corners and picturing the dwindling numbers on his ATM receipts, how being unemployed for six months had drained more than just his bank account.

Since the law firm terminated him—after five years of eighty-hour workweeks—his days were driven by Ellie's needs, rising daily not to meet clients and peruse legal briefs, but instead, wearing old jeans and wrinkled T-shirts that were easy to wash the stains from, his time and energy was bent to his daughter's fascinations and whims. His thoughts were all that remained his, and more and more, growing with exponential detail and intensity, they were about Serena: ten years ago, for just one night, they had been lovers. And, now, here in view, her presence was so remarkable that it couldn't be just a coincidence. He was sure there was a meaning to this.

"Birds, Daddy?"

"Yes, sweetie, we're going." Kyle pushed the stroller forward, swinging them in a wide circle of the field trip group.

Cincinnati's Natural History Museum felt tremendous, its curved ceilings and half-moon archways far above his head the remnants of the train and bus station this building had once been. Layered over the turn-of-the-century architecture was the museum veneer: thin, clean carpet in a muted blue; a series of raised and lowered platforms of individual displays and interactive models; tracks of light angled to showcase maps, diagrams, and statues; and throughout the room, a series of oak and redwood trees that rose above the lighting, their artificial branches spreading wide and disappearing into the dark ceiling. In the Fossil and Re-Creation Center, the displays created a panoply of mechanized noises. Roars of polar bears standing tall and menacing on their hind legs. The heavy roll of boulders. The cracking of ice.

Serena handed the folded map to a boy, maybe five years old, and then they joined a group of children so large, Kyle wasn't sure how he hadn't seen them earlier: the children's chattering voices, the tiny slaps on shoulders and hands, squeaking shoes, zippers ripping up and down jackets, cries of "Gimme!" and "Nyuh-unh!" Serena appeared to be one of three adults, all women, all probably field trip volunteers. At the back of the group, the teacher held up her hand and called for attention.

Kyle steered closer: Serena was still gorgeous. She had jet-black hair that tumbled in waves to her shoulders. Her face was perfectly symmetrical, and even now, years since he had last seen her, her skin was flawless. Though her hair hid them, he knew that her earlobes were connected, a feature he found on other women elfish and repulsive, but which made her somehow more striking. Above her left eye was a scar that cut a razor of pale skin through her dark eyebrow. She'd fallen from a tree when she was nine. Eight stitches.

The wheels of his stroller squeaked. Kyle never realized he was holding his breath.

He pushed the stroller down a wheelchair ramp, and into one of several sunken areas in the room, and they were standing face-to-face with the re-creations of two massive dinosaurs: a stegosaurus, its huge plates rising out of its back, tail raised against a tyrannosaurus rex, their skin and eyes so vivid Kyle could actually picture them moving. Above, pterodactyls loomed, lit up by small track lights angled along the ceiling. Sharp, bony teeth protruded from their triangular mouths, their eyes following Kyle like an optical illusion.

"Lemme out! Lemme out!" Ellie tugged at her safety belt. He unstrapped her, and lifted her out of the stroller.

"Down! Down! Down!" He placed her on her feet, and she ran to the nearest display. On floor level in front of her, pterodactyls stood on a rocky terrain, watching over their eggs and their newly hatched babies whose beaks were lifted to the sky. The faces of the smallest pterodactyls, Kyle thought, were softer than the parents', probably to appeal to children. From a hidden speaker, a mechanical pterodactyl shrieked.

"Birds, Daddy!"

"I see, sweetie. Aren't they pretty?"

"They're big."

"Pterodactyls were very large birds. Some as big as airplanes."

Ellie, mesmerized, wrapped her fingers tight around the wire guardrail. He knelt down and watched her absorb this idea.

"Do they move?" Ellie asked.

"No, sweetie, they're just statues."

"Oh," she said. Statues. What was that like? Hearing a word for a first time, not knowing what it was but somehow, in the way children do, storing it, ready to use it in some unexpected fashion months from now. Ellie crept down the guardrail, keeping her small hands latched on the steel wires as she walked. She was loveable then, unlike the times when she cried and howled and chattered, times that had been growing in frequency, times that made being a father a torturous, horrible thing.

"Are you tired? Do you want to ride in the stroller?"

"No, I okay," she said. Her eyes expanded again as she spied a small, sloth-like creature trapped in mud. "Eeyore!" she yelled, pointing.

Her high-pitched squeal made several adults turn, including Serena. A fist closed inside Kyle's chest, squeezing the air against his spine. Had she seen him?

"Let's look at Eeyore," he said, steering Ellie. His eyes remained on Serena, who looked at them with indifference and then back at the group of kids. She must have been too far away. He bent down and ran his fingers through Ellie's hair, and watched her large, pretty eyes take in the donkey.

"Is that really Eeyore?" she asked.

"No, sweetie, that's a statue. Remember what a statue is?"

"Uh-huh. Make-believe. Right, Daddy?"

He craned his neck and looked at Serena again: a woman he bought coffee from for a few weeks when he was in college. He remembered seeing her in the bar that night so many years ago, the awkwardness of their hello outside the coffee shop, the way he knew after a few minutes she would invite him home with her, and then standing in the kitchen of her drafty apartment he was surprisingly conscious of how much he wanted this moment, this one unplanned, raw experience, right before they made love three times. After, Kyle traced the scar on her eyebrow and listened as she explained leaping for and missing a branch attached to a friend's tree house. In the morning, he slid his jeans up over his legs and as she slept, he went into the kitchen and poured a glass of cold water and wrote a note on a paper towel and wrapped it around the water glass, a note with no phone number or request to see her again, and set it gently on the nightstand and he leaned in, and—though he isn't sure if this happened, he prefers to remember it this way—she whimpered softly when he brushed his lips against her temple, pushed a strand of her hair away, and left. Walking down the street that cool morning, alive and confident in who he was in the world, he decided he would never call her, wouldn't set foot in her coffee shop again, just because he could make such a choice. Nine years later, one night with Serena had become a physical ache, a dream he could call up and see and touch. What he was perhaps only half-aware of was his need for the feeling not in her apartment, but the certainty of walking away, the clarity of a still-uncharted life ahead of him. Kyle conjured that moment now with a richness far beyond anything a museum or book or anything else could possibly imagine.

He took Ellie by the hand. "C'mon, sweetheart."

"Where we going?"

He stood, his left arm draped downward, clutching his daughter's hand, which was caked in something confectionary. Where was Serena? He pivoted, searching for the flock of children.

He snaked around groups of adults, ignoring Ellie's

stumbling footsteps. He crept forward, tugging his daughter along with one hand and with the other, twirling his wrist, loosening his fingers, trying to shake the tension from his body. He smoothed his hair, licked his lips, and concentrated on slowing his breathing. This is stupid, he thought. No: daring. Bold. Assertive.

They passed women in business suits sitting on benches with their hands folded in their laps. They looked tranquil, as if they had just escaped the office, if only for an hour. For a moment, Kyle thought of work, all the long hours at the firm, the expectations of being made a partner one day, and the suddenness of the downsizing followed by days of disbelief: businesses always needed attorneys. Wasn't there a promise from law school and the firm, a promise of a piece of the future, a promise that hard work would provide stability? He forced this question from his mind by bending down and scooping up Ellie, her eyes darting around at the constant din of volcanic eruptions and screeching dinosaurs. He strode toward Serena with his shoulders held back and a half-smile on his face.

A museum guide was explaining to the children how The Cave had a real, live colony of brown bats inside, and that they were to stay in their groups, not wander off. Serena stood on the outskirts of the group, her arms folded across her chest, an expression of pleasant boredom on her face. Her jeans were low cut and expensive; her white blouse—silk fabric, good stitching, a stylish collar—had the top three buttons open, revealing her smooth skin.

"Excuse me," Kyle said. He set Ellie down, loosely holding her hand high to his hip. "Serena?"

She glanced first at Ellie, then him, and feigned polite recognition. "That's right."

"Do you remember me? I used to come into the coffee shop in Clifton. It was a long time ago. About ten years."

"Oh, sure, Insomnia. That was a long time ago."

"It was one of my hangouts in college. I always used to get a double espresso." He grinned. "I'm Kyle."

"I stopped drinking caffeine after I graduated. I was jittery from drinking so much, and really, it does horrible things to your skin. Even the smell of those places bothers me. The ubiquitous modern coffee shop." She smiled at her own observation, and tapped her fingers absently against her necklace. Narrowing her eyes, she took one step back and reappraised him. "Did we work together?"

"No, I was a regular."

"I see. Well, I don't mean to be rude, but there were probably five hundred customers every day. I'm sorry, it was a very long time ago."

"That's okay." Ellie leaned away, playing some sort of balancing game, and his shoulder dipped to handle her sticky hand. "I just recognized you and wanted to say hello. Are you with your son?"

"Yes, my Avery." She turned her head in her son's direction, and absently brushed back a strand of hair, revealing an understated, expensive diamond earring. To her son, Serena gave a smile so genuine and breathtaking it made Kyle, with painful acuity, aware of his insignificance. In his thoughts, he never saw her as anything other than the pretty girl at the coffee shop, and it startled him that in his mind, she had always been unchanged.

Serena studied Ellie. To Kyle, she asked, "Are you on a field trip, too?"

"Yes," he lied. "A day care group."

"You have the day off."

"You really don't remember me?"

Serena smiled cruelly but said no more. If she didn't remember him, she certainly seemed to recognize him for what he was now. He focused on the scar cutting through her eyebrow, and didn't notice when Ellie wiggled free from his grip.

"Well," he said, offering a curt nod. "It was good to see you again."

"I'm sorry I don't remember you. Did you say your name was Kyle?"

"Yes. I'm Kyle."

He held her gaze. Remember me, he thought. Please remember me. If his memory of their night together was to continue to be liberating for him, it had to be shared. He waited for a glimmer of acknowledgement. Instead, she nodded blankly, then glided away to rejoin her son's group. She stood at the entrance to The Cave, shepherding the children, and then they all entered and she was gone. Pressure mounted behind Kyle's eyes, his shoulders curving forward as if a great weight had been placed against his neck, and a little dizzy, he lowered his chin. Something terrible had just happened that he couldn't quite understand. He turned the palm of his left hand upward, as if the answer would be in a book he held, and discovered Ellie had let go.

She was gone. He blinked. This was impossible. She couldn't vanish like this. There seemed to be a large radius around him, several square yards of bland carpeting where no one stood and Ellie should be. He took a step forward, and scanned around the legs of the nearest people. Curls, curls, curls: her blonde hair should stand out. He crouched to the floor and spun in a slow circle, seeing nothing but knobby adult knees, and he repeated her name in a soft panic, as if calling to a scared animal.

"Eleanor?" Kyle said. "Ellie?"

He stood and walked quickly to the stroller. He peeked inside and found it empty. His heartbeat echoed in his ears and he slammed his hand down on the stroller. Racing by a group of seniors, surveying the entire room, he hurried into the next corridor. He yelled her name again. Did you see a little girl, he blurted out to anyone, with blonde hair and purple pants? They shook their heads. He jogged from room to room and his hands began to shake. What if someone took her? What if some pervert preyed on children in museums, paying admission to wander the rooms and find little girls looking for birds and Eeyore and promising them that Winnie and Piglet are just outside? He screamed for her, his voice shrill, piercing, terrible.

"Sir?" Kyle whipped around. An old man with deep-set eyes

and impossibly white teeth placed a hand on Kyle's elbow. "Did you lose somebody?"

"My daughter. She was right here." He shook his head in disbelief, and the stranger's strong grip on his elbow tightened. "I don't know how I lost her."

"Let's walk to the front. Security will do a page and we can wait by the front door. Children wander off. She's just fine, I'm sure."

The old man was too calm, somehow hypnotic. He lead them, striding with military precision, to the museum entrance. Kyle explained to the security guard what happened, where he was with Ellie, and with glazed eyes the guard nodded and pushed buttons on his computer. Six monitors showed various rooms of the museum; even in black and white, the pictures were remarkably clear. The guard tapped buttons slowly, and Kyle fought the urge to shove him aside as he panned through the entire building, floor by floor, until Ellie appeared on the screen, standing in front of a pair of interactive monitors, her hands hovering over a series of buttons. It was as if she somehow knew they were seeking her, and she was mocking their search.

"That's her!" Kyle said.

"Sector 11," the security guard said. "I'll take you there." He picked up his walkie-talkie and radioed to that area that they were on the way.

"See?" The old man said. "She didn't even notice you were gone."

"I turned away for one moment. Just one."

The man—his shoulders wide, his beard neat and trim—spoke in a clear, sonorous voice. "It's for women, you know. Watching children."

"What?"

"You shouldn't be here. Being here is a horrible thing." And with that, the old man fished a plastic lighter from his shirt pocket and dipped away, disappearing into the rotunda crowd. Kyle turned to the security guard, searching for a witness to this strangeness. The guard merely made an impatient smacking sound with his lips, wet and fishy.

When they found her, Ellie was standing transfixed by the blur of water bombarding a coastline, trees bending until they snapped loose, small cars spinning down flooded streets. The audio was broken; her eyes were wide. Kyle scooped her up and buried his daughter's head under his chin.

"Baby," Kyle said. "Baby, baby, baby."

The security guard nodded at Kyle, turned on his heel, and left.

"Sweetie, in public, you have to stay with me. You can't wander off like that."

Ellie wiped her mouth. "Daddy, look! Storms!"

He looked down. Animation showed how low atmospheric pressure over warm ocean water and the air above it loop together and, according to the green arrows, push air up into a vortex, creating the eye of the storm. Everything in the eye of the hurricane remained calm; outside, the ocean churned, creating triple-digit winds that turned the sky into a nebulous threat of purple-and-black clouds. Then the picture changed, and a coastline, building by building, was ripped apart. They watched in silence.

Kyle slumped on the edge of Ellie's bed, watching her sleep with the stuffed pterodactyl he bought for her at the museum gift shop tucked under her arm. His wife Molly was a financial advisor and often met her clients late in the day when they could leave work an hour early and beat traffic to her office. Her bonus and recent promotion was a badly needed cushion after he got laid off. Once, they had wanted four children; now, Molly was uncertain if she wanted another child, let alone several, and Kyle's image of a family was beginning to fade. He thumbed the stray hairs back off Ellie's brow. He stood slowly, careful not to make the mattress rise too fast, crept downstairs, and opened the sliding door to the backyard. Outside, the late-evening sun was beginning to set, and it was that time of autumn when the days were warm but as soon as the sun set, it became unbearably cold.

He stood on the patio, and remembered when he was a teenager at St. Xavier, and the starting quarterback of Cincinnati's number-one team. He missed the certainty of football's controlled aggression. He pictured the dogwoods at the end of his yard as goalposts, and he moved with quick hops, bouncing backwards, feeling the pass rush and stepping forward, the sound of pads slamming into one another, hard grunts and curses, the brush of meaty hands pawing at him. The crowd roared. Eyes downfield, elbow up, the wide receiver running ahead, making the cut but not yet open, and here it was, the anticipation of the crisp pass, the knowledge of where his teammate would go if he placed the pass just right, firing the football into the air, the ball spinning perfectly against the Friday night lights, and his teammate, hands out and in perfect stride, catching the ball and racing into the end zone. The cheering crowd; the band playing the school fight song; the public address announcer's voice muddled but elated. Kyle carried on the shoulders of his lineman, the crisp autumn smell of work and victory. He imagined all this with startling clarity, and its vividness made his chest ache with longing for this glory, this purpose.

Kyle pulled out a chair from their lawn set, and dropped. With his foot he dragged another chair close, the metal scraping the concrete, and propped up his legs. The sound of the scraping was still echoing in his ears, the tiny vibrations in his calves, when he heard the garage door mechanically tug up the rails and come to a jolting halt. Molly was home.

When they had first moved in, they would make dinner together, talking in the dining room long after their plates were empty and the food in the kitchen was cold; later, she was reading books on motherhood, shopping for baby furniture online. Now she came home and collapsed on the couch, exhausted, barely interested in him or Ellie, and she would recite the events of the day with a dispassionate anger, as if she was the sole survivor of a horrific act of mass violence and was reciting the facts to a historian. He shifted on the cold metal and waited for her to find him. The sliding door pushed open.

"What are you doing out here?" she said.

"Sitting."

"It's getting cold."

"Then bring me a blanket."

He could feel her standing there, considering the demand. Then he heard the door close and reopen, then her shoes clacked on the concrete and an afghan was around his shoulders, its thick fabric settling against his neck.

Molly walked to the chair opposite his and placed her hands on her hips. The setting sun was behind her, forcing Kyle to squint, the tints of gray in her blonde hair visible in the light. She was pear-shaped, and the extra weight from pregnancy hadn't fully come off, giving her figure a more natural and pleasing appearance, almost as if motherhood was what finally grew her into her body. Her eyes, hard and small, seemed to expect denials and evasions, and in her tailored charcoal suit, she appeared in control. Seeing her this way, Kyle missed wearing a tie, the snug fit of the silk knot around his neck. For a moment, her jaw tensed and the veins in her neck stood out. Then, with what seemed like enormous effort, her face softened, and she gave him a playful smile. "Guess who I saw today?"

"That was today?" Kyle leaned forward. "Who came back?"

"This time it was him."

They were one of Molly's first client couples. Handsome in middle age, with fine jewelry and expensive haircuts, these clients were both on their second marriage, and during the initial screening with Molly, they held hands, smiled at each other's jokes, agreed on their financial goals—retirement, college funding for their four pre-teen children, vacations every year, setting up their investment properties as a limited liability corporation, and so forth. But ten minutes after they left together, the wife called back, returned to the office, and admitted to owning nearly fifty thousand dollars in accounts hidden from her husband. Over the years, Molly discovered that he too had assets his wife didn't know about, and periodically, she met with them individually to discuss their secret accounts.

"What happened?" Kyle asked.

"I knew one of them would call. They came in separate cars. Five minutes after they left, he called from the parking lot and came back upstairs."

"What did he want?"

"Nothing interesting. He still has accounts in the Caymans, and he just wanted to check their status. He said once they were for his youngest son to go to college, but I doubt it. I don't think the money is actually for anything."

Kyle drummed his fingers on the table. "I took a philosophy class in college, and we had to do a thought experiment. Did you ever do one of those? Where you imagine something to prove a theory? Anyway, we had to imagine having twenty million dollars under our bed. But the thing was, we couldn't tell anyone we had it and we couldn't spend it."

"So the money is worthless."

"Exactly. It's just paper in a box. There's no value when it can't buy something."

"But it has. It bought my client peace of mind."

"Happiness?"

"Maybe not happiness. Something else." She flattened her hands and spread her fingers as wide as she could. She pursed her lips, concentrating on her knuckles, and the tension ebbed back into her face. "Why are you sitting out here?"

"You already asked me that. I don't know." He crossed his arms. "Ellie and I went to the Natural History Museum today."

"The pterodactyls? Did she like them?"

"Loved them. I got her a stuffed one from the museum store."

She eased back into her chair. He squeezed his hands together and waited for the lecture about overindulging their daughter and spending money he was no longer earning.

"I had a Popple when I was a girl. Remember those?"

"Popples?" Kyle cocked his head. "You never told me that."

"Sure I did. I had this Popple, orange with blue ears. I called her Maggie."

"Are you sure you told me this?"

She waved a dismissive hand. "Of course. I slept with that thing until I was almost ten. Sometimes Maggie was a bear. Other times, I curled her into a ball by rolling her into her front pocket. Imagine you could fold a kangaroo into its own pouch and make it a ball. It was like that. I bet my mom still has it somewhere in my old room."

"Isn't it weird how much Ellie loves dinosaurs?"

"I don't think so. I had a Popple."

Kyle shrugged.

"Hey," she said. "What's wrong?"

What was wrong was that she asked this question without placing a hand on him, or leaning across the table and rubbing his forearm, without coming behind him and wrapping her arms around him so she could breathe in the faint scent of his spicy, thick aftershave that still lingered this late in the day, and he could again feel significant. What was wrong was that he didn't quite know that he felt all of this. He tugged the afghan around his shoulders.

"I lost Ellie today."

"You lost her?"

"We were at the museum and I got really interested in a display, and when I looked back down, she had wandered off."

"Is she okay?"

"Fine. She didn't think anything of it."

"She isn't hurt."

"She's fine. I'm upset. Could you ask about me, just once?"

He stood, knocking over his chair, the metal shuddering against the concrete. He marched into the house and snatched the nearest glass. From the freezer he grabbed the vodka and took a long drink. The vodka's burn down his throat was a relief. Why hadn't Serena remembered him? He filled the glass with ice and poured another, and stood in his kitchen, his breath and the sounds of the outdoors—the hum of a lawn mower, the squawks of birds—creeping into his ears. When he returned, Molly sat unmoved with her arms folded across her chest and her lips drawn tight.

"Do you wish my hair was longer?" she asked.

He sensed she already knew the answer. When they were young, he had liked to sneak up behind her and brush her hair aside and kiss the nape of her neck, wrap his arms around her. She had cut it short after Ellie was born: she hated getting their daughter's tiny, sticky hands tangled in her hair.

"Longer?" he repeated.

"Like when we first met."

"I love you no matter how your hair is."

She frowned. "That wasn't very convincing. And that's not what I'm asking."

He focused on some distant point at the end of the yard. She stood up and went inside; when she returned, she was carrying the vodka and a glass. She poured a large drink and left it untouched on the table; Kyle held his glass in his lap with both hands as if it could save him.

"A guy in my office made a pass at me about a month ago."

Kyle snorted.

"Why is that funny? That's not possible?"

"No, sorry. I didn't mean it like that."

"Yes, you did." She picked up her glass but didn't drink. "It was at the end of the day and we were reviewing some client agreements in my office. The door was open. I'd leaned over to write something and he slid his hand over mine. I locked our fingers. And then, with his other hand, he gently ran his fingers into my hair, right above the collar."

"What did you do?"

"Nothing. That was it. We looked at each other, and I could feel that I was smiling, and then I said something dumb about going home, and he nodded, because he's married too, and that was it. And then I came home."

"You didn't kiss him?"

"Aren't you hearing me? I came home. You asked me what I did, and what I did was come home."

"And you think you shouldn't have."

"You aren't listening. I came home. To you. To Ellie. And what do I get? Vague accusations about, Christ, who knows what?"

"You have no idea what I go through every day."

She tapped the rim of her glass, and stared at him. "That's bullshit," she said evenly. "You're being ridiculous right now. I'm sorry you got laid off, I really am, because that's hard on both of us. But whatever existential crisis you're going through needs to stop. Right now."

Kyle pushed the blanket off his shoulders; he wanted to feel cold and be able to complain about it. Somehow, he lost all sense of what it was that made him sit outside in the first place, what it was that hollowed and angered him about his life.

"There was an old man," he said, hopeful and aware of how manipulative this would be. "He didn't tell me his name. But I was running around the museum looking for Ellie and he helped me. He was so calm. It was like when I was a boy and watching TV with my father, and resting my head against his belly, and how soothing it was the way his chest would rise and fall, rise and fall." He folded his arms across his chest and gave what he believed was a sad smile. "That's how it felt today, soothed, like all the things I was worried about would be okay."

"Jesus Christ, what are you talking about?"

Kyle fumed. His head throbbed and he set his empty glass down on the table. The ice rattled like broken piano keys. He lowered his head and scratched his fingers back over his scalp, wishing he could tear the skin from his skull.

"I'll start dinner," she said. "Come inside when you're ready to start acting normal."

She stood up, and after Kyle heard the door close, he walked into the yard, the grass swishing against the cuffs of his pants, the lawn's unevenness now obvious. The three dogwood trees were spaced evenly apart, and the grass was green, neat, and dark. A few autumn leaves sprinkled his lawn. Where did those come from? He glanced at the other backyards, and couldn't see the splashes of brown and orange and red. He saw a uniform, solid green. When the season did turn and the leaves bled fully into their dying colors, he would only see change when every tree was dropping its leaves, when the fall could no longer be ignored.

He turned. Upstairs was all dark. A sliver of light appeared. Ellie's door had opened. Downstairs, through the kitchen window, Molly was preparing dinner, ducking in and out of sight, hot steam rising from the kitchen sink invisible beneath the frame, and he wondered what it was she was making. The ray of light above was gone. Then, directly in front of him, through the sliding doors, Ellie appeared. Several lights were flipped on, throwing a soft glow on the family room, and she turned on the television. She sat down on the floor, holding something in her hands. Kyle was aware then that he always moved on someone else's time—his wife's, his daughter's—and the idea of being left alone to choose suddenly frightened him. The lit windows of his house looked tangible and close. Above, the darkness upstairs, like a great nebulous sky devoid of clouds, hovered over his family, framed in the spotless, unmoving glass. He saw his life with a new brilliance. He saw that living in dreams was a dangerous thing. Kyle moved forward, closing the visual of his house, which had appeared unreal and too large, walking onto the concrete, past the blanket and his empty glass, and pulled open the sliding door. Neither his daughter nor his wife acknowledged his presence, and inside it was warm, the air thick with a smell of oregano and garlic that Kyle did not notice. He moved toward Ellie.

She sat cross-legged on the floor, the pterodactyl in her lap. On the screen, cartoon characters Kyle didn't recognize argued about which direction to go: toward a waterfall or into the forest.

He bent down, his arches tugging painfully away from bone, and his knees popped and groaned as if carbonated. He put his hands on Ellie's shoulders and rested his chin on the crown of her head.

"They're lost," she said.

"Who?" He pressed his lips to the back of her head, closed his eyes, and imagined nothing.

SPARRING VLADIMIR PUTIN

At the beginning of President Clinton's second term, I was waking up in a different European hotel room almost every morning. Ohio, the state of which I'd been governor for eight years, had just elected my handpicked successor in a landslide. I was one of those New Democrats who believed we were going to change the world with our progressive policies and union-friendly wink and nods, with our sly, wannabe-JFK charm. Kicking off my damp sheets, shaken awake by my own nightmares about shadowy figures outside my window dumping poison into the ventilation system, I stared beyond my tangled legs, over the neat piles of luggage, and into the adjacent room where stacks of classified documents and dark brown folders lay on the dining room table. I blinked and remembered the cities I had just seen: Oslo, Tallinn, Riga, Minsk. Squeezing the bridge of my nose, the fear of a hangover sending me in search of vitamins and tomato juice, I vaguely remembered I was flying to Ukraine.

Climbing the stairs to a government-issue Boeing, ready to fly from Vilinus to Kiev, I clutched my attaché case to my chest. Inside was a day-old copy of *The New York Times*. I hurried to the tiny cabin in the back of the plane, closed the door, and poured a hair of the dog. Buried on page seventeen next to a half-page ad for a Neiman Marcus sale was the news I was looking for: Tony Erpenbeck, perhaps the sole reason I had become mayor of Cincinnati twenty years ago, had just been charged with federal bank fraud, tax evasion, and regulatory violations of building and safety codes in three states. Erpenbeck was the guy who swung the union votes in west Cincinnati to get me elected mayor and, in return, I looked the other way when he violated building and safety codes for his regional development empire. Now, Erpenbeck told the press that he had acted on the orders of Matt Bowman—my handpicked successor as governor who had won in a landslide, a friend from high school, a political ally for thirty years, and the go-between I had used to secure the deal with Erpenbeck all those years ago. Bowman wasn't yet talking but I knew that if he did, he would be talking about me.

"You aren't supposed to be reading that," a voice said.

I looked up. Alain Hellmuth stood in the cabin doorway. He was the point man on this trip, my liaison whose job was to report back to the White House that I was cooperating and waving the Stars and Stripes. He was a thin man with a paunch, wispy hair, and frameless glasses, and in every nation I visited he remained stuck to my elbow, a navy blue White House planner tucked under his arm. He loved using words like "feedback" and "monetize." I hadn't heard him come in. To test my ears, I rattled the ice cubes in my glass of scotch.

"Too late now," I said. "Am I in any additional shit, or is this goodwill trip the end of it?" I was supposed to be assigned the ambassadorship to Ireland. I was supposed to be living in Dublin, with a small cottage in County Kilkenny my wife and I could escape to on the weekend, invite our children to take a break from college and visit the Emerald Isle, raise sheep and goats, go dance a few jigs at local pubs. Instead, someone's Big Idea shuttled me out of the country on a contrived five-week swing through Eastern Europe to shake hands with mid-level politicians, assess the fundamentals of each nation's precarious economy, and solemnly tour an endless array of World War II memorials, while the whole budding scandal in Ohio would, in theory, be handled by the Clinton administration. So far, they appeared to have slippery fingers.

"These things are under control," Hellmuth said. "You don't need to worry about it. You need to focus on this trip. You can relax, and provide us with a lot of good information."

"You guys know this." I picked up the Lithuania NSA and Economic Viability Assessment and flung it at Hellmuth's feet. "I'm not evaluating anything for you. Capitalism good, socialism bad. Join the EU. I know the drill." I finished the last finger of scotch.

"It's a little early for that," Hellmuth said.

"I honestly have no idea what time it is."

"Nine-thirty in the morning. And you've been here for four weeks."

"I'm bad with numbers."

Hellmuth sat down across from me, our knees almost touching. I listened to the ignorable hum of the jet engine, and curled my toes on the rug.

"David," Hellmuth said. "I know this is frustrating for you. You will be our next ambassador to Ireland. I promise you that and, more importantly, the President has promised you that. These confirmations take time, especially after a nasty election when the Senate wants to pick apart every single nominee. This is the kind of trip that looks good and makes people happy. We saw how you controlled Ohio for eight years—these meet-and-greet trips are what you excel at. And you know why you sometimes need to do a little acting for the crowds."

This was true: I won Ohio with a slew of barnstorming and impromptu speeches, my pretty wife Lucia at my side, an American flag in the background. I was the first Democrat governor of Ohio in twenty-four years, and my administration accomplished the following: a hold on taxes, wins in education reform, a couple of court appointments that made everyone happy, and a steady stream of white-collar jobs into the big C's— Cleveland, Columbus, and Cincinnati—all while keeping the farmers happy with a sly dose of pork from the boys in Washington. Once, I had been bulletproof.

"I haven't seen Lucia in four weeks," I said. "It's January! We wear three pairs of socks, wool overcoats, scarves, hats, and I'm still freezing my ass off."

"You're going home in four days and of all the countries we've visited, Ukraine is the most important to us. Russia wants to keep the countries on its borders, particularly the ones with access to open waters, under its thumb."

"And you want me to tell you that Ukraine can be the next Ireland in fifteen years. Yeah, I got it." I cracked my knuckles. "I spent the last three months reading up on Ireland. You know, the Celtic Tiger, their tech boom we don't want to miss out on? Connect with Boston, our biggest tech hub outside of Silicon Valley?" I slumped deeper into my chair.

"You know," Hellmuth said, crossing his legs. He stared at a point above my head and forced a dreamy look as if he could see Disney sheep leaping over the moon. "I'm always charmed thinking about your name. When I think that you were named for Davey Crockett. And that last name! Joyce. Wow." He shook his head. "Very Irish. It could be a great asset in Dublin."

I sobered up: I used flattery before threats a thousand times, a song-and-dance routine as familiar to me as the face I saw in the mirror every morning.

"What's your point?" I asked.

"Don't embarrass yourself, David. You've been given a very easy penance." I blinked at that, and tightened my jaw. "Slam dunk the last days of this trip and your problems, our problems, go away. You'll be in Dublin by St. Patrick's Day. But you need to play ball."

It had been a few years since I had been on the short end of the political stick. Unsure what to do, I simply stared at the bridge of his nose.

"We touch down in about ninety minutes," Hellmuth continued. "Go shave. Do your exercises, call your wife, whatever you need to do, but get it together." He stood, smoothed his tie, and left the room.

I stood up, and looked around the small cabin. Two chairs faced two others; there was a small sink to my right with cabinets above. The doors behind me led to the main cabin, the opposite doors led to the small sleeping bunk I had on the plane. I went into that room, and looked at my sad sack of Samsonite luggage, the three bags I had been living out of for a month. I had, barely, enough room to do my tai chi exercises, which had been my morning ritual for nearly a dozen years. In my youth, I had been a national champion in judo; at some point in my political career, for appearances, I shifted my studies to tai chi. Once a year I let a photographer take shots of me on the back lawn of the governor's mansion so that I could charm women and the twenty-something collegiate crowd with my quasi-Zen and better-than-average looks.

I folded the small, uncomfortable bed up against the wall, removed my socks, and took fifteen deep breaths. I bent down to my toes, held the stretch in my hamstrings, then raised my arms high over my head and held that until I was no longer conscious of where I was. I moved smoothly, the stale cabin air batting against the back of my throat and into my lungs, the coarse carpet beneath my feet rubbing my soles as I pivoted. I exhaled, feeling the wonderful looseness of my muscles.

I showered, then called Lucia. No one answered the phone. Like me, she felt the absence of our youngest of three children, Amy, who had just left in the fall for her freshman year at Harvard, a fact that left my working-class roots pulsating with pride. I pictured my empty house. When I left, the kitchen island lay buried under a stack of travel books on Ireland; beneath those was our last phone bill with the rather large three-figure balance cataloging our recent flurry of phone calls back to her family in Gweebarra. On mornings like this, standing with my ear pressed against a slim phone that rang and rang, I remembered my wedding, the hundreds of family and cousins there, all Irish, most of whom I had never met, kissing me on the cheek and dancing with me and my wife. I set the receiver down, waited a moment for my loneliness to pass, and prepared myself for Kiev.

The plane taxied to a stop and the stairs led down to the tarmac. The runway and airport looked gray and abandoned; I turned in a circle and looked at the surrounding area, flat and devoid of life. Nobody met the plane. I looked back at my group; twelve bureaucrats in navy suits stared back like spooked wild animals. Someone made a phone call and twenty minutes later, four black Suburbans with tinted windows showed up and we were shuttled off to the embassy. We took Khreshchatik Street and drove past the metro station and the recently renovated Golden Gate, an old fortress structure from centuries ago, and entered Independence Square. A small church sat on its northwestern corner, across from the train station. Next to it was a McDonald's.

After checking our bags, we promptly headed over to the Rada, Ukraine's parliament, and introduced ourselves to President Leonid Kuchma. He was a portly man with thick jowls and bloodshot eyes; his hands twittered nervously as he spoke, and I got the sense that he was somebody's figurehead. Ukraine was, like so many other nations I had seen, a banana republic. Kuchma led us down the hallway, and introduced me to Victor Pinchuk. His face was greasy and his thinning hair looked like it had been combed back with mud. Kuchma stood straight, tried to appear sober and confident, failed at both, his eyes growing bleary as Pinchuk began to talk. It was pretty obvious who was in charge.

Pinchuk owned a conglomerate called Interpipe Group, which held interests in industry, media, and banking; his core product was steel pipes. His empire also dabbled in politics—he was a deputy in the Rada, hence his corner suite, the walls covered in official-looking photos of him shaking hands with diplomats and secretaries of state. He employed, he told us (repeatedly), over thirty thousand people, and had power over the rest of the country through his political heft in the parliament.

I nodded at him. "How do you reconcile your business interests with your political interests?"

He shrugged. "If I am a businessman, first I will think about my shirt, because my shirt is closer to my body. In my country they call it corruption. In yours, they call it business as usual, yes?"

He had a point, and I didn't particularly feel like arguing with him.

Pinchuk took us on a tour through the Rada, a stately building designed in a blend of Roman and Byzantine influences. From what I had gathered from my meeting with Pinchuk and Kuchma and my late-night reading nursed by a couple of brandies, the Rada was a coterie of wealthy powerbrokers and oligarchs. Heading to the second floor, I looked down onto the parliament floor and watched a small cluster of politicians trip over themselves to move away from a man in a gray suit. He strode past them like a lion hunting prey, his eyes bouncing from aisle to aisle, his straight posture and swinging arms conveying power. The Ukrainians, through smiles and cowering, seemed to love and fear him. He glanced up at my entourage and locked eyes with me; I thought he wanted to rip out my jugular. I nodded slightly and he cocked his head, looked ready to yell something that would incite a riot, changed his mind, and disappeared through a set of double doors. I looked back at my entourage to see if they had witnessed the same thing I had; they appeared still shackled to Pinchuk's long diatribe about who knows what. Pinchuk then led us outside, and directed our Suburbans to his steel factory on the western edge of town.

We trudged through the drab factory, and I did my best to treat the whole thing like a stroll through a Democrat enclave in Cleveland; Hellmuth, the shift from the Ukraine winter into the stifling factory fogging his glasses, and I appeared to be well-known by the manufactured crowds standing along our path, chirping my name—Mr. Joyce, Mr. Joyce, welcome! Bring us jobs they'd say, and when it came time for me to eddy by and shake a few gloved hands, they smiled ear to ear. Hellmuth shot me looks like I was Truman himself, unshakeable and misunderstood by everybody, and up we'd go, rising to the next crowd of underpaid workers cheering themselves hoarse, each man rolled off the line to impress the American. Somewhere, a band pumped through a few bars of the Ukrainian anthem and the factory managers stared at us like we were furniture movers. The local politicians, reeking of booze, yawned. Pinchuk glanced at his workers like they were litter blowing across a vacant street.

"In all the world," Pinchuk said, leading us up steel steps to an office. "Rich people are very unpopular." He had continued in this vein the entire trip and though I was unsure whether he was trying to convince me or just pander to his entourage, I smiled and nodded at the proper inflections of his voice and thought about what Lucia would be doing at home just then. We entered the floor manager's office, a rust-colored room whose scratched windows looked down on the factory floor. Pinchuk continued to pontificate about his work: an AIDS foundation run by his wife, an orchestra hall he had built in Dnipropetrovsk, a theatre in Moscow, and something he referred to as a "cultural center" in Kiev. I bit my tongue and muffled the urge to laugh.

There was a knock on the door, and without waiting for an answer, it opened, and the man in the gray suit entered, surrounded by three additional men in black suits. He smiled and seemed more at ease compared to when I had seen him earlier. Pinchuk started speaking Russian to the smallest of the three men in black who, when he addressed me, spoke in perfect English and called himself Yergushov. He presented me to his boss, the man in gray, Vladimir Putin.

His grip was vise-like, but his palm cool and artificial. I had no idea who he was, but he looked younger than me, perhaps in his forties, and I guessed he spent a great deal of time outside exercising. He had an aquiline face and a look of general amusement with the people around him.

"A pleasure to meet you," he said. "I hear your youngest daughter recently enrolled at Harvard. Congratulations."

"Thank you," I said, trying to remember if my intel junket had said anything about a Russian diplomat swooping in. "I wasn't aware you'd be joining us."

His laugh was like a broken muffler, spastic and metallic, and he smiled at us as if there was no greater pleasure on earth than my weak attempt at politeness. The Ukrainians laughed on cue. It didn't take much for me to figure out they were scared shitless. I glanced at Hellmuth, and with my eyes asked: who the hell is this and why don't you goddamn know?

"Diplomacy can be so boring," Putin said. "A few surprises, that is what politics needs. Besides, our countries, though allies, are very much competitors, wouldn't you agree?"

"I think both of us are competing with China now."

"Yes, that is true. I'm sad to say that we are not the superpower we once were. But that will change soon."

We toured the design and architecture offices on the opposite end of the plant, why, I don't know. Putin's equivalent of Hellmuth did the majority of the yapping, with Hellmuth himself making pointed remarks punctuated by pointing gestures. Hellmuth made a call on his cell phone, then looked at me blankly, letting me know he was digging up what he could on our new host. Pinchuk fell into a sullen silence, and I was thrilled I no longer had to stare at his unctuous smile. Putin seemed as pleasantly bored as I was, and as soon as the tour was over, we decided to ride in the same Suburban back to the embassy. The security forces looked at us as if we had asked to roll in mint jelly and run through the streets of Kiev in kilts.

So our conversation was delayed until we arrived at the embassy. I excused myself to change shirts, and in my room, on the dining room table, found a slim manila folder about Putin. I flipped quickly: He was KGB for twenty years, working out of East Germany. Law degree, expert in sambo, which is some kind of Russian judo. For the last three years he was St. Petersburg's first deputy chairman of the city government and chairman of the committee for external relations. Yeltsin had just made him the first official business manager of Russia. I tossed the folder on the table and chewed the inside of my cheek: the folder said I was in deep shit.

I changed from a white shirt to a blue one, skipped the tie, and hurried back downstairs to a large banquet room, the tables set with gold and crystal dinnerware and the oak-paneled walls covered with oil paintings of dead Russian luminaries. I hurried past the politicians, brushing aside smiles and extended hands, ignored the food, went straight to the bar, and asked for a bottle of vodka and two glasses, then worked my way over to a corner to wait. Putin found me after three drinks, sat down, and threw back two shots as quick as lightning.

He knew all about my problems. He made a crack about homebuilding, and I asked what gulag he had been raised in. I told him about what it was like having a vicious ex-wife and a wonderful current one and trying to understand what the younger me hadn't been able to see in the first place. He talked about espionage, the way a person breaks, the distinct pleasure he got in making someone talk. I praised the political machine I had built, the way a few animalistic approaches like staring a man down and leaning in when talking to a state senator could make my bills undefeatable. He bemoaned licking the boots of incompetent politicians, doing the "yes, sir" dance for twenty years, all the while wishing he could get a few of those clowns into his interrogation rooms with no windows or cameras or witnesses. In short, I liked him right away.

"What is your wife doing now?" Putin asked.

"Lucia works for the Columbus Arts Foundation. Community theatre, grant writing, stuff like that." I chuckled. "Like Pinchuck."

"Fuck that guy," Putin said. He laughed his muffler laugh. "Ten years ago I'd have had him in a room with no windows, and in five minutes," he said, holding up his left hand, "I would have him signing his miserable life over to me."

He balanced his glass on his right knee. As he talked about mind games and torture, I studied his right hand. His grip on the glass, tenuous and weak, like dying worms baking on the sidewalk after a rainstorm.

"More?" he said, nodding at my glass. My tolerance had soared over my last month of drinks at every meal, but I felt the vodka corroding my stomach. Still, the idea that he was weak, that I had found a button on the button-pusher, made me agree with a frat boy's reckless confidence.

"I'll get it," Putin said, dismissing an aide. "I need the fresh, cigar-filled air." I leaned back in the club chair, oddly aware of how comfortable and expensive it was, and tried to focus on how to play Putin. I couldn't shake the one thought that despite my intentions, my need to please Washington by securing some victory on a scoreboard that didn't exist wouldn't vanish: I really liked my unofficial counterpart, my new buddy, Vlad the Interrogator.

Putin appeared, heading toward me, carrying two bottles of vodka in his left arm. His weakness, then, seemed amplified: he dragged the entire right side of his body. From his walk, I imagined he had spent years hiding it. I couldn't imagine how this man, his right arm swinging like a dead fish, his right leg hobbled, could hide it so well. If I hadn't known to look for it, I would never have seen it, but right then, watching his flushed face, his broad grin that I knew I was mirroring, I could see Vladimir as a boy, training to get stronger and fitter, limping through cold Russian winters, battling his body, fighting who he was to be something his own muscles and bones told him he would never be.

Halfway through the second bottle, I decided to hell with it and asked.

"What happened to you?" I said.

"What do you mean?" Alcohol hadn't weakened his studied English accent. I felt like drool rushed down my cracked lips like a broken faucet.

"Your body. Your hand." I pointed. "What happened?"

Putin sat up erect, and he seemed as sober as a priest.

"I'm guessing polio," I said.

"I do not know what you are talking about."

"That's cool," I said, waving my hand. I sucked down another shot, and poured another for both of us. "I'm amazed, that's all. You hide it well. That's what I admire. It's amazing, really. I mean it." I wondered why I was telling him the truth.

Putin crouched down, and rested his elbows on his knees. He waited.

"Neurologically," I said. "It's unheard of. Not a whisper of it in my files. You being KGB, all our CIA Virginia farmboys, and nothing, not a single note about any kind of disability or injury. How did that happen? I'll tell you—they aren't seeing it. They aren't looking for it. They're judging, not understanding, not understanding character." I sipped my vodka. "Character. A constitution. Uncorruptable and fearless."

Putin's jaw relaxed. He nodded slowly, then lifted his glass and clinked it against mine.

"Thank you, David." He swallowed his drink, and eased deep into his chair. I did the same, and we sat quiet, amid the noise, under the curious exchanged glances of the aides protecting us, sitting out of range of hearing.

The weight of the moment, and the vodka in my stomach, too great, I leaned forward and grinned.

"Did I ever tell you I was named after Davey Crockett?"

Putin squinted at me. Then he let loose his Russian laugh and I told him the story.

We finished our last bottle, and with the help of some aides, stood on our shaky feet, allowing them to lead us to the elevators. Putin and I whistled *The Ballad of Davey Crockett*, and then we began to sing it, making up the words we didn't know (which were most of them). We laughed and stumbled and said our hearty goodbyes with a firm handshake and shoulder slaps, and once Hellmuth deposited me on the couch in my room and left, closing the door with a heavy wooden thud, I staggered to the bathroom and made a pre-emptive strike on a hangover by shoving my finger down my throat and vomiting up a liter of high-quality Russian vodka. I then passed out on the floor next to the balcony windows.

In the morning, I woke with my head pressed against the cool doorframe. I rolled onto my back, and looked around the room. At the dining room table, Hellmuth ate breakfast and read the current *Le Monde*.

"How did you get back in here?"

He smirked and looked up from the paper. "Don't you understand that you're the puppet and I'm the puppeteer? Haven't you caught on?"

I stood, sat down at the table, and took his plate of food. My stomach rumbled, and I pushed the poached eggs and wheat toast back to Hellmuth.

"I like Vladimir," I offered.

"That's super," Hellmuth said, clearing his throat. "Putin would like to be our tour guide today."

"Where to?"

"The monastery caves. It's in the old part of town."

"Good idea?"

"You'd rather tour more steel factories?"

I shrugged and looked out the window. Across the river, I could see old Kiev: the Byzantine spires and churches of the ancient caves. I felt an urgent desire to fly back to Ohio and never seek public office again.

"How soon?" I looked at my watch—it was almost ten and I had no idea what time I had passed out.

"Noon," Hellmuth said, looking over his glasses. "Your drinking buddy doesn't like to get up before eleven."

Two hours later, Putin and his entourage met us in the lobby. He had a *USA Today* folded under his arm. The line of Suburbans waited for us outside, and this time, they were prepared for Putin and me to ride in the same van.

"You told me you practice tai chi, yes?" he asked.

"Not this morning," I said. Through the tinted windows, I could see the unsmiling faces of people scurrying to work, their heads wrapped in thick scarves and bulky hats.

"Head hurt?"

"No, I'm fine. Just didn't think of it today." This truth puzzled me; my shoulders, in knots from sleeping on the floor, tightened and I shifted my back for relief. "I passed out on the floor," I admitted. Putin laughed hard, even snorted once.

Our caravan took us out of the new stretch of Kiev; the wide boulevards narrowed and our large caravan squeezed through the narrow streets once designed for pedestrians and street vendors. The taller structures faded away and the city sloped toward the Dnipro. Small freighters dotted the western side of the river, and the water was a spectacular color of blue. My head aching, I tried to remember where Chernobyl was from Kiev.

The eastern side of town was a different world; modern structures vanished, and the Byzantine architecture was everywhere. The smaller huts in sandy brown colors dotted the landscape, sliding toward the river as if all the concrete buildings had thirsty roots; Russian Orthodox architecture, particularly churches, sprouted on boulevards, and all the brick buildings had beautiful stone archways. The engraved dates on the cornerstones dated back several centuries, and large, glimmering domes peeked through the horizon.

"You'll like this, David," he said. "Very peaceful. Very tai chi." I laughed—Putin was busting my balls.

Our caravan pulled up to the back of the museum. The driveway was nestled between small, formidable hills. Our security forces swept the immediate area, then held the doors for us. Putin met the curator, shook hands, posed for pictures. I remained in the background. I felt like I was watching the Ohio version of myself, the false obseqiousness of a politician charming a crowd. I witnessed myself, and became awashed in revulsion and anger. I hated what I saw in myself, what was mirrored in Putin.

The museum was the monastery caves of Pecherska Lavra. Putin guided our group through the collection of golden treasures of the Gaimanov and Tolstaya graves. I had no idea what he was talking about. Still, I was impressed by how much he seemed to not just know, but that he loved being a guide. He possessed a genuine awe for these ancient people whose lives were nothing more than museum attractions, and I couldn't help but feel that our lives were destined to be the same: something on display for tourists, the fanatical, the lonely.

Putin talked endlessly, and with time, his aides and my aides stopped listening and conversed quietly among themselves; I was his lone audience. He lectured on the burial mounds of Samaritan queens, the Persian influence on the region, the skill of Kievian jewelers which, he said, could be seen in the temple pendants and golden shoulder bands, and more recently, in the miters and chalices.

"How many people get this personal tour?" I asked.

He shrugged. "My wife used to listen, when we lived in Germany. She finds it amusing now, like a parlor trick. But she does not enjoy the museums as much."

"Is Lyudmila back in Leningrad?"

"Yes. Classes start soon. And your Lucia? Did you talk to her today?"

I hadn't called my wife since I touched down in Kiev. I made up a yarn about Lucia traveling to Boston to visit Amy. Putin seemed pleased with this answer.

We entered a dark room lit only by archaic lamps in the corners, a restored Tolstaya grave of a Scythian king buried with his son. Vladimir was silent. To the right, underneath a glass case, was a short akinaka sword and its gold sheath, decorated with jewels. I stared at the akinaka, its steel gleaming sharp and lethal. I looked at the hilt, and wondered how heavy the sword was.

Vladimir walked over and stood next to me.

"Did you fight in wars?" he asked.

"Two tours in Vietnam."

"I remember seeing *Patton*. The movie. Toward the end, Patton looked over the wreckage of the war and he remarked how much he loved it. He hated himself for it, but he did love the battle."

"Do you feel the same way?" I asked.

"I am not big on guns." He shrugged. "The Cold War was a war with no battles, no fights. I was an intelligence officer. It was not the same."

I thought for a moment. "What about judo?"

He tilted his head back and looked to the ceiling, as if he had just finished a deeply satisfying meal. "A great sport. Hand-to-hand. Strength and balance."

"I last did it a few years ago. A group of Chinese businessmen were coming through Columbus, and thought it would be fun. I cracked a rib."

"Since?"

"Just tai chi."

He nodded. I looked at him, and sensed, I was certain, contempt, a withering disdain for a slightly older statesman who he believed had let his best years pass him by.

"I'm still good," I said. "My strength is still there."

"Is it?"

I looked around the room, and his eyes followed. The grave's treasures reflected the king's warlord life: golden plaques and pendants, a massive pectoral victory shield detailing triumphs, swords and iron spears, stolen jeweled chests of Scythian life. For a moment, I thought we could shake off our ties, remove our shoes, and try to beat the hell out of each other right there. Putin seemed to be weighing something very carefully. I swung my head back around, and stared him down.

"Tonight, we will spar," he said. "There is space in my hotel. I will make the arrangements."

There always is that rush, the adrenaline, when bullets fly and the ground explodes, and while you and your platoon are still alive and not missing any limbs or screaming for a medic, before the body count and severed limbs, there is something primal in it that I did, I must admit, love.

I said, "I look forward to it."

Around six, a bellhop delivered to me a judogi. The white

cloth of the jacket and pants was thick and pristine. The black belt was of the same quality. I tried on the uniform, and it fit perfectly. At first I was annoyed that Vladimir could find a uniform in my exact dimensions, but then I remembered he was ex-KGB, and admired how quickly he could get information. I looked in the mirror. Before leaving for Europe, I wore overpriced workout gear made for health club members and rich tennis-playing executives. I tried to picture what my face looked like in a combat zone—calm, perhaps, or furious, or scared—and I had no idea.

After dinner in my room, Hellmuth and I took our group to Putin's hotel. Like all the hotels in Kiev's business district, it had a stately quality, European and glamorous. We were directed to a banquet room at the end of a long hallway of thick red carpeting with tiny intricate square patterns, and the walls were decorated with armaments and artwork of past rulers and noblemen of the region. We entered the room from the far-right corner; in the middle was a large blue mat. Folding chairs were set at each corner; Putin's corner and my own had a small table next to the chair. Neat rows of metal folding chairs surrounded the mat on all four sides. Our small group of twelve Americans was bunched around my corner, and after spending four weeks with them, I finally noticed how exhausted they were, how, like me, all they wanted to do at this point was go home. I guessed roughly two hundred people had filled the room: dozens of Rada members, influencial oligarchs, Putin's small entourage. Against the far wall, several tables had been set up for food and drinks; large platters of cold cuts, plates of caviar, dozens of bottles of alcohol, and in the center, a large roasted pig with an apple in its mouth. Cooks and waiters shuffled out the heated trays of hors d'ouevres. I felt like a circus freak.

"Your idea or his?" Hellmuth asked. "I'm still not clear on that."

"Mine. I think." For a moment, I couldn't remember who suggested it either. I tried not to think of my career. "Should I try to win?"

"Do you think you can win?"

We studied the room for a quiet moment.

"Have you ever punched someone, Alain?"

"I sucker-punched our high school quarterback. He took out the girl I had a crush on. I broke his nose. The other guys on the team kicked my ass."

"But you broke his nose."

Alain bounced on his toes. "Damn right I did."

"Did you ever get the girl?"

"Nope. I met my wife at Yale. First and last girlfriend. We've been together for twelve years."

I wondered if Lucia was at home, or if she would have gone to a movie or dinner with some friends, and what time it would be in Columbus if I called her when I got back to my room that night. I smiled: I was beginning to like Alain.

Then, cheering; we swiveled our eyes to the opposite corner. Putin had entered. His contrived insouciance was gone and he ignored the suits and the bodyguards and the criminal mob in the audience to stare at me from across the room with the same animal ferocity as in the Rada. As the cheers from the opposite side of the room carried Putin—and his six surrounding bodyguards in gray suits and sunglasses with Kalashnikovs hanging from their shoulders—Hellmuth remarked there were no reporters. Near Putin's corner, on a folding chair in the first row, a young man in horn-rimmed glasses sat with a notebook perched on his knee. I pointed him out to Hellmuth, and he said he'd find out. I went to my corner, and sat down. On my table were three white towels, a stainless steel pitcher and a water glass, and a blue band; I attached it to my belt. Hellmuth returned with a smirk on his face.

"Putin's unofficial biographer," he said. I looked over at the scribe. He stared at me for what felt like a long time, then he giggled and scribbled furiously on his notepad.

Someone clapped two wooden sticks together three times, and the crowd took their seats. Two officials sat erect on their stools in opposite corners. The third official, an Asian man with a pointy chin, stood in the center of the ring and signaled us forward. We sat facing each other, insteps flush against the mat, and bowed, necks and backs straight. We were two meters apart. The ref signaled to us, and we stood.

He had been practicing; his technique was more fluid and natural than mine. I shuffled defensively, made some weak moves to counterattack, and basically stalled. He scored two quick half points, and when I realized his grappling technique was much better than mine, I stayed defensive, with the occasional feign to throw him. I was still fast enough to avoid getting pinned too quickly, but eventually he did, taking me down by throwing me in a knee-wheel move, and as soon as I hit the canvas, Putin moved me into a headlock, then pinned me on my back. The whole thing lasted maybe three minutes. We returned to our starting positions and bowed, my head spinning as I lowered it toward the ground. The crowd cheered.

"Again?" Putin asked. He looked like a hunter who had just bagged his first six-point buck.

"Sure," I said, a little winded. Judo events normally have quiet, respectful crowds, but fueled with alcohol, nationalism, and the obviously superior Putin, the crowd roared even louder. I tried again, once more becoming defensive, trying simply not to get pinned. The Russian cheers sounded boastful, and though I couldn't understand them, I believed they were mocking me, jeering me to be a man and fight and take my whipping. Putin scored a half point when he tossed me over his hip. I landed with my shoulders up, broke his grip on my collar, and tried to counter. He kept locking my arms as I tried to wrestle him to the ground; we both hit often, neither of us scoring points.

But in the middle of this local brouhaha, with a half point against me, I succeeded in countering Putin's attack. I caught his right hand and shifted his balance forward, bent my knees, lifted him onto my shoulders, pulled my left hand down to my chest and threw Putin over my body in one fluid motion. He hit the mat hard, and from the look on his face, it was probably the first time he'd really been rattled in years. The ref held his hand straight out: he had scored an obvious victory a *waza-ari*, a half point. Furious, I asked him what the fuck was his problem, but he didn't seem to understand English or care what I said and looked at me blankly. Putin took his time getting to his feet, his thick legs staggering, and when he attacked again, I grabbed his shoulder, buried my foot in his abdomen, rolled backwards and threw him even harder. Match over.

For the small American crowd it was like I had just stormed Iwo Jima. After Putin hit the canvas and the official signaled a full point ending the match, the crowd's noise got louder and louder and the Americans roared with approval only to be drowned out by the Ukrainians' and Russians' furious yelling, the entire room exploding with noise. We sat and bowed; as we walked to our corners, I focused on the rhythmic slapping of my feet, my cadence a little giddy with a touch of John Wayne swagger.

I looked for the biographer. A Russian in a navy suit whispered harshly to him, and the scribe left the room. A DAI officer waved the kitchen staff into the room and then locked the door. The cooks held items in their hands—frying pans, knives, pewter plates—and stood against the back wall, straining their necks to see into the ring. Everyone was standing in the aisles, screaming. I ignored my stool and stood with my hands on my hips. Hellmuth offered me a shot of vodka. He said, "You deserve it," and I said, "Yes, I do," and sucked it down. I smacked the alcohol from my lips.

Yergushov appeared next to us; he was sweating profusely.

He said, "Putin requests one more match."

I looked across the mat. Putin stared at me.

"A rubber match," I said. Yergushov didn't understand. I ignored him. I stood up, looked at Vladimir, and nodded.

He nodded once and stood. The crowded roared. I could see hands exchanging colored bills and actually felt the hot breath of all the spectators around me. The cooks made a wretched noise by banging their culinary equipment, creating a rhythmic clatter with the occasional scratch of a knife against a stainless pan. The Americans began hollering for another pin. Putin's marble head looked cracked by his own sweat, his face red, the veins in his neck bulging. I wish I could say I had a moment of revelation. I wish I thought of flying back to Ohio, or that I pictured cities like Galway and Cork, traveling there with Lucia, walking the serene beaches of Kilkenny, her sinewy arms locked with mine, or smelled her rich perfume and the way I buried my face in the curls of her hair when I slept at night; or maybe even imagined a romantic train ride south through Ireland, and large banquet tables filled with food and the chatter of the Gaelic language sprinkling my English and the smiles and laughter of dozens of family and friends and their families and friends, my fighting over, a life of lazy nothingness.

But that isn't the truth.

What was true is that there is nothing more honest than a fistfight. What was true is that I loved the combat. I strode back onto the mat, sat down with a great calm, and we performed our bows. I stood up, stared at his sweaty marble face, and mouthed *I'm going to kill you.* He gave me a smile, nodded, and said *And I you.* I would guess that he too took a deep satisfaction in that moment, with no more handshakes and deals and politics, but some kind of gladiator mentality that is stupid only to those who have never fought, and as we took our stances, we each seemed ready for our finest moment, arms flexed into fists, poised, fingers coiled like snakes.

The ref dropped his hand.

EXIT 17 DOES NOT EXIST

Ali arrived at work to find the front window of Maverick's shattered. The large, accordion-like bars she slid to the side each morning remained upright, and along their hinges, glimmers of broken glass refracted the sunlight. She stepped closer, shards crackling under her feet. Inside the ledge were two bricks, and the lock on the bars was untouched. They weren't even trying to get in.

Ali turned. Though she was wearing sunglasses, she placed her hand over her forehead, and peered around the lot. She focused on the storefronts, mentally repeating their names like a chant—*Hader Hardware, Ponderosa, The Hi-Fi Saloon, Skyline Chili, Buckeye Valley Medical Association*—looking to see if there were any other break-ins or damage. Then she lowered her hand, realizing she didn't really give a damn what happened to any other store, and pulled out her cell phone. She sat down on the sidewalk, and called the police. She twirled her phone in her palm, dully accepting there was nothing she could do now, and to pass the time and not think about her brother Jerry, she instead imagined what insurance forms she would need to fill out and wondered if they were downloadable off the website or if she would get a fax from an agent today and whether this would increase her rates yet again, the numbers rising and falling in her mind like cartoon characters. A patrol car arrived, and both the officer and Ali seemed bored with the details. She hadn't touched anything, she said, and she unlocked the front door, and walked in behind him.

"Just vandalism," he said. "We'll file the report, but I'd be surprised if we catch anybody. Probably kids. A thief really after something would have broken your front door."

"Christ, that's the second time this summer kids have fucked with my store. What's their problem?"

The officer shrugged. The radio at his shoulder squawked, and he turned his body away from Ali to speak.

After he left, she took her camera from the office and snapped photos of the damage. She barely glanced at each picture before pressing the button and capturing the next image; she didn't need to spend any time contemplating what this meant, why someone would do this, didn't need to see this as some sort of social realist artistic statement. There was no sense, no beauty, in this. She took pictures of the floors, the window frames, the front door, a survey of the pettiness of it all, and with each picture, Ali felt more and more like none of this mattered. She set the camera next to her computer and retrieved the vacuum from the back closet. She was unwrapping the cord when Leo, her only employee, showed up for his shift.

"The fuck happened?" he said.

"Some kids threw a rock at the window."

Leo drummed his fingers on the counter. "Did they get in?"

"Bars on the windows took care of that, chief."

Leo lived in his father's basement, the two of them alone for the last twenty years since Leo's mother left them for a real estate developer in Florida. Leo cooked and mowed the lawn, and his father smoked cigarettes and listened to the Reds on the radio, sipping cold cans of Hudy Gold beer from a cooler he kept restocked next to his recliner. Leo's thinning black hair was shaggy, and he favored black T-shirts of comic book characters. Today he wore a Punisher shirt, and Ali smirked at the irony of it, a comic book shirt, and believed all of it—the walls, the crammed tables, even her own thoughts—remained only to haunt her.

"I think there's a shipment in the back," Ali said. "And if

you'd check the webpage for orders, that would be great."

He headed toward the office, then stopped.

"Are you okay?" he asked.

She thought of the hundreds of appropriate and contradictory answers, then said, "I'm fine, chief. But thanks."

"I like your new haircut."

Five days ago, the day after her brother died, Ali had her hair cut short around the back and sides, leaving it long in the front, hanging in front of her eyes, hiding her face, and forcing her to brush her hair back and tuck it behind her ear. Jerry used to yank her ponytail, even when they were both adults, and she felt that leaving her hair uncut would be like having a ghost limb. Leaning back, tilting the stool onto two legs, like Jerry used to with the kitchen chairs when they were kids, Ali waited for something to happen. Anything. She stood up, leaned on the counter, flexed her bare arms. If only a customer would enter the store, stare at her sinewy arms, the way her breasts pushed against her tank top, then she could savor someone's desire, even if it meant being his exotic Asian fetish.

Ali stared at the sliding bars. When they didn't remind her that she was located in a shitty north Cincinnati neighborhood, when she could imagine better things, they somehow reminded her of the old movies she and Jerry watched as kids, sneaking into the basement, choosing one of the Beta films her father owned, and how they would lie on the floor shoulder to shoulder, the sound turned low, her footed pajamas almost able to reach the television stand, the way Jerry's shoulders tensed and her own stomach knotted during the dramatic scenes they had both watched dozens of times before. She particularly loved *The Getaway*, the first film her father had seen when her parents emigrated from China to San Francisco; she had been named after Ali McGraw.

She ran her hand along the handle of the autographed Tony Perez bat—a 36 oz. white ash Louisville Slugger model her brother got from the Big Dog back in 1980—displayed on the counter edge since she had opened the store. On the glass top under the bat, Ali had taped a photo of Perez holding her, four years old and grinning, on his massive right shoulder. Jerry, nine years old then, had taken the picture.

"Chief?"

Leo popped up from the comic book section along the opposite wall. Ali hadn't seen him come to the front, and she wondered how long she had been sitting and doing nothing.

"I'm going next door to get a sandwich," Ali said. "Do you want anything?"

"Just a large soda."

She nodded, took her purse from behind the counter, and walked two storefronts to Jersey Mike's. It was too early for the lunch push. Her friend Joyce was behind the counter scraping mustard out of a large plastic jug and into a narrow black condiments bottle; a blue bandanna held back her thick red hair. She asked Ali about the vandalism.

"Like they're gonna catch anyone," Ali said. "All this is going to do is jack up my insurance rates."

"Kids. God, this neighborhood. I swear if my kids start doing that shit someday." Joyce pounded a fist into her hand, smiling as she shook her head. "What can I get you?"

She ordered two turkey sandwiches and two sodas; Leo would eat eventually and she decided to buy lunch for him. Ali stared out the window. Two kids pedaled by on stunt bicycles. Blurry kids on bikes always caught Ali's attention.

"Jerry was going to Taos in October," she said. "He entered a bike race."

Joyce asked Ali how she was doing. Ali gave the canned answer: it's hard but she manages; she misses him; it was an accident; she's okay. And so on. Joyce slowed down, cutting the tomatoes delicately, squirting mayo on the bread in patient streams, and Ali sensed her friend was waiting for more.

"I'm tired of seeing cop cars," Ali said. "They're everywhere. With the store today. And with Jerry." She stared at the Formica counter. According to the police toxicology report, Richard Mulkey, the driver that killed Jerry, had a blood alcohol level of .24 when he exited I-71, swerved up the ramp, accelerating, and plowed through a red light and into Jerry's driver-side door. Mulkey, who had been out on bail from his third DUI charge, suffered nothing more than a broken nose.

Joyce set the sandwiches down and removed her latex gloves. She leaned on the counter, then took Ali's hand.

"Jerry was great," Joyce said. "Remember he came to all our soccer games in high school? How many brothers do that?" She frowned, shook her head slowly. "Honey, I'm so sorry."

Ali was quiet. She bought her store, Maverick's Cards and Comics, almost five years ago. As soon as she had the keys, Ali and Jerry had celebrated by sitting on the floor in the back office, empty except for one metallic desk, and drinking cheap champagne from red plastic cups, reading comic books, and laughing as they drunkenly flipped playing cards into a baseball cap.

"You should come by for dinner," Joyce said. "We haven't done that in a while."

Ali looked at her and wondered how they could be the same age. Joyce had two young, noisy children, and as nice as Joyce was, spending time around her family made Ali consider celibacy.

"I'd love to," Ali lied. "Maybe after I get back from the card show this weekend."

"I always liked Jerry's work," Leo said. "Those graphics he did for our website, you know?"

Ali stopped chewing. They sat at the end of the counter farthest from the door. She'd forgotten Jerry's drawings and graphics were on the store webpage.

"Jerry could draw," she said. "He wrote his first comic when he was ten. It was about this rabbit cop named Presto. He captured criminals and stuffed him into his top-hat jail. Just like that, they disappeared forever."

"A rabbit named Presto," Leo said. "Like that would sell."

"Yeah, okay, it was stupid. But then, when he was older, he wrote this comic called Ghost, which was this guy who could shift to different levels of invisibility."

"Either he's invisible or he isn't."

"No, that's what was cool about him. Ghost didn't have control of it, not completely. He studied martial arts, in part to kick ass, but also to control his mind. See, he had some illnesses—bipolar and autism, mild forms of both, or something—and he couldn't always completely vanish. Only partly. Other times he could."

"That doesn't make any sense."

"Fuck what sense it made. It was the drawings. Jesus."

Leo nodded. "You're right. I'm sorry."

Tears pressed behind her eyes. This is what she hated about her grief, how it could be set off by anything. The day before, flipping through her mail, a white envelope from a wildlife preservation charity made her cry for twenty minutes.

"Jerry was good," she said slowly. "Talented, really talented. You know what my parents made him do? Graphic design. And they started me in calligraphy classes, you know, just in case I had any bright ideas."

"Were you any good?"

"No, I was terrible. Which made me love comics more. And all his baseball cards. God, he came here all the time. He hated when I tagged along. I'd have to stay behind him and his friends by almost an entire block. His last year of high school, he started letting me come along. I thought it was cool that I got to ride shotgun in my brother's car. We'd just browse and he'd listen to me complain about being an eighth-grader."

"Beats being a ninth-grader. Freshman year sucked."

She looked around her store. The comics lined the wall to the left of the door; by the window, where the comics began, six-year-old Ali had grabbed her brother's sleeve and cried, told him the kids made fun of her for being Chinese, and why can't we go back to San Francisco? In the middle of the store, large folding tables were covered in purple felt tablecloths and stocked with action-hero figurines and cards like Pokemon, Yu-gi-oh!, and Magic the Game; they used to be overflowing with baseball cards, and while shuffling through an open pack, Jerry explained the mathematics behind PECOTA baseball statistical analysis to a twenty-three-year old Ali. Comic books curved down the far wall to the back office. The back walls displayed, behind locked cases, sports cards, and comic figurines lay scattered on the tables, along with buckets of cheap baseballs, buttons that played *Take Me Out to the Ballgame*, and Starting Lineup figures. There, in the back of the store, Ali had admitted she once a bought a $200 belt (when she was twenty-one), and she told Jerry about her first serious boyfriend (twenty-four), and Jerry told her about his new website and design company (twenty-six).

"Are you thinking of selling?" Leo asked.

Ali looked at the floor and the worn electrical tape that sealed the telephone and credit card wires to the thin gray carpet. She said nothing.

The 12th Annual Great Midwestern Sports Card and Memorabilia Show was held in Chicago. Placing her purse and a blueberry muffin on the passenger seat, Ali slipped into her car before dawn, left Cincinnati, and arrived at the Palmer House early in the afternoon.

After dropping her bag in her room, she took the stairs to the convention rooms in order to absorb the hotel and push aside the familiarity of her store and her apartment. Stairs seemed to be located everywhere; the ones around the elevators were made of steel and echoed as she walked; others were carpeted in a dark purple-and-red checkered pattern; some led nowhere, or stopped abruptly at a particular floor. The first floors of the Palmer also felt disorienting—multiple "ground" floors with different entrances, luggage shops and shoe stores in one area, restaurants in another, wide open spaces with couches and people in dark suits, corners with more stairs leading to more levels. She felt she was trapped in an Escher drawing.

She entered the conference room through the far-west wing. Dressed in faded low-rise jeans, a brown leather motorcycle jacket, and yellow track shoes, Ali hoped to feel cooler than the people in the room, to be something more than just an average collector. Looking to her right, she noticed how the larger stores with more money and more space were lined against the walls; the small stores in the middle formed five long, neat rows. She smiled, pleased she didn't bother to buy a table and drag Leo and his van loaded with merchandise up to the Windy City.

She eased down the aisles, hands in her pockets, feeling like one of the shoppers of her own store. Some of the people behind the tables were like Leo—black comic book T-shirt, blue jeans, gray trainers, greasy hair. Others looked like professors, the faint smell of charcoal drifting off their brown blazers, and teenagers with wispy beards and acne-spotted cheeks slipped by, popping gum, their shoulders hunched. A tall woman with red hair snorted, and the noise made Ali turn and stare at the woman's unabashed laughter. An elderly man wearing a Prada cap, his BluBlockers hanging from his neck, eased by, shuffling a pack of football cards rapidly through his fingers. The garbage cans overflowed with Mountain Dew bottles and Cheetos bags.

"Looking for something in particular?" a man asked.

She looked up from the table she had been perusing, which was covered with white boxes of comic and baseball cards. The man, unshaven and barely taller than Ali, smiled eagerly. She thought he was cute in a harmless, generic way.

"No, not really," Ali said. "Just checking out the competition, I guess. I have my own store back home."

"Where's home?"

"Minneapolis," she lied. She offered her hand. "Ali Lin."

"Silas Kearns." He pointed to his small pile of autographed baseballs, held in square, plastic cases. "My company is trying to move into sports memorabilia. We also do jerseys, you know, the throwback stuff, and old hats. Signed scorecards, stuff like that. We need to hit the big shows, get our name in people's mouths."

"What about comics?"

"Not our specialty. We love 'em, but we're interested in making a little money."

She looked at the beige cashbox behind Silas. On the top was a green rectangular magnet: Exit 17, Sea Isle, New Jersey.

"Are you from Jersey?" she asked.

"Nope, born and raised in Oregon."

Ali pointed at the cashbox.

"Yeah, I got a bunch of those from a friend who grew up out there. The exit doesn't exist, and my buddy thinks it's ironic or Zen or something. There's no exit seventeen and no one remembers why. One of those things that's been around so long no one remembers the story."

"But there's an exit thirteen?"

"I think so." He smiled. "I mean, that would be really superstitious. Here," he said, taking the magnet off the cashbox. "Take it. I have a bunch of them at home."

Ali palmed the green magnet, touched the corners with her finger, felt the plastic push into her skin. She looked up. "Thanks," she said.

They chatted for a while, and Ali, pleased he was so short that he almost had to look up at her, accepted his invitation to join him and several other collectors for dinner.

Other than Silas's, Ali forgot their names almost instantly. Ali caught Silas glancing at her regularly, and she pictured him as one of the boys in her store, all grown up, his chance to finally be an equal to the Asian girl who owned Maverick's. She smiled when he looked over, then steered her eyes back to whoever was speaking about the Fantastic Four or the West Coast Avengers. She asked the waiter for more water, and squeezed the lime around the glass, conscious of Silas watching her. At times, Ali interjected praise for whatever manga novel was being discussed, but otherwise preferred to listen.

At the end of the night, she and Silas took the same elevator. He pushed the button for the seventh floor, hesitated, and looked at Ali. She could see the hope in his eyes, the shy smile curling around his lips, and felt momentarily cruel. "Ten, please."

They rode the elevator in silence. When Silas stepped out, he turned and started to speak, but Ali cut him off.

"We'll have breakfast," Ali said. "Lobby at eight?"

In her hotel room, Ali went straight to the minibar next to the television. She opened it and stared at all the small bottles— bourbon, whiskey, scotch, their labels shiny, their size making them irresistible, their cost making them unattainable. Shaking her head, she began to sob, and with weak legs she sunk down to the floor, crying and choking loudly, until the strange thought that her tears could be heard through the walls silenced her. She stared at the floor until her breaths became steady. How silly, she thought, caring what others think. She went to the bathroom for a glass of water, and then she sat down at the desk, picked up the phone, put it down again, and wondered who she would have called and why the hell she had lied to Silas about where she was from.

Ali carried a bag of donuts and muffins and two cups of coffee to the pavilion room, where Silas sat waiting. She flopped down cross-legged on the bench, pulling off bits from her muffin slowly, making sure she had a blueberry in each bite.

"Have you ever been to Oregon?" Silas asked.

Ali shook her head. "My parents just retired to San Diego. Lots of Chinese Americans retire there."

"You're Chinese?"

"As opposed to?"

Silas blushed, bit his lip. He stared at his shoes.

"It's cool," Ali said. "I can't tell Germans from Poles anyway."

He laughed, and she reached out and touched his forearm.

"It's really okay," Ali said. "Honest. I'm not offended."

She lifted her hand from his arm, tore off another piece of

muffin. "Kids used to call me Alien. You know, Ali Lin, *Alien?* They said I looked like E.T., too. The little blonde girls were the most vicious. Most days, I just wished I was invisible, you know, so no one would see me, no one would talk to me."

"Did you get in any fights?"

"My brother protected me." She looked around the room and started counting the number of people.

"Older?"

"Jerry's five years older than me. He's a graphic designer." She held Jerry's death close, let it surround her body like a life preserver. She clung to the private source of her sadness.

Silas took a second donut. "So he must like comics, too."

"He loved them as a kid. He still likes them, but not as much. He kinda passed them off to me and they became mine."

"You two sound close."

Across the room, a man laughed, and in his hand, a large cup of orange juice, filled with ice, shook.

"We are," Ali said, finally. "Jerry's my best friend."

"I've got three brothers, and they used to beat me up. I'm the youngest."

Ali looked at Silas, and listened to him talk about their backyard basketball games of two-on-two, and gravel-scraped knees and fistfights and playing guns or war and wondered how Silas hadn't heard her, hadn't heard Ali, her real self, speaking about her brother. How another person couldn't sense the sorrow that Ali knew she was drowning in.

"What panel are you going to at nine?" Silas asked.

She held his gaze for a long moment. "What panel are *we* going to, you mean?" She decided, then, to spend the day with him, and she did, going with him to discussions by small press owners about distribution costs, lectures on the various Spiderman serials, and after buying a couple of classic Batman comics and some Willie Mays cards and sitting through another round of dinner with people she didn't know or want to know, Ali slept with Silas. She let him believe he seduced her, pleased at his effort, his obvious lack of grace and style, and finding herself pleasantly unaware of who she was or why she was bothering. When she was certain Silas was asleep, Ali slipped out of the sheets and dressed. She stood at the foot of the bed, feeling vacated and empty. She walked to the closet, where several of Silas's authentic jerseys hung. Concealed in the dark, her breathing softened, and everything about herself became indiscernible. Without thinking, she took three at random, opened the room door, and left. She returned to her room, shoved them into her bag along with her clothes and the various free gifts she had picked up—buttons, bumper stickers, unopened packs of baseball cards from the 1980s—took a quick look around the room, then went downstairs and checked out.

At home, she opened her bag and took out her prizes: a white 1956 Cincinnati Reds Ted Kluzweski jersey, a powder-blue 1980 Kansas City Royals George Brett, and a purple 1966 Minnesota Vikings Fran Tarkenton. She looked down the long hallway of her apartment, and walked to her open kitchen. She remembered how Jerry helped her find the place, a bowling-alley style apartment across the street from an elementary school, and how much she once savored the late-night quiet that now unnerved her. A pair of large sliding doors gave the room light, and opened onto a small porch that looked at nothing but the backs of other apartment buildings, and the brick houses that always looked wet and muddy. To the left, where the apartment opened up and was wide and beautiful, she had a large plasma television, a Bose surround system, and in neat, orderly shelves next to the television, a collection of DVDs loaded with her, and Jerry's, favorite films—*The French Connection, Bullitt, Midnight Cowboy, Mean Streets, The Conversation.* She turned, faced her front door. She looked down at the jerseys in her hand, the way her fingers clutched them. How white and pale her hand appeared. She trudged to her bedroom, stepped over the piles of clothes around her closet and hung up the jerseys and then, rubbing her arms as if she were cold, drifted slowly backwards, keeping her eyes fixed on her closet as if expecting it to vanish, and collapsed on her bed, gazing at what she had done. She reached down to the floor, slipped her hand into the pocket of her coat, and pulled out her magnet. She closed her eyes and dreamed of fluorescent lights and car crashes.

"Damn, boss," Leo said. He whistled. "Cool jersey. How much?"

She sat down on the stool behind the counter. She had chosen the Brett jersey. It was too big, but she had found an orange T-shirt to wear under it.

"Nothing, chief," she said. "I stole it."

He laughed, and waited to hear the actual price. Ali stared at her hands and felt a sudden shame, and wished she had lied.

"You're serious?"

She tugged at her knuckles, squeezed the skin together.

"From who?"

"Some guy I fucked."

Leo walked behind the counter. "Did he hurt you or something?"

She closed her eyes, briefly making the world vanish.

"Ali, go home. Let me take care of the store. Take the week off."

"I need to be here. I know it was wrong. Okay? I know that."

She opened her eyes and stared at the thin carpet.

He said, "I'm going to check the website. I didn't do it this weekend. I'll be in the back." She nodded and kept her eyes focused on the ground until she was sure he was gone.

Ali passed the morning by flipping through the current issue of *Beckett Baseball Card Plus*. Kids started coming in after lunch, dropping their bikes on the sidewalk like litter, and entering the store smelling of chlorine. She noticed how freckles broke out on their faces as the summer grew longer, their hair lighter in color. A red-haired kid came to the counter, snapping Ali out of her desire to stare out the window and study the steam rising off the macadam. He asked to see a box of commons. She stood, reached for a box on the second shelf from the top. She led the boy down to the far end, away from the door, and placed the box on the glass counter. From his cargo shorts, the boy pulled out a notebook sheet with "Upper Deck 2002" scrawled on the top and a long list of card numbers he didn't yet have to complete the set. Ali and Jerry had collected cards the same way, buying packs instead of sets. She began to tremble; she sank behind the counter, sat on the floor, and felt another seismic wave of grief in her lungs.

She heard voices, and the boy said, "Hey, man," and then Leo was there, crouched down next to her. Each breath hurt, like she was swallowing rocks. He stood, and asked the boy to run to Jersey Mike's and ask for Joyce. Ali heard the bell chime, then once more a moment later. Joyce was beside her, her arm around her, and Ali leaned into her shoulder and waited for her sadness to pass.

With time, she stopped crying. Ali rubbed her temples. She wiped tears from her face with the back of her hand. Joyce ran her fingers through Ali's hair and made hushing sounds. The three of them sat for what felt like a long time. Then, Ali put her hands on the ground, and Joyce and Leo helped her to her feet. She rubbed her palms into her eyes.

"I want you to come to dinner," Joyce said.

Ali headed for the door, and they followed. Outside, she sat on the windowsill and inhaled the humid afternoon air. Across the road, in the opposite strip center, a check-cashing store and two closed storefronts dully gleamed. On the corner, the remains of an abandoned gas station waited to be leveled.

"I'm just tired," Ali said. "I'll be fine." She glanced at Joyce, then Leo.

"I want both of you to come," Joyce said. "You need to."

Ali ran her hands up and down her arms. She wondered what Jerry would do.

Joyce put a hand on her shoulder and kneaded. "It's just dinner. You've been over lots of times." Ali remembered. She remembered the way Joyce's two kids shouted, running through the house with plastic bats and dirty dolls, the way Joyce's husband sat with his legs up and a hole in the crotch of his jeans showed his green boxers, the house's regular clutter of items: out-of-date L.L. Bean catalogs, neighborhood newsletters, various navy and beige backpacks, sandals and shoes and bits of clothing (gray hiking socks, ski hats, cardigans with large brown buttons), and a colorful array of toys. Ali felt suffocated there. But now, breathing in the sweltering afternoon air and hearing the roar of the cars race by, she thought about how tired she was of crying, of fighting for some unseeable victory. She believed her own identity was slowly vanishing.

It was warm inside Joyce's house. Tony, Joyce's husband, came into the living room and shook Leo's hand, gave Ali a sympathetic nod. Ali looked around and found the house neater than she remembered. Joyce led them to the dining room table and sat them down. Joyce and Tony went into the kitchen, and brought back a tray with two cups of coffee, a bowl of sugar, and a small cup of cream. Ali could smell pot roast cooking. She heard Tony shuffle through the kitchen and turn off some switches.

"Do you want something stronger to drink?" Joyce asked.

Ali looked toward the kitchen. Joyce's daughter stood in the doorway sipping from a plastic cup. The little girl had blonde hair and bright blue eyes. Ali thought of whiskey and the clink of ice cubes, and couldn't remember the little girl's name.

"What are you having, sweetheart?" Ali said to the girl.

"Chocolate milk." The girl's eyes widened. "Do you want some?"

"I sure do. Will you show me to how to make it?"

The girl asked her mother *Can I? Can I?* and Joyce smiled. Ali followed the girl to the kitchen. The girl stood on a stool and took a yellow plastic container from the cabinet near her head. She explained to Ali how you should use three scoops, even if the directions say to use only two, and Ali handed her the milk and watched the girl use a long, narrow spoon to spin the tiny grains to make one thick glass of chocolate milk.

"Taste it," the girl said. "Do you like it?"

Ali rolled the milk around her mouth. "I love it."

"I hope you like pot roast," Tony said. Ali sat next to Joyce, across from the children. The girl smiled at Ali as she drank more and more chocolate milk. The little boy was quiet, absorbed in playing a hand-held video game, and the room filled with the warm smell of bread and pot roast. Joyce offered the basket of bread to Ali, and she tore loose a large, warm piece. She picked up the butter and spread it over the bread. It was delicious, and Ali chewed slowly, feeling her shoulders relax.

The children began to ask questions about the police and the robbery, and Joyce answered for Ali, who promised them free comic books next time they came by to see their mom at work. She'd still own the store then. She knew that now, that the store, despite all its worries and concerns, was something she loved, and like her brother, could never truly abandon her. She would never have to let Jerry go. When Joyce touched her elbow and squeezed in thanks, Ali smiled. The food was passed around in white ceramic dishes, and after loading up her plate, Ali ate roast, cutting it into small strips and dipping the noodles in gravy. She inhaled the smell of food, listened quietly to everyone talk. She listened as Leo and Tony talked about the Reds and the children told their mother that they learned at school how to make paper kites, and looking at Ali, their eyes wide and excited, they said that next week, they were going to write notes and attach them to balloons in the hope that kids from other schools would find their notes and mail them letters. Ali pictured the children, holding bright blue balloons, a handwritten letter attached to a long red ribbon, and freeing them into the air, their hands held high as they let go, shouting as they released them into the sky, excited for their balloons to vanish.

A SURGEON'S STORY

I know something about killing.

I know about the way people can kill with their own hands: shooting, stabbing, suicide, vehicular homicide. Also, I know about the way people die from the mysterious failings of the human body: aneurism, heart attack, pneumonia. I know these things because I am a vascular surgeon, a profession of accuracy and precision, and I have been employed at Massachusetts General Hospital for seventeen years. Raised in Salem, educated at Yale, I considered the crisp, cool weather and the proud stoicism of New England to be a part of me that courses and cuts through my body like the hills and streams I love to hunt in. I have always been fascinated by the thrill of hunting; equally, I have always been intrigued by saving lives. Once, I believed these were opposite ends of a spectrum, and to be a part of both worlds created for me a greater understanding of them both. Yet due to my interactions with Stacy Douglas, a third-year Harvard medical student, I realized I had never truly understood myself. She forced me to see there was no dichotomy between surgeon and hunter, between protecting and taking life, and I now understand the natural unity of my profession and my passion. My name is Leonard Cromwell.

My father taught me to hunt when I was eight years old. We rose before dawn on Saturdays and Sundays, driving in the darkness of early morning, the blast of air coming through his open driver's window mixing with the pungent smell of his cigarettes. We crept through the woods, rifles on safety, my eyes trying to follow his and learn as he scanned the woods for deer and their tracks. He'd motion to me silently, two fingers to his eyes, then at me, his hand swooping out toward a higher ground, then his hand flattened, and curled into a fist. I tried to see him then as the soldier he once was, his face drawn rigid and severe, his motions unwasted and precise. His directions led me to the best alcove, where I would patiently wait for the buck to cross my path and when it did, I would focus through my scope on the smallest hair on his coat, one between his front legs and high on his chest where his heart raced with apprehension as I unlocked the safety. The entire world stilled like the quiet of a late-night snowfall, and then I squeezed the trigger.

My father dropped into Europe with the 101st Airborne; he was injured in the first campaign and spent the rest of his military service in a hospital in England. Mother told me that he had been the only man of ten to survive a frontal assault on an enemy position. He had scars across his sternum from the bullets. He never spoke of it directly. My father was pleased that I was too young to get drafted into Vietnam and while certainly proud of his military background, he never encouraged me to enter the armed forces myself.

"War," he said, "is something I would never wish upon anyone. There are better ways to build character."

Somehow, the picture of my father parachuting into France entered my mind the first time I entered surgery. My father must have had an extraordinary sense of fear as he dropped his chute and picked up his rifle, scanning the Normandy forest, unsure what to do and yet certain of what lay ahead of him. I felt the same trembling rush of adrenaline in my first week on surgical rotation. That first week I was preparing to watch Dr. Edward McAllister remove a spleen and repair the intestinal walls of a car-accident victim; I hadn't seen the patient come in, but had heard that his wife was DOA and that the front seat smelled like the bottom of an old whiskey barrel. Dr. McAllister entered the room with his scrubbed hands and forearms held vertical, as if he were carrying a small, wounded infant in his great arms. His forehead was cratered with thought lines; his office was lined, along with medical journals and reference books, with Greek and Latin literature, and he was affable and charming when he shook my hand earlier that morning. Intelligent, articulate, and kind: I had never heard a colleague speak poorly of him. A nurse slipped gloves onto his arms. He strode to the patient, then cocked his head.

"What is this?" Dr. McAllister's voice had risen an octave. He turned his ear closer to the small cassette player in the corner of the room. A movement from Beethoven's seventh symphony was playing. I waited, curious.

"What is this?" he said again, his voice cracking like a pubescent boy's. "This isn't Debussy, is it?"

A nurse shook her head. Her eyes, the only part of her visible, dilated, the lines around her sockets tight.

"Debussy!" McAllister shrieked. "Goddammit! Change the tape! Change the tape!"

I looked down at the patient. His eyes were closed, and the breathing mask covered his nostrils and mouth. Large, rectangular white sheets covered his body, and his pale, hairless feet sprouted out toward the edge of the table. He did not seem to mind the noise. The nurse scurried to the cassette player, ejected the tape, and fumbled through a stack of cassettes arranged neatly next to the machine. Meanwhile, McAllister continued to scream, continued to blow into a childish tantrum.

"I can't work like this!" he yelled. "I can't! No! What are you doing? This is my room! Mine!"

His voice split and cracked, and he waved his arms like a child demanding a cookie, ready to drop to a kitchen floor and pound his fists. He stopped, stared at me, my arms rigid at my sides as if holding my own legs down. His lips trembled slightly, and he raised his hand and pulled his last three fingers slowly into a fist, his pointer finger extended at me.

"Stand in the corner," he said.

Without so much as a nod, I walked to the far corner and stood. The cassette machine now played a movement from Debussy's fourth symphony and the nurses gravitated back toward the patient. McAllister remained with his forearms held away from his body, as if his own racing heart would contaminate them. Head down, above his patient, ready to begin, his eyes darted up at me, wide and vibrant. His entire body snapped erect and the nurses stepped backwards as if an alligator had suddenly risen out of a lake and smacked its jaws at them.

"I said in the corner."

"Dr. McAllister, I am in the corner."

"Nose against the wall. Do not look at me."

"But I'm supposed to observe."

"Nose!" His voice raised another terrifying pitch, like the heroine of a horror film. "Against the wall!"

I turned. My chest tightened, and I felt very cold, the pale green tiles directly against my face, the stainless steel trays against my legs, their cold metal chilling my skin through my surgical scrubs. My shoulders shook with fear and with, I knew then, genuine envy and awe.

After that successful surgery, Dr. McAllister walked me out of the room, draping his broad arm across my shoulders, his composure returned to the benevolent doctor we all knew, and explained to me in detail how he went through the stomach wall, the removal of the spleen, and the amount of internal bleeding the patient experienced. I could feel the whole operation, see it in my hands as we walked down the hallway, and as he spoke, emphasizing his points with the same cutting and pointing directives my father used, the smell of antibiotic scrub drifting from his palms, I knew I would be a surgeon.

My life has been unremarkable when not hunting or at the hospital. This is not a disappointment to me. My father long wished for a small piece of land and a quiet life, but the memories of what happened to him in France and a few bad investments, along with a tendency to drink, prevented him from achieving either of these goals. I know little about things beyond my profession. I was married once and divorced a few years later, without children, ending as amicably as the end of a marriage can. Once, I longed for children, but I believe my time for that has long passed and I do not regret it. I have enough money, and other than the professional journals and a large collection of classical music, I have no hobbies.

Prior to our incident, I had seen Stacy Douglas several times in the hospital, but we had not spoken. Interns and medical students appear and vanish with such regularity that to distinguish between them is futile. I no more care about who they are than I do about the patient on the operating table; my goal is to save lives, and much beyond that is outside my nature and not appropriate for me to pursue. However, I must admit to remembering Stacy Douglas and noticing her before we first shook hands.

Stacy Douglas is from Revere. I do not say this to be elitist or derisitory toward that poor, oft-mocked region of Boston. It is just something that catches the attention of any Bostonian. Stacy Douglas was a fair-skinned girl with dark hair and blue eyes, pretty in that rather generic way that young women nowadays seem to be, with the high-pitched, nasally voice of the impoverished class in Revere. Who she was could never be hidden.

"Consider this man," Dr. Pete Anderson said to her as a means of introduction, "our star pitcher." Dr. Anderson pointed at me, finger and thumb extended like a firearm, grinning with his affable fraternal charm.

"Dr. Cromwell," she said. "It's a pleasure to meet you. The star pitcher?" She laughed her polite, hyena laugh. "I love the Sox."

"Football," I said to her. "Football is the key to surgery."

"I see," she said. She smiled, toothy and awkward, unsure what I meant. I looked at her thin hair, her bangs.

"I'm sure you don't. I didn't when my father told me."

Dr. Anderson, amused, took a step back. Stacy studied me like she was reading Sanskrit.

I continued. "Europeans don't play football, my father said. He thought that's why they don't win wars. Football requires controlled aggression. You have to remain calm under enormous pressure, avoid being misdirected, and know when to attack. My father was talking about warfare but the same principles can be applied to medicine."

"You played football." She said it flat, as if setting it to memory.

"No. I never liked the game. But what my father said was appropriate." I nodded, as much to her as myself. "Don't forget that. Controlled aggression."

"Lots of broken bones in football," she said, smiling, still failing at charm. "I'm considering orthopedics."

"Our unique skeletal structure is a beautiful creation." With effort I kept my eyes off her face and neck and studied the row of charts next to the nurses' station. I remembered how Dr. McAllister once said that our skeletons remain behind to educate the generations not yet born, that what remains of us is bone. Stacy Douglas nodded, frowning in concentration, and I tried to imagine myself as a mentor, putting my arm around her shoulder and guiding her down the hallway, explaining a surgical procedure, and the idea dried my tongue.

With an obsequious smile, Dr. Anderson led her away—Stacy was on an inpatient care rotation then—and I watched her walk down the hallway. She seemed frail, like a young deer, its sense of danger and discretion not yet refined. I felt embarrassed at the unsolicited advice I had just given. My father's advice was now my own, a kind of appropriate strangeness that came over me when I spoke to the residents. I was never sure how to articulate to Stacy, or anyone else, that knowing what to seek, cut, and repair was, perhaps, the simplest part of the operation; years of study of anatomy gave every competent student all the knowledge needed to repair sinew and bone. The distinction, I wanted to tell her, was demeanor and control.

Surgery does not mean difficult: it means repair, it means damage that the body alone cannot heal. I was scheduled to perform a sternotomy, a simple replacement surgery removing the aortic valve and substituting it with a natural-tissue valve. The patient's sternum lay bare, the smell of iodine drifting off his chest. I reviewed the x-ray of his heart and lungs, and then the platelet count from his blood test. The anesthesiologist, assisted by a resident, was behind a drape monitoring the patient's vital signs.

The patient's ribs were spread apart with vise-like retractors while my assistant cauterized the bleeding tissue. The circulating nurse departed for more sponges and replacement blood; the scrub nurse unwrapped packages of sterile utensils. The perfusionist had four cannulaes in hand, two large and two small. I connected a large cannula to the patient's inferior vena cava, the big vein returning spent blood from the body to the right atrium, detoured into the Stockert machine, then pumped by the right ventricle to the lungs. The patient had been under for thirty-four minutes.

I prepared to insert the fourth cannula into the ascending aorta.

"I can't see," Stacy said.

Ignoring her, I clamped the aorta, made a stab incision, and inserted the cannula.

"Excuse me," Stacy said.

"Ms. Douglas," a nurse said. "Do not bump me."

"I need to see what's happening."

"Ms. Douglas," I said. "Quiet, please."

She was silent then but tension cut across my shoulder blades, like cheap wood sagging under the weight of heavy, dusty books, unnerving me. With great concentration, I steadied my hands, trying to ignore the nasally cadence of Stacy's voice still on my mind.

With a stab incision into the right atrium, I inserted a

cardioplegia cannula into the coronary sinus. The internist placed the fourth tube into the ascending aorta. Stacy cleared her throat.

"Quiet," I said. "Please."

"Just my throat."

I hissed, "Ms. Douglas, I said be quiet. Observe, do not speak."

Above the surgical mask, her eyes burned at me with what could only be called contempt. We continued the procedure. The first valve clamped, I attempted to proceed to the second clogged valve. My hands, now unsteady, began to visibly shake with anger. I lowered them and they struck and rattled the surgical table to my left.

"Dr. Cromwell?" a nurse asked.

I turned. I stared directly at Stacy Douglas. "Why can't you be quiet? Don't bump the table, don't ask me how I am. You do not talk. Are we clear?"

"Yes."

"No, we aren't. You spoke again."

Her brow furrowed and those eyes—those young, angry eyes—tightened in disdain.

"I answered your question. Don't bark at me like a dog."

This is where I ruined myself. This is where I committed such a horrible, inexcusable act, and yet, I remember and feel it too succinctly, with such clarity, that it must be so entrenched in my nature, so natural to who I am, that I am now grateful to have discovered it. To have discovered what, in essence, a base and violent person I am.

I stood upright, walked around the patient, and with an open hand, slapped Stacy Douglas hard across her right cheek.

She stumbled back a step, her head turned away, almost like a cartoon character in how she spun and stepped backwards. Her left hand touched her cheek, and then she looked at me with such horror, such disappointment. The room, other than the beeping of the heart monitor, was silent. At the time, I gave no thought to what I did. Other than the operation, which I proceeded to complete successfully, I do not remember the rest of my time in that room. I can give concise details on the specifics of the operation, but only from the incident report do I know the rest: Nurse Stallworth took Stacy Douglas out of the room, lead her to the women's locker room, and crouched down in front of her asking again and again if she was all right, and Stacy, seemingly in shock, nodded she was fine, her strong fingers delicately against her cheek, her expression one of complete surprise and amazement. The three remaining nurses in the operating room exchanged glances and, as they testified, my demeanor was controlled, normal, and professional once Stacy left the room. None of the three made any comment to me at the time of the operation from fear, they stated, of being assaulted.

Again, I remember none of this. Only the procedure. Once the operation was complete, and I was scrubbing down, only then did the awesome humiliation of what I had done sink in. I struck a student. I hit—in anger, not defense—another person. Alone, I sat down on the bench, the wood cold beneath my flanks, the stillness of the sterilized room permeating my skin. I began to sweat. Staring at the stainless steel sink, warm water bursting from the faucet, I tried to imagine how I could have done such a horrible thing.

Surgeons are not the same people when we enter the operating room. When we enter, we cross a threshold that is difficult to comprehend. The detachment we feel is total, like when the prophet understands the teacher and the entire world of knowledge and servitude frees him to transcend. It is a trance that should never be broken. And the petulance we feel when that trance is broken creates the most feral rage. Inexcusable, of course, but my only hope then was to better understand what I had done, not to justify.

I stood. I changed clothes, sliding on my trousers and a dress shirt, oddly conscious of how expensive they were. Using a Windsor knot, I added a tie, laced up my shoes, and walked down to the office of William Horton, Mass General's chief of surgery, and confessed.

I am aware of the hypocrisy of my light reprimand. These are the facts: Stacy Douglas did not wish to press charges. The appalled nurses were aloof and distant toward me; I do not think I have ever worked with any of them again. And my record as doctor and surgeon, my history of financial support to the hospital, the university, and my charity work, allowed me to get the lightest of sentences: one month unpaid suspension, individual letters of apology to Stacy Douglas and all four nurses, and enrollment in an anger management course. That was all.

The humiliation: doctors giving me sympathetic nods, female nurses and administrators giving me the most vicious, hateful stares. All deserved. It only lasted a day, however. Inquiries were made into the incident, statements were given and typed and reviewed, and I offered my resignation. This was refused. After he laid out the conditions of my suspension in his office, Bill Horton walked me to my car. Our footsteps echoed on the parking garage concrete.

"We protect our best doctors," Horton said. "I won't lose you over one incident."

I looked at my palms, seeing again my hand smashing into Stacy's cheek.

"I hit her," I said.

"We understand that. And it's unacceptable." I could not look at him. "But it was an isolated incident. Ms. Douglas isn't pressing charges. There is no lawsuit. You go to counseling and you return to your duties in one month. That's the end of it."

I leaned against the trunk of my car, the weight of my own body suddenly an incredible burden.

"Listen," Bill said. "We've been friends a long time. I know you. I know you don't have a malicious bone in your body. This time off can be good for you. Meet a nice woman. Get away from this place for a while."

Bill had never understood my devotion. He liked being in

charge; he was as much an executive as he was a doctor. He was political in a way the chief is required to be. His love was for the discipline and execution of a well-organized hospital, not for being a physician. We shook hands, and I lied, promising I would call.

At that time I was not able to explain it to Bill Horton. Yes, there was a tremendous humiliation. Yes, I had struck another person. These are both stains on my honor and I regret them. But what I was beginning to feel, what I could not articulate standing there in the cavernous parking garage, was a sense that I no longer knew how to be a surgeon. I sensed, with a growing calm, that something in me had permanently changed, or far worse, never been there at all, that the interconnected nature of saving lives and taking them, of being a benevolent doctor in the hallway and a petulant, gifted operator in surgery, never truly existed. The blurred distinction of life and death that I hoped I gained some understanding of was a construct of my weakness, of my flaws.

This realization of an error in my hypothesis about being a surgeon came in parts. For once, I had nothing to do. I avoided the hospital and the bars and restaurants and clubs of my fellow doctors. Off call, I turned off my beeper and unplugged my phone. I left my house to go to my anger management courses, which met on Tuesday and Thursday evenings in the city, and the grocery store. I borrowed thick, scholarly biographies from the library, read them in two days, and checked out additional ones. I read about Lyndon Johnson. I read about Gandhi. I read about Peter the Great, Queen Elizabeth I, George Washington, Thomas Jefferson. The flaws of these dead leaders, laid out in pages and pages of leaden prose and footnoted meticulously, demonstrated how our weaknesses are always there, always on display for the rest of the world to perceive and judge. This only dismayed me further. How had I never seen my dishonors before?

Pressed, however, I do not believe I could explain with any sufficient clarity what my flaw was. I sipped my bourbon and stared into my backyard; snow capped the broken branches in my yard, the black trees were coated in thick, icy white, and I noticed small depressions in the snow, tracks of, most likely, a rabbit or a neighbor's dog. The reading lamp above me was the only light in my den. I flicked it off, gathered my coat, and left.

The Edisto Bar & Grill was a regular stop for me on hunting days. Always open, I'd slide into a booth and eat slowly (an omelet with green peppers and ham, hash browns, two English muffins, two cups of black coffee) as I pictured my path into the woods, my lingering thoughts of the hospital or charts or patients vanishing as I imagined snow crunching beneath my boots, rifle in hand, listening for the signs of deer. It was three weeks into my suspension and I hadn't been hunting once. I eased my truck into a parking spot and entered.

A booth by the window was open. The waitress placed a cup of coffee and a plastic glass of water on the table. I ordered what I always ordered and wondered what I would do after I ate. Crawl home and sleep? Drive aimlessly? I looked at my watch—it was four-thirty in the morning. Days had blurred into nights and I lacked any sense of being grounded in time, in a schedule, in responsibility.

She saw me first. I did not notice her until she stood next to me at my booth.

"Hey, Dr. Cromwell."

I looked up at Stacy Douglas. Her eyes were wide with alcohol. Her thin hair was pulled back in a dirty ponytail. She wore a sleek skiing jacket, thick khakis, and a dark turtleneck.

"Can I sit down?" she asked, sliding into the seat across from me.

"I don't think that's a good idea."

"We're far from the hospital. No one will see us. And I already ate, so you don't have to buy me breakfast. Or dinner. Whatever. Why do they make us work sixteen-hour shifts? I just got off at midnight, and you know the strange thing? I'm completely awake. That's so bizarre."

The waitress set a cup of coffee down in front of Stacy and smiled at me. Stacy poured sugar and cream into her coffee but did not drink it.

"Are you all right, Dr. Cromwell? No one has seen or heard from you."

"I'm on suspension."

"I know. I thought they were your friends though."

"Of course they are."

"I didn't want to say anything. They made me give a statement and sign a confidentiality agreement."

I wished she would leave. I wished she had never existed.

"The nurses, I mean," she continued. "They said I shouldn't stand for something like that. Nobody should hit anybody. But you were right. I shouldn't have been talking. I got in the way. I didn't belong there."

"That's no excuse for me."

Stacy slumped in the booth. She picked up her stirring spoon, stared at it, then dropped it loudly against the saucer. Truckers paid their tabs, the old cash register ringing shrill and loud as buttons were struck. I believed I could hear each and every fork and knife touching plates and clattering loudly on the tables.

She said, "I'll never be a good surgeon, will I?"

"I have no idea, Ms. Douglas."

"Sure you do. You can tell me."

Turning my head toward the grill, I watched T-bone steaks and fatty bacon overcook and crackle.

"I'm not sure I have the hands," Stacy said.

"That has nothing to do with it."

"Then what does?"

The waitress brought my food, setting the thick plate down with a disinterested thud. I picked up a fork and stared at the warm, greasy food.

"Do you live around here?" I asked.

"Me? No. I'm here with friends." She turned. "Actually, it looks like they left. I guess."

I chewed slowly. "I don't know anything about you."

Though it was not my intent to discover it, Stacy proceeded

to lay out her history to me. Her parents had owned a restaurant, Lanterns, and her father was the chef and her mother the bookkeeper and hostess. The restaurant had been a historical landmark; John Adams had dined there frequently. They lost the restaurant during an electrical fire and the insurance company accused her father of arson. Years passed as the lawsuit worked its way through various lawyers and courts; her father jumped from catering job to catering job, and then developed food allergies. His wife was diagnosed with multiple sclerosis. Unable to find steady work, he took a job as a school janitor because the benefits package covered his ailing wife. Stacy was their only child. A National Merit Scholarship got her into UMass-Boston; determination got her into Harvard Medical School. Doctors, she said, saved lives and made money and didn't ever have to worry about taking a job cleaning toilets and mopping floors for ungrateful, surly teenagers.

"Money," I said. "Prestige."

"Safety." She reached for her cold coffee and sipped. She shrugged, and then drank a mouthful.

I said, "That isn't a reason to be a surgeon."

"It is for me."

Outside, a soft snowfall began and I realized Stacy hadn't been here with her friends but had hunted me down and waited. I could feel the outside stillness, the calm that a silent snowfall created in me when I crept slowly through the New Hampshire woods.

"I can't explain surgery. But perhaps I can show you what I mean."

She looked at me with an untrammeled expression. Then, as if hiding, her eyes glazed over and she shrugged. I placed a twenty dollar bill on the table and we left the Edisto. I held the passenger door while she climbed in. Her shoes were sturdy, waterproof boots and watching her slide in and fasten her seatbelt, it dawned on me she might not have any friends at all. She was alone in the world. I closed the door and decided.

Once we were on the road, she said, "I thought you had a Benz."

"I only drive it to the hospital. Otherwise I prefer my truck."

"I thought about what you were saying. About skeletons, about bones? How come you aren't an orthopedic surgeon?"

"Not where I belong. I repair arteries and veins. It's who I am." Unconvincing, even to myself, I added, "It's where I belong."

She looked out the window, wiped the damp glass with her hand. "I've been thinking of dropping out of school."

My eyes remained on the road and the thickening flakes of snow.

"After you hit me, I started thinking more about quitting. Not because you hit me. It was how I acted in surgery. I didn't have the mannerisms. Wrong temperament. I behaved like a little girl."

"I never should have struck you." I turned to look at her. "That's inexcusable."

"I know." Her breath fogged the glass, and she did not bother to wipe it anew. "But that's not what I'm saying. I'm not talking about when you hit me. I'm talking about why you hit me. I didn't belong in there."

We drove in silence. I pulled into my driveway and killed the engine.

"Stay here," I said. "I'll be right back."

"I'm not getting out?" She slid her lean fingers over the seatbelt.

"No. I'm picking up supplies then we're leaving."

"Leaving?" She frowned at my dark house. "I thought we were staying here."

I looked at her then. She smiled, first trying to appear sexy and brave, but it melted quickly into uncertainty when I stared back in amazement at what she thought I had brought her to my house for.

"That's not why we're here," I said. I could feel my cheeks

burning red from embarrassment.

"I thought you wanted to." A strand of her dark hair fell across her forehead and she turned her eyes down to her knees.

"No, Stacy. That's not it." I searched for something appropriate and could think of nothing. She sniffled and wiped her nose on her sleeve. "I don't think of you in that manner."

"Then why am I here?" she said, raising her nasally voice, her eyes tearing. "Why are you doing this? I thought that's what you wanted."

"We're picking up supplies," I said. "We're going hunting."

We drove in silence. I perceived the sound of all my equipment rattling in the trunk: the two hunting rifles, the box of shells, the slim, dull buckles on the orange hunting vests, the thick soles of my boots. I'm certain I did not hear these things, but we drove in the dark and the sounds of the road and the quiet roar of the truck engine died away and I believe both of us focused only on what was in the trunk.

The parking lot was empty. Gravel and snow crackled under the weight of the wheels; the headlights, swinging across the lot and toward the woods, illuminated the snow and the sharp glimmer of ice covering it. Dawn began, and the sky seemed lighter, coloring the black trees in thin hues of purple. I killed the engine and we sat in silence.

She whispered, "I've never shot a gun before."

"It's easy," I said, my voice soft. "Remember you don't pull the trigger, you squeeze it."

She nodded, and I opened the door and walked to the trunk with the eager quickness of a teacher. I slid the two soft rifle cases down the truck bed and opened one. From a long beige case I removed my Winchester M94, a .30/30 with a custom stock, and slid the hammer back. Stacy eyed the rifle with her intense, curious expression. I held it at arm's-length. She took the rifle in her upturned palms.

"Keep the stock firm against your shoulder," I said. She

raised the weapon tentatively. "Don't worry, it isn't loaded. Get used to the weight. When you squeeze the trigger, there will be a kick. If the stock is against your shoulder, you'll be fine."

"I won't hit anything."

"That is not the point. Look through the scope."

She raised the barrel of the rifle, her left hand holding it steady and sure. She aimed for the woods.

"Do I look through one eye or two?"

"Whatever is more comfortable. Just remember that with two eyes it will take a moment for your vision to adjust. And if you use one eye, always use the same one. Left or right."

Her wide eyes stared into the barrel. She closed her right eye, then reopened it, and closed her left.

"Right eye," she said.

"Are you cold?"

She shook her head. She seemed sober, relaxed, focused. I touched my chin with a gloved hand, wondering if my face once possessed the same intense concentration. What I felt was the burning sensation of jealousy, wanting to possess something—youth, and the myriad possibilities of a life yet unlived—long beyond my years, and even at her age, I imagined my future with such precise certainty that my mind never had the opportunity to consider other lives or professions. I became conscious of my age. I would be fifty-one years old in April; I had been working and breathing in hospitals for over half my life. Anger curled my fists. It was a wonderful, delicious feeling.

We dressed. I gave her a faded Red Sox cap; after adjusting the plastic knobs to a smaller size, she slipped her ponytail into place. I tugged on my worn camouflage cap and gave her an orange vest. I laced my hunting boots, pulling hard on the laces. In my hands, I felt I could tear the rifle apart as easily as ripping paper.

"Ready?" I asked, breathless.

"Definitely."

Now dawn had fully come; the dark outline of trees became

visible, and even the slim grooves of tree bark became distinct. The falling snow had ceased, and the rising sun lifted the darkness like a veil. I felt Stacy Douglas behind me, maybe five paces, and I could see, even with my back to her, the way she gripped her rifle, prowling the woods in the way I imagined my father did when he was in Normandy. There was no wind and I could feel the temperature rising. Around us were thick pine and spruce trees and a rocky, sloping path. We crept for nearly fifteen minutes, and stopped at the lip of a low incline.

Just beyond us, past a lump of small boulders, the thick spruces reemerged. The wind that had not existed for the last half-hour picked up ever so slightly, pushing across our faces toward the east and I felt a deep, angry chill run through me. At this moment, I felt incredibly alive. Across the tops of trees, I could see the entire valley, and oaks and redwoods poked through my view, reaching for the clouds, and I remembered how wondrous the world is. How many days had I remained in my home, the heavy biographies in my lap, pinning me to my chair? I inhaled the cold air deeply, its icy texture chilling my throat. Below us, through the thick snow, were fresh deer tracks.

I turned to Stacy, flattened my hand, and we lowered ourselves, still hidden in the tree line, into a crouch. I pointed a finger at her. Then, with my flattened hand, directed her to a spot to my left. She nodded. I leaned close, my lips nearly against her ear. I inhaled her scent, a mixture of alcohol and fried food and strawberry lotion, and I wanted to wrap my hands around her head, pull her close and press my forehead against the crown of her head with my eyes closed as if in prayer and thank her for this wonderful sensation of rage.

"I'm going down the hill," I whispered. "Off to the right. You'll see the antlers."

"I can't do this," she said. She kept her eyes downhill, and her breathing came hard. "I'll miss."

"Aim for the middle of his chest. Aim for the smallest hair on his body."

She looked at the rifle in her hands. I do not know what thoughts entered her mind then, but her breathing became steady and controlled and she closed her left eye and looked through the scope.

Gently, I said, "You have to remove the safety."

Her left hand remained still. I slid my hand over hers, enveloping it. I guided her hand back down the barrel of the rifle to the safety latch. Her fingers raised, shaking my hand loose. On her own, her hand continued, and she pushed the safety off. Her expression was one of serene concentration.

"Good girl," I said, and stood, slipping off to the right and into the trees. I walked down the woods, bracing myself with my feet, feeling with delight the heavy breathing and pounding of my body. I slid to the right, farther, making sure I would steer the buck in Stacy's direction, and waited.

The buck was gorgeous. His proud, large antlers rose from his head like wings; his thick, shiny coat was spotless, and I admired his utilitarian legs, lean and strong. He swung his head, looking for the sound I was making, then froze, unmoved in that remarkable stillness that wild animals can achieve, the type of stillness I only see in human beings when they are anesthetized and under the harsh light of the operating room. He strode away from me, to his left, where I wanted him, and into Stacy's line of sight.

From my vantage point, I could see all if it: the buck striding into her sightline and Stacy aiming the Winchester down at him, her body unmoving and still. It was the most astounding moment of my life. I knew then that I had done something that I had never done before: I created. My life had been one of killing and repairing, shaping what is already there and tearing it down with the high-powered speed of a small metal bullet or putting it back together with synthetic thread and incisions and shapely cutting tools. But, then, standing in the cold woods, I watched Stacy Douglas, the ambitious Revere girl, stare down the scope of my rifle and in a moment of amazement, I knew that I had created a surgeon, and I felt my own breathlessness and hers become one as her steady hands wrapped around the rifle, knowing the stillness she felt was just like my own, and the shot's echo in the valley told us both that she had found her mark.

THE UTILITY ROOM

As the couple rose from the car, Ellen leaned against the living room window, gazing into the shadows on her lawn, just as she was the day her ex-husband moved out, loading a moving truck with the help of one of his friends, a man who smiled sheepishly at Ellen and kept his eyes down the entire time. Now Ellen could see the man and woman walking toward her house with their heads held high, the sunglasses on their faces hiding their eyes, moving up the driveway with the easy gait of a couple gliding down a beach. Her fingers tightened on the keys in her hand, two of them, the receipt from copying them today still in the pocket of her cardigan. This is what my life is like, she thought, at twenty-five and divorced: observing the happiness of other people from afar; a life as a serial video store customer staring out from windows.

They had asked to come through the back door. As a signal, Ellen had left her garage door open. She parked her car in the center now, taking both small spaces with her sedan. It struck her that she drove a Camry, a married person's car. She looked down at her hands and imagined them dotted with age spots, and to vanquish the image from her mind, she pressed the keys into her palms, the sharp edges digging into her skin. Their knock, three loud raps, jolted her attention, and she rushed through her kitchen to the mud room and yanked the door open.

"Ellen Boyle?" the woman said.

"Yes." Boyle was her maiden name, and the sound of it still

struck her as foreign. "You must be Brenda and Percy. Please come in."

Ellen stepped aside, and the couple entered. She wondered if they noticed she hadn't used their last names. She had assumed they would be, in some way, pernicious and slick: Percy in a jet-black suit and gleaming gold cufflinks, Brenda in expensive heels with gaudy rings that clinked loudly when her hands moved. But they were neither of these things. They were plain. Percy had a slight paunch, wore pleated khakis and penny loafers. Brenda was slim, her hands pixyish, and Ellen suddenly felt very protective of them.

"Thank you for seeing us, Ellen," she said, "on such short notice."

Ellen nodded. "Can I get you something to drink? Water? Coffee?"

"No, we're fine."

"Okay, then," Ellen said. Uncertain what next to say, she shoved her hands into her pockets and again, as it had regularly since Nicholas had moved out, the urge to cry gripped her like a fist. Once, this mud room had a small television and wicker furniture that they had dragged out onto their back patio for summer barbecues. Just last year they had even redone the tiling. Now Ellen could feel the February chill pass through the windows and the cold tile under her feet; the room, empty of all furniture and with only two cardboard boxes marked "Goodwill" in the corner, felt as still as a mausoleum. "Why don't I show you the room?"

Ellen led them into the kitchen and turned right. The utility room was here, tucked between her living room and mud room, along the long stretch of her corner lot. After she saw the ad and spoke to Brenda, Ellen had moved a queen-sized bed from the guest room—now her unfurnished study—and went to the attic for the night table and the mini fridge positioned in the corner. Beneath the windows, there was an armless chair whose origin she couldn't remember. The closet was empty, and along the opposite wall hung vintage travel posters of Budapest and Shanghai, places Ellen had never been and, she now knew, likely never would. She had vacuumed and dusted, even considered painting the room. But why bother? Why would they care?

"Here it is," Ellen said.

She hovered in the doorway, feeling like an intruder in her own home. The couple went to the windows and looked into the yard; as if on cue, the shadows from the trees vanished as bright sunshine broke through the sky and threw warm rays on the bed. It is a well-lit room, she thought, watching as the white walls absorbed the light and made the space welcome. Percy sat on the bed. He leaned over and opened the top drawer of the nightstand, then closed it again. He had nice dark hair and a pleasant face. Ellen would have never thought of him as an adulterer.

Brenda eased around the room, studying every object like an appraiser, absorbing it all as if the experience of this silent survey would be a memory to cherish. Perhaps it would. Ellen shifted her shoulder, digging it into the doorframe. Was Brenda the adulterer? Were they both? Ellen hadn't asked. She had asked so little of Brenda and Percy that only now, absurd as it was, did it occur to her that she knew nothing about the couple at all. She only knew they were paying cash, the first three months up-front.

Brenda came around the bed, and Percy stood up. She walked to him and pressed her palm against his shoulder. Ellen recognized this touch—an intimate one, a silent thank you. She used to touch Nicholas this way when they were first married and thought of themselves as adults, a couple who used body language and hidden codes to navigate parties, express lust or impatience or call for help with the brush of fingertips. Palm against the shoulder: a grateful touch; for his existence and his presence. A rush of raw anger flashed through Ellen. Where had these gestures gotten her with Nicholas? Where was this understanding of intimacy, of what was unspoken, when she was still married? Ellen hugged her chest.

"So?" she asked. "What do you think?"

"It's perfect," Brenda said. She looked down at the mattress. "Thank you."

"Twice a week, yes?"

"Do you want to know the days?"

"No," Ellen said. "I'm at school during the week. It doesn't matter."

"Because, sometimes, we might have to switch days."

"It doesn't matter."

Ellen stepped into their room—already: *their* room—and handed her both keys, which opened the door to the garage. From her purse, Brenda removed a bulky white envelope. When Ellen squeezed, the bills inside collapsed together.

"You should count it," Percy said, his voice soft and shy.

"I feel like a mobster," Ellen said, fingering the hundred dollar bills. Percy smiled. Had she made a joke? Was a white envelope with fifteen hundred dollars funny? And did it matter, if it helped her pay her mortgage every month?

Brenda sat down next to Percy. Ellen stared at the couple sitting on the mattress from her old guest room, their hands pressed together on his lap, serene for just a moment in their own world, in their small room, in the presence of nothing else but a woman who rented them a private place to make love for an hour, twice a week.

"So you're a pimp?" Jeannie asked.

"I guess so. I kinda feel that way."

Ellen and her friend Jeannie sat on the coffee shop patio, sunlight streaming through the tree branches, on an unseasonably warm February day. Across the street, seminary students tugged outside by fifty-degree weather that simply couldn't last sat on park benches and frowned down at the massive books in their laps; on blankets spread out against the grass, couples ate sandwiches and drank from thermoses. Dogs raced across the stretch of lawn, their owners lazily slapping a leash against their thighs as they strolled through the park, their paths chosen at random. Ellen wiggled in the metal chair and thumbed her ceramic mug.

"What are they like?" Jeannie asked.

"Friendly. They're just like us, only middle-aged." Ellen watched a bearded man race by on a bike, questioned where he was going. "I wonder if he has children."

"Maybe she has children. Maybe she's the bad one."

"Maybe neither of them is. I really don't know. I didn't ask. I know their names, and when they left, I wrote down their license plate. It's amazing how much information you can find out about someone online. Even got their credit history. They seem like regular people who just want to pay cash so there's no paper trail for their spouses to find."

Jeannie shrugged. "You have her phone number. Why don't you call and meet her?"

"No phone calls. What if her husband answered the phone? Besides, what would I ask her? 'Who's this guy you're fucking? How many children do you have?' I can't do that."

"Wait, remind me. They found you, or the other way around?"

"I found them on Craigslist. This is better than a roommate—they only show up during the day when I'm at work, and I don't have to sell the house. I mean, half my mortgage, in cash? Financially, it's perfect. It's a good business transaction." She closed her eyes and pinched the bridge of her nose. "Christ, I sound like Nicholas."

"Have you heard from him?"

"No. The divorce is settled. Maybe if there's tax stuff next year, but otherwise I don't have anything to say to him. I heard he lives in the county." Ellen pulled her knees up to her chest. "I heard he has a girlfriend."

"Sweetie," Jeannie leaned in and put a hand on Ellen's forearm, "I'm so sorry. What happened? He didn't call and tell you that, did he?"

"Gossip. The fifth grade teacher's husband saw him at a bar, he told her, she told me, why, I don't know. They said she was young."

"We're young."

"She meant college-aged, twenty-one. Maybe." Just then she was grateful that Jeannie was unmarried. Ellen stared at her left hand, and the sight of the pale skin where there once was a diamond ring set against a plain gold band made her furious. Jeannie tugged her chair closer, put her arm around Ellen's shoulders. She leaned in and rested her chin against Ellen's arm.

"Why am I even upset?" Ellen asked. "I don't love him. He's gone. I never see him."

"Dating anyone?"

"I can't. I went out with that chemist twice, remember?" Jeannie nodded. "On the second date, when he touched my hand at dinner, I jumped, knocked over my wine glass. His fingers were so cold, like he had dipped them in ice or something. Nicholas always had warm hands." Ellen shrugged. "I'm just not used to being touched like that."

"Being single sucks."

"I'm divorced," Ellen spat. "It's not the same thing at all."

Jeannie leaned away, unwrapping her arm from Ellen, her chair scraping the concrete as she pushed off, her eyes finding something interesting in the park again, and grabbed her latte. She sipped, and said nothing. Ellen regretted her words and stared intently at Jeannie, hoping for eye contact. She hadn't meant to insult her. It was simply true: the freedom of being single and unmarried wasn't at all like being abandoned for "irreconcile differences," hearing the gossip of him now in the arms of a bubbly twenty-one year old, emptying their home of photos and splitting the wedding gifts, fighting over possession of items they once bought as a couple. She wasn't single; Ellen believed she was discarded, trash rotting along the edges of a distant highway. Her single friends might as well have been from a different planet.

In the spring, when she came home from work on Mondays

and Thursdays, the windows in the utility room were always open. The top edges of the bedsheets and comforter were neatly turned down, like in a hotel. Sliding open the drawers, finding nothing, Ellen walked around the room, sniffing the air, searching for the scent of sex. She opened the fridge: four bottled waters and a bottle of chocolate syrup. Ellen checked the rug for syrup stains and found nothing; crouched down, she ran a finger around the seal, the cuttingly cold air blowing against her ankles, and she stood up and pressed the fridge closed. She cranked the window in, latching it, knowing next week she would once again find this room opened to the world. Why do they leave the windows open when everything else in the room remains so neat and exact?

On Thursdays, Ellen would find the sheets in a small pile by the door. The trash can was always emptied and relined with a plastic bag from the grocery store; the hall bathroom remained spotless. Other than the windows and the clump of sheets on the floor, it was as if they were never there at all.

In June, on the last day of school, all the teachers went out for drinks, a celebration of their one week off before they began summer classes or the other odd jobs many of them would have for the next ten weeks. Ellen had found work as a study hall monitor for Saint Louis University. She was to sit at a desk in a large lecture hall from nine to four, have people sign in, and then act disinterested as the athletes and marginal students sent text messages and downloaded music while she spent her entire day sipping bad coffee and perusing library books and magazines she brought with her in a tote bag: books on starting a small garden in her backyard, how to provide nutrients to the soil, what to grow, when to plant; articles on money management and investing and budgeting, the things that she had foolishly left to Nicholas; books on Western history, immigration, the Mississippi River. All her curiosity and wonder from college, an entire part of herself, had vanished in her marriage, swept aside by the role of wife and the demands of creating the foundation for a family she never had.

"You are so lucky," one of the other teachers said. "I'm working at a summer camp again. How did you get that?"

"Beats me," Ellen said. She didn't want to admit she knew a friend of Nicholas's that had promised her the position last summer.

They sat outside; the weather was still pleasant, not too hot for a St. Louis summer, and in their group of eight people, all of them comfortably drunk and vulgar now they were away from elementary school ears. Ellen leaned back into her chair. She craned her neck, stared straight up into the warm, dark sky, feeling the pleasant buzz of her gin and tonics drying her tongue and relaxing her muscles; the stars above her, constant and unblinking, filled her with a wonderful sadness. Here, among her colleagues, friends perhaps, she had never felt more alone. Maybe this was how Brenda felt at night, washing dishes and listening to her children play in the other room, the steam from the sink clouding her kitchen windows, the hot, soapy water blistering her skin, a drone of baseball announcers from the television in the family room where her husband sat. Or like Percy, perhaps in his office at home, planning how to send his kids to college, the stereo playing soft baroque music, and he would raise his eyes and stare into a silent fullness of his imagination and picture, somewhere across town, Brenda. In their homes, filled with people, they too were alone. Ellen swirled her neck, facing the other teachers as they erupted with laughter; all she caught of the joke was that St. Peter had said something about seeing a house.

Blurry-eyed, she gazed to her left. Across the patio, a man smiled at her. He had brilliant teeth, gleaming like a searchlight. Ellen blinked. The man waved, ducking his head slightly, and the gesture, so shy and childlike, touched her. She continued to stare at him, waiting. He looked at his friends—all men, dress shirts stripped of ties and their sleeves rolled up—down at his beer, back at her, back at his friends. Pleased she was wearing a skirt, she smiled and twisted her hips in his direction, crossing her legs at the knee, pointing toward him with her toes.

Finally, he got up, walked across the patio and stood over her. She didn't stand; he didn't seem very tall, and Ellen was suddenly afraid she might tower over him.

"Your glass is empty," the man said, pointing.

"Gin and tonic."

"I'll be right back."

The clacking of his shoes on the pavement carried him away from her, and she leaned forward, trying to hear his steps, studying his dark pants, his posture. He returned quickly, handing Ellen her drink and easing into a chair that someone had vacated.

"I'm Daniel," he said.

"You have beautiful teeth."

"Thanks. I'm a dentist."

Ellen laughed loud and obnoxious at such a perfect joke.

"No, really," Daniel said. "I'm a dentist, practicing for the last three years. I guess I did an okay job of putting my own braces on."

She smiled this time. "You must have. I'm a third grade teacher. Our year just ended and we're out celebrating." She nodded at her glass. "I guess you can tell."

Daniel, it turned out, was as plain as vanilla yogurt, and she adored him for being so ordinary. His appearance was clean and neat; his haircut was inexpensive and a little sloppy, and the skin under his jaw sagged, and yet his smile was soft, his eyes crinkled with kindness, and she could imagine looking up at him, tilted back in a dentist chair, and feeling completely relaxed. When his friends hollered that they were leaving and they exchanged phone numbers, he pulled out his business card, flipped it over, and wrote down his home number, and this gesture, like his smile, Ellen found perfect in its sincerity and simplicity. She pressed the card between her hands, watched him walk to the parking lot, and waited for him to turn and wave, as she knew he would, and though she wasn't certain, she figured that when he called her and made plans for dinner, she would do so while picking out her outfit, hearing his voice while staring at her clothes, the closet doors open, and struggling to decide which of her heelless shoes would be cute enough to go with a summer dress.

Brenda had left a note, saying they had borrowed two glasses, and apologized for doing so; they would bring their own next time. The note stated they had rinsed the glasses and set them in the dishwasher; Ellen lifted a glass out and sniffed, but she had no idea if it had been filled with water or whiskey. Ellen peeked in the utility room and verified the windows were open. A summer breeze nudged the curtains from the wall, and Ellen watched them flutter away from the outside world, careless and free. She cranked the window closed.

On their first date, Daniel parked in the driveway. Through the open windows along the side of the house, Ellen heard his footsteps as he walked around to the front door. She stood still, listened as he rapped on the screen door, and from her vantage point, looking down the main hallway, beyond the end table and closed doors, he stood visible through the glass, the porch light shining down on him. She felt a wave of happiness that had been absent from her life for months. A shiver of delight ran through her for this moment free of solitude and loneliness; she knew everything else that evening would pale in comparison. She walked shyly down the hallway, eyes on her feet, smiling, and let him in.

"You look terrific," Daniel said.

"Thank you," Ellen said. "Do you want a drink before we go?"

He slid his hands in his pockets and turned his head toward the living room. He appeared to be thinking hard about the question, as if he had never before been asked such a thing. It struck Ellen then, sweetly, that he was nervous.

"No, I'm okay." He took a step into her living room. "I love your place."

Ellen removed her sweater from a coat hanger. To her, it was still a room with all the small pieces of her ex-husband removed:

photographs of them gone but for the traces of dust around where the frames used to stand, the smaller television she pulled from the basement to replace Nicholas's big screen, the preposterous number of unlit candles she placed around the room to make it feel like her own. She rubbed the fabric between her fingers, focusing on its thick texture.

"I like the chair by the window," she said. "It's a good place to read."

Daniel studied the oversized red chair, and tilted his head to study the scratch marks near its legs. "Do you have cats?"

"No, I'm allergic. The chair was from a yard sale. After I got it, I vacuumed it a couple of times, and it was fine."

He moved toward the front door. "I can't believe what people get rid of. So much of it is still good."

Ellen nodded, followed his lead, pleased when he held the door for her. She locked up, the latching of the deadbolt thrilling. The keys dangled from the door and she held her hand away, watching the keys jangle together, a night at home literally locked away, her breath held tight within her chest, savoring this moment, which felt monumental in a way she couldn't entirely understand. It's one date. Nothing more. She slipped the keys into her pocket, and walked alongside Daniel to his car.

They drove into the city, the cars racing around them as Daniel drove slow, staying in the right lane, taking them into St. Louis. He said they were going to a Turkish restaurant. The restaurant's exterior was a dark brown wood, the kind of bland design appropriate for a late-sixties dentist office. They parked on the street and crossed the tiny, gravel parking lot, all seven of its spaces full, and entered through the front door.

Inside, the teenaged hostess smiled, and with two menus in her left hand, she gestured to her right. Beyond the hostess, behind a half-drawn curtain, Ellen could see the small bar, the patrons all male, wearing leather jackets, smoking pungent cigarettes and drinking vodka.

The hostess led them to a booth in the far-back corner,

giving Ellen a wonderful view of the room. Wide swaths of warm red draperies hung from the ceiling, and table lamps gave each booth an inviting glow. The small cluster of tables in the center of the room were candlelit, illuminating, it seemed, nothing but couples, their bodies leaning toward each other, fingers intertwined, a bottle of wine on the table. Exposed beams were chocolate brown, and from tiny speakers around the room, Turkish music played. Servers ducked in and out of the kitchen; distantly, Ellen could hear the sizzle of food, and a spicy aroma lingered in the air. The tension slid out of her shoulders; she rested her forearms on the table, and resisted the urge to be too forward and reach out, like all the others in the room, and take Daniel's hand.

They ate slowly, talked for hours, and finished their bottle of wine. When they stood to leave, he took her hand. In the parking lot, leaning into him, feeling slightly drunk, Ellen blinked at the bright yellow lights across the street. Focusing her eyes, steadying herself against Daniel's body, she pointed.

"Ted Drews," she said. "I didn't know we were that close."

"Wanna go?"

"Absolutely."

They crossed the street, and hopped into one of the long lines, surrounded by a sea of loud, laughing teenagers, smiling parents and their baby strollers, dogs with wagging tails, the on-duty cops laughing and joking with the men they knew. With their ice cream in hand—Daniel had butter pecan, she had cherry vanilla—they found a concrete bench looking over the busy street. Cars raced by intermittently, and teenagers laughed as they dashed across the street to and from their cars. Ellen remembered then the first time she had come here with Nicholas. They had just moved here, and he insisted it was the best ice cream. She found it unremarkable, told him so, and the night, like this one, was important in how unimportant it was, how casual and effortless their intimacy had been, their lives in front of them heading endlessly into the horizon.

"Hey," Daniel said. "You just went a million miles away."
Ellen blinked. How long had she been sitting quiet?

Finally, she nodded. "I guess so."

"So, I have to ask you something."

"Okay," Ellen said, steeling her stomach. She could feel the disappointment edge into her face, waiting for Daniel to screw this up.

"If we have triplets one day, can we name them Huey, Dewey, and Louie?"

Ellen snorted, and ice cream dropped onto her lap. Embarrassed, she laughed harder, tried to blot the ice cream with her napkin. Daniel handed her his napkins.

"Let's just call the third one," Ellen said, "something evil. Like, Leftovers. Really give him a complex."

"I like it. Or maybe just call them One, Two, and Three. Maybe in French so they get picked on in school."

"That would definitely happen." Ellen shook her head, relaxed. "There's this girl I had this year, and her family is German. Her last name is Schnitzel and no one could pronounce it right, and the boys started calling her *Shitheel*. They can be so cruel, and yet—and this is terrible to admit—really clever, too. It bothered her for a few weeks and then she started wiping her shoes on their pants and all the boys developed crushes on her. Isn't that bizarre?"

"Kids are tougher than we give them credit for. I get the same with my patients. Their parents terrify them with their own fear, and then they find out a cleaning is really easy."

Ellen balled the napkins in her hand. They finished their ice cream, and Daniel took their paper dishes and threw them away. When he returned, he took both her hands, sticky and warm, and leaned in. He kissed her gently, first her lower lip, then her upper, then fully, and after, pulling away, he gazed at her mouth, avoiding her eyes, still just a little shy.

As Ellen and Jeannie stood in the foyer, their shopping bags still dangling from their hands, Ellen's laughter froze. Down the hallway, Brenda stood holding an envelope. Color rose in Ellen's cheeks, embarrassed to be caught coming into her own home, and as she set her bags down, furious that she felt so.

"Sorry," Brenda said. "I wasn't expecting anyone."

"Summer break," Ellen said. "We have today off."

"I see. Well, I was going to leave a note, but I might as well talk to you in person now." She flipped the envelope over, studying it as if she had no idea how it had appeared in her hands.

Ellen walked into the kitchen. "Problem?"

"Yes and no. This is your last payment. The keys are tucked inside, too. We won't be coming back here."

"Did I do something wrong?"

"No," Brenda said. She placed the envelope down on the island and flattened her trembling left hand over it. A large bandage wrapped her index finger. "I'm sorry. I didn't mean to be obtuse. You're not an employer. This has always been such a cryptic arrangement, hasn't it? I mean that Percy and I broke up. We won't need your room anymore."

"Oh," Ellen said, looking beyond Brenda's shoulder and into their room. "I'm sorry to hear that."

She shrugged. "It's for the best."

Jeannie's heels clicked softly behind Ellen. She turned. Jeannie waved meekly.

Ellen looked at Brenda. "Do you want to have a drink?"

"Yeah," she said, "that's a good idea."

"Let me use the bathroom."

Ellen left them alone, and closed the bathroom door. She put the toilet seat down and sat; chin in her hands, she suddenly remembered that she hadn't introduced Jeannie and Brenda. Her stomach turned over. Why was she nervous? She wasn't the adulterer. And this was her house, not theirs. She leaned against the toilet tank and sighed, the porcelain chilling her lower back. She knew nothing about Brenda. What had happened here, in this house, her house, over these last six months? To them, to her, she wasn't even sure what she was considering other than the acidic burn in her stomach. Alone, she sat still for what felt like a very long time. Finally she stood. She flushed the toilet and turned on the faucet, clutching the sink as if she could rip it from the wall. In the mirror, her reflection peered back at her, her blue eyes wide with worry. Of what?

As she opened the bathroom door, she could hear laughter. She followed the noise as if enchanted, leading her into the kitchen, curious, and she watched Jeannie pour what must have been their second martini; on the island was both gin and vermouth. A third glass, without olives, waited for Ellen.

"Oh, hey," Jeannie said. "You okay?"

"Better now," Ellen said, picking up her drink.

Jeannie nodded to Brenda. "Ellen started dating again."

Brenda gave Ellen a genuine, kind smile. "Good for you. That must be so exciting."

"Yes," Ellen said. What else had they been talking about? "He's a nice guy, Daniel. We've only been out twice, but still, I think it'll turn into something."

"I'm jealous. All that wonderful stuff to look forward to. That's such a rush."

"Are you all right? I mean, with Percy."

"Yes, I suppose." She looked at Jeannie, who shrugged. Clearly Jeannie had already asked Brenda this. "I wasn't looking for anything like this, and when it started, I never really expected it to last. That made it better, in some way, because I really loved every moment we had." She swirled her drink, stared down into the stem. "It was never going to last."

A thousand questions ran through Ellen's mind, none of which she felt were appropriate to ask. She wondered if she would ever see Brenda again after this, after this day, these drinks, these next few minutes of conversation. Crossing her arms, the martini glass resting gently against her elbow, she again looked into the utility room. The drapes drifted away from the window, shifting with the breeze.

"What should I do with the room?" Ellen asked.

"You could rent it out still," Jeannie said.

"I suppose." She looked at Brenda. "I think of it as yours. My ex-husband had his things in there. I never really spent any time in that room."

Brenda said, "Maybe an office? A game room?"

"Beer pong," Jeannie winked.

"When I was younger," Brenda said, "I was great at that game."

They laughed, and the stories of their college days, their drunken stupidity and reckless happiness, began, each story funnier and bawdier and more absurd. As they spoke, pouring additional martinis, the afternoon turning to evening, Ellen failed to keep her mind in the conversation, stirring a malleable question as if it would finally solidify: what would she do with that room?

Daniel put the car in park, but he didn't turn off the ignition. Ellen slid her hand on top of his.

"Turn off the car," she said. "Come in."

They entered through the mud room, Daniel's hand on her hip. She laced his fingers in hers, and in the doorway to the kitchen, she pulled him close and kissed him. She wrapped her arms around his neck; he pressed his hips against hers. Their feet stumbled together, and Ellen spun from him, around the edge of the doorway, away from the kitchen, and with Daniel still behind her, she found herself facing the utility room. His breath was hot against her neck, his right arm rewrapped tight around her waist. Through the open windows, the streetlights illuminated the untouched room.

"Here?" Daniel said.

What had Nicholas kept in this room? Ellen couldn't remember. She somehow pictured it as cluttered, filled with boxes and an ugly, crooked desk and a dusty stereo system playing loud rock music. But she found that there was so much missing: when she tried to remember one specific memory of the room, one object, one moment with Nicholas, anything, she found that she could remember nothing at all.

"Ellen?"

"Yes," she said. "This is my room." They yanked the bedspread away, and their bodies become urgent: buttons fumbled over, moans and grunts and gasps uttered fast, shoes kicked off with the laces only loosened, belt buckles snapped, and Ellen kept her hands on him, clutched the back of his neck, guiding him down on top of her. She squeezed her eyes shut, and opened them again, staring up at the ceiling. With the windows open the room was so bright, and Ellen focused on a single streetlamp, its light shining on a street beyond her that bent and turned, its destination still to be explored.

UNION TERMINAL

From the living room of his Mount Adams condo, Patrick studied the lights along the Ohio River, the silhouettes of people moving from their cars to the riverside restaurants, the darkening buildings of Cincinnati, the brake lights of cars burning bright, and he imagined the phone in his hand as an anchor sinking into the riverbed, holding him in place. The phone rang; he turned his palm up, slow and curious, as if he had never seen a cell phone before in his life. The screen read, "O'Connor, William." Patrick closed his eyes, and with his free hand squeezed the bridge of his nose. For a moment, he considered ignoring the call, then hit *Accept*.

"I need you to come get me," his father said.

"Dad, I just drove back from the other side of Dayton. I'm beat."

"I'm having a hard time breathing."

Patrick turned from the window. "How long?"

"Since I got home."

"Call James."

"Why would I call your brother when I have you on the phone already? Listen," he wheezed. "I don't need an ambulance and goddamn sirens. Just a ride to the hospital."

Eyes open, Patrick stepped back toward the window. Even as the evening dusk darkened the city, he could still see the steam rising from the concrete, the hot waves of air escaping from the sewers at the edge of each street. He drummed the glass with his knuckles.

"I'm on the way," he said.

Patrick, five years old and bundled into his winter coat, clutched his three unopened packs of baseball cards. With his gloved hand between his shoulders, his father steered him toward the passenger seat and out of the January cold.

"Thanks, Dad," he said once the car was started and heat rushed against his feet. He had no idea why his father was nice enough to stop for baseball cards, but he knew better than to ask.

"No problem, sport."

"Can we go to McDonald's?"

"Sure. Gotta make a stop first."

His father was a large, barrel-chested man, with thick shoulders and strong hands. In school, Patrick had seen a picture of Paul Bunyan, and told the class he looked just like his dad. Patrick placed his feet atop his gym bag, pressing his sweaty uniform and shoes into the floor. His kindergarten team had won their first game of the season—he had even scored. As the teams lined up at midcourt to slap hands and mumble "Good game," he looked up into the stands, and searching all the parents and older brothers, found that his father had, once again, not come.

His father lit a cigarette, and cracked the window. Wind whistled through the gap; the radio was tuned to a classic rock station. Patrick opened one of the packs and held the cards close to his face in order to see who he had. He pulled the hard gum from between the cards and jammed it into his mouth.

On a block that Patrick didn't recognize, his father killed the engine. The houses in front of them were massive, with long lawns that dipped from the house to the street; porch lights illuminated pristine railings clear of beer cans and ashtrays. Patrick knew that the insides of these houses had rooms that boys his age weren't allowed to enter. His father reached behind him into the backseat and grabbed a small, navy duffel bag that Patrick had never seen before.

"Listen, sport," his father said. "You stay here. I'll be back in ten minutes."

"Where are you going?"

"I said, you stay here. Got it? Go through your cards."

His father opened the car, taking the duffel bag with him, and against the blackened streets, his father blended in: his dark pants, his dark coat, his dark cap. The door creaked closed, his father softly pushing his weight against it to latch, and then he disappeared from view.

Patrick worked the gum; when removed from the pack, it was always tough like plastic. He opened the other two packs and shoved the gum into his mouth, working the pieces together into one soft wad. He shuffled his cards, looking out at the lawns. There was a great darkness between the houses, like alleyways in his neighborhood, and he was beginning to worry. Where did Dad go? It was beginning to get cold, too, and he wished his father had left the keys so he could have the heat on and listen to the radio.

His father seemed to be gone for a very long time. Patrick sat up on his knees, his cards tumbling to the floor, and peered into the darkness. His stomach churned. He knew not to cry—his father sometimes beat him for crying—but he was beginning to fear his father wouldn't come back. Where would he go in the middle of the night? Patrick's breath fogged the icy window, and despite himself, he could feel tears pressing against his eyes.

The trunk flew open, and Patrick cowered out of sight. He peered over the headrest; his father pushed the duffel bag, now large and shapely, into the car. His father shut the trunk and hurried around to the driver's door, got in, started the car, and drove away quickly.

"Where'd you go?" Patrick asked.

"Just an errand, sport." The hair around his ears was slick with sweat and his cheeks were red, the way he looked when he mowed the lawn on a hot Saturday afternoon. "Ready for McDonald's?"

"I guess." Patrick slumped in his seat.

"Put your seatbelt on. Man, what a night. I can taste those fries already, huh?"

Patrick nodded; he was hungry. His father had a crazy smile on his face, his eyes distant, as if he was wrapped up in a dream. He didn't understand it, but if his father was happy and sober, what more could Patrick ask for?

He found his father sitting on the front porch, his hands on his knees and his thinning gray hair uncombed. He had shaven his beard when he went to prison but kept his mustache, which now covered his mouth. At his feet was an old rotary phone and several empty cans of Schlitz. Patrick lifted the phone, and followed the snaking cord to the screen door; he set the phone in his father's recliner, then tugged the front door locked. In the car, his father was silent, and with his eyes closed and his head against the seat, shook his head at all of Patrick's questions about the pain. When Patrick pulled the car to the curb of the emergency room, his father whispered, "Wheelchair."

Patrick spent the next four hours in the waiting room on the ninth floor of Christ Hospital in Mount Auburn. He worked off his Blackberry, answering emails and checking invoices, attempting to not think about the scratchy, incessant wheeze of his father's breathing. Finally, a cardiologist asked him to step into the hallway. Arms folded across his chest, Patrick listened as the doctor explained that his father's heart was functioning at twenty-five percent of its capability, and several valves were damaged and leaking. Unfortunately, because of his father's physical condition, they were recommending his father lose thirty pounds before he have an operation.

"He's a poor candidate for surgery," the doctor said.

"What if he loses the weight?"

"Quadruple bypass. And even then?" The doctor shrugged. "It's not good."

"No, I get it," Patrick nodded. "Poor candidate for surgery."

"Mr. O'Connor, your father's liver and lungs are a wreck. He's fifty-three years old and has the body of a man twice that age. I'm surprised he's alive at all. Even if he diets, your father might not last long enough to have the operation."

A nurse led Patrick down a bright, sterile hallway to his father's room. A small, bare dresser stood opposite his father's bed; a television hung in the corner. Windows along the far wall provided a view down onto the trees surrounding the hospital's small rose garden.

"How are you, Dad?"

"Fair," his father said, looking out the window. "This room must cost a fucking fortune."

"Your insurance coverage is paying for all this anyway."

"You mean, *your* insurance." He turned his head. "How was the trip?"

"Long. But I think I got a new contract up there. Should be nice long-term." Patrick sat down in a chair next to his father's bed, the heels of his shoes pinching his ankles. "Don't worry about the money."

"Who's worried? I'll be dead soon."

From his father's chest and the clean, thick bandages around his hands, wires ran to a series of machines along the wall. Numbers on the monitors, some large and some small, blinked and changed in the corners of each screen, the picture brilliantly clear and bright. Patrick figured there must be some way to dim all the screens at night so that his father could sleep. His father's gray mustache was now neat and trim, and the color had returned to his cheeks; his thick fingers were linked together and rested on his large stomach, rising slow and steady with each breath. He leaned slightly forward from the plush pillows, as if coiled to swing his legs out of bed at any moment.

His father asked, "Did they tell you?"

"Your heart is weak," Patrick said. "The doctors are recommending a diet of fruits and vegetables, 1300 calories a day, nothing fried or fatty."

"Christ." His father snorted. "That's not gonna happen."

It was well past midnight, and Patrick was exhausted—leaving early this morning for Dayton, then south again after lunch to his company's offices in St. Bernard, then east across town to home, all the way north to Loveland to get his father, and then out to the western edge of the city—and worried about the paperwork surely waiting for him on his desk tomorrow morning. He straightened his spine. He had been taking care of his father for years now; Patrick always saw his college graduation and his father's arrest occurring within three months of each other as a cosmic irony he could recognize but not understand.

"Fruits and vegetables," his father said, leaning back against the pillows. "Fuck that."

Riverfront Stadium was built in 1970; perfectly round and made of concrete, it was divided into four tiers of seats, organized by color. Patrick and his father would often sit in the red seats, the highest tier, to watch baseball. Between innings of each game, Patrick counted the vacant blue seats, the ones closest to the field, and tried to imagine why anyone would cough up the chance to sit so close.

Once, when Patrick was seven, his father lumbered home holding a white envelope. He winked at his son, and popping a can of Hudy Gold, said, "Blue seats, sport. Grab your glove."

"What about James?"

"He's at the McGraths', playing with Tim and Corey. Not invited. C'mon, son, just you and me."

They had four tickets. Before entering, they stopped and scalped two to a black man with thick, large glasses. The scalper had a large handful of tickets, and gave Patrick a wink. Once inside, his father used the cash to buy two beers, a soda, and hot dogs, and they settled into their seats. From their row, Patrick could peer across home plate and directly into the Reds' dugout. He studied the Reds players: who sat next to whom, who was near the bat rack, who spit tobacco or sunflower seeds the farthest. He didn't notice the young couple that sat down next to them—white, the man still in an Oxford shirt from a day of work; the woman in sandals and her sunglasses tastefully resting on top of her blonde hair—or when two uniformed policemen came down the aisle and asked to speak to the two men.

"Back in a flash," his father said, finishing his beer. Patrick traded a glance with the other man's wife. She gave an uneasy smile.

The two men returned five minutes later. His father's red face and scowl told Patrick all he needed to know: it was the same look he wore when he brought out the belt, buckle dangling at his knees. Instinctively, Patrick hunched his shoulders when his father growled, "Come on, let's go."

They didn't speak as they went back outside the stadium and repurchased tickets. Red seats. They trudged up the long concrete ramps to the top tier. When his father was angry, Patrick tried to slink away from home, leaving him on the porch to drink, hoping that when he returned, his father would be too drunk to give him a beating. But here in public with nowhere to go, they simply watched the game in silence for three innings. Finally, his father said, "Those tickets were stolen."

He continued. "If anyone asks, we bought those tickets from the black guy. Okay?"

"Who would ask?"

"If anyone asks," his father repeated, "we bought those tickets from the black guy. Understood?" He cleared his throat, and seemed suddenly calm.

Patrick nodded. Where did Dad get stolen tickets?

His father shook his head at the field. "The team could have at least given us free tickets, rather than make us buy more. Greedy fuckers." Then he hailed the beer man.

After leaving the hospital Tuesday night, Patrick met his younger brother James at the Mount Adams Grill. Yesterday he had left five messages before James had finally called him back; he showed up unshaven but, to Patrick's surprise, on time. His brother was cursed with the combination of his mother's thin build and his father's fierce expression. He had their father's pugnacious nose, strong cheeks, and broad forehead, so despite his withdrawn nature, he always wore the expression of a man eager to pick a fight he knows he can't win. Their mother, who Patrick only recalled from photographs, often seemed as if she was on the verge of an illness: a head cold, the flu, stomach pains, bronchitis, or the bone cancer that eventually killed her when he was ten years old.

They had a round of beers and talked about the Reds' losing streak before settling into their own lives.

"How's Kate?" James asked.

"Good. She's still in London."

"You broke up?"

"Doesn't bother me. Work takes up all my time. How's married life?"

James lit a cigarette and shrugged. He took long drags, and when his cigarette was half gone, he stubbed it out, then folded his fingers together as if in prayer. "So how is he?"

"Bad. This is probably it."

"Your message said he was having an operation."

"He's waffling, and the doctors want to run some more tests. Regardless, it won't buy him much time. He doesn't take care of himself."

"He's only fifty-three."

"His insides are mashed potatoes. Bad heart, high blood pressure, renal failure, sleep apnea. He's overweight, too."

"But they're gonna operate anyway."

"They've scheduled more tests. I don't know what Dad wants to do."

James nodded and finished his cigarette. He scratched his chin.

"What happens if he dies?" James asked.

Patrick stared out the window. "I'll take care of it. I'll sell the house. He doesn't have much else."

"What's it worth?"

Patrick narrowed his eyes; his brother lit a fresh cigarette. They sat silently and listened to the early evening noise of the bar: the post-work crowd, the clink of liquor bottles behind the bar, the eagerness in the broadcasters' pre-game report.

"Not much," Patrick finally said. "It's in Loveland."

James nodded and ordered a fresh beer. They waited for it to arrive and for the waitress to walk away.

"Listen," James said. "I was wondering if you could help me out."

Patrick nodded. "How much?"

"Five hundred?"

"I'll wire it today." Patrick leaned back in his chair. His brother stared out the window. "You in trouble?"

James shook his head, keeping his eyes averted. Patrick let it go, not eager to peel back their unspoken agreement, how often he took care of his brother with a loan that they both knew would never be repaid.

They ate burgers and fries and reverted back to conversations about sports. Finished, their plates cleared away, Patrick asked James if he was going to visit their father.

James said, "I don't like hospitals."

"It isn't for you. It's for Dad."

"Right. No, I get it. I just don't like them."

"Dad asked to see you," Patrick lied.

"Bullshit," James said, sounding like their father. "I know that isn't true." James sipped his beer, and Patrick noticed for the first time how thin his brother looked, the paleness of his skin. He looked like a skeleton. It struck him then that his brother had been drinking before he showed up. James ran a finger around the base of his beer glass, his hand steady. "Do you ever think about how our lives would have turned out if Mom had lived?"

"I don't know," Patrick said. "Honest? I don't remember her well. Do you?"

"Not really. I'm just thinking. Someone there to deal with Dad. Maybe he wouldn't have been such an asshole, you know?"

James slouched on his stool, leaning to the side like a dried-out sandcastle. Patrick reached forward to lay a hand on his brother's forearm and before he could touch him, James pushed away from the table, tilting his stool onto its back legs. He smirked, looking like their father again. "Let's just pay the bill and get the fuck outta here."

Walking out into the street, Patrick checked his messages. Clutching his phone, descending the steep incline to his car, sweat instantaneously forming on his skin from the July heat, Patrick tried to picture the London his ex-girlfriend lived in: the bridges and tunnels, the ageless architecture, the accents, the mild weather. He couldn't hold the image. The possibility of anywhere else but this was beyond his imagination.

The next day, on a restless night of sleep, Patrick worked until noon, and then returned to the hospital to discover another cardiologist had examined his father, and that this doctor had suggested that rest and medication might work.

"Always get a second opinion," his father declared. "Always. This cardiologist told me that my heart is a mess, but he doesn't think I need surgery. Just time to heal."

For years, his father worked on a factory line for General Electric; in the evenings, he came home caked in sweat and smelling of copper. During the summer, when he was feeling good and his breath was blustery with cheap beer, he propped his steel-toed boots on the porch banister, rocking gently, and told Patrick about Cincinnati, the history of its German immigrants, the pork industry, how the streets used to overflow with animals herded to the slaughterhouses on the riverbanks. It was the easy repose of his father's stout body, grinning as he spoke, and how he brushed his mustache with his cigar-like fingers that made the stories so captivating. His father loved talking about the lifts, the commuter system that brought the workers out of Cincinnati's downtown and into their homes in the surrounding hills—Mount Auburn, Mount Healthy, Price Hill. The lifts had been gone for decades; Patrick had only seen the shells of the abandoned stations, but his father made them alive, telling romantic stories of men in fedoras and hardhats side by side, ready for another honest day of good work.

Patrick had been a senior at Ohio State when his father was arrested for robbery: three armed robberies and three breaking and enterings, each carrying a twelve- to eighteen-month sentence. His father had been caught when he tried to sell rare coins that were a little too hard to come by, scaring the collector into making an inquiry call to the police. His father never did have a good explanation for what he did other than it was an easy-money thing, both to the cops and the neighbors that let James stay with them so he didn't have to switch high schools during his senior year. Despite remembering the holes in his past through therapy sessions, even today Patrick struggled with the picture: his father in a mask, a .38 in his waistband, a toolkit of picks and screwdrivers and glass cutters in a small duffel bag.

"Heart surgery," his father snorted. "To hell with that. I just need rest. I can take sick leave, right?"

"We can work something out," Patrick said.

"Can't avoid death. I don't need any operation."

When he won his college scholarship, his father asked him why he thought he was so much smarter than everyone else. When Patrick started his own company, distributing filtration and lubrication materials to coal mines and construction companies, his father, calling collect, said the business would fail. And when Patrick expanded into Indiana, Kentucky, and West Virginia, his father questioned why he was so eager to leave his hometown. Finally out of prison, his union job gone, his father worked odd jobs until Patrick hired him as a security guard at one of his warehouses, a job with no responsibilities and good medical coverage, which both of them resented. The supervisor had called two months later, embarrassed and apologetic, about the smell of alcohol on his father. Patrick instructed him to ignore it. Maybe, Patrick now thought, if he had done something then, or maybe in the years before, he wouldn't be standing in a hospital feeling responsible for things he couldn't control.

On Thursday morning, Patrick followed the instructions James left on his voicemail the night before, and pulled to the curb outside his brother's house at eight. Somehow, he knew to stay in the car and wait. After a moment, his brother stepped onto the porch, followed by his wife, a rail-thin woman with dark red hair. James turned so that Patrick couldn't see what he was saying, then gave her a chaste kiss, and came down the stairs. He set his bag in the backseat, then slid into the front next to Patrick.

"Are you sure you want me to take you?" Patrick said.

"We said goodbye here," James said. "I don't really want her to see me go in."

"But she knows you're going?"

"Of course she knows. How else would I explain it?"

They drove in silence, heading east out of the city. The skyscrapers vanished into long stretches of apple trees and open pastures on both sides of the road, which narrowed quickly from four lanes to two. It took nearly forty-five minutes to reach the facility. The driveway was gravel, the stones crackling under their tires, and the house was an old Georgian revival with a deep, broad porch of immaculate white peppered with black metal chairs. Ashtrays lined the railing, empty paper cups of coffee standing next to them like sentries.

"Here we are," Patrick said.

James nodded, but did not get out of the car.

"Do I need to check you in or something?"

"Nope," James said. "I just walk in there. If there's something you want to say, you need to say it now. I can't receive any phone calls for the first week."

"What if something happens to Dad?"

"You can leave a message. Can't do anything about that now

anyway, can I?" He ran a thin hand down his face, and licked his chapped lips. "I kinda hit bottom this week. Maybe I was waiting for this and just didn't know it."

Patrick wondered if his brother picked this moment to disappear from the world, this moment when their father was most likely to die. Or perhaps he really had just reached his breaking point. Patrick couldn't quite find the right words to ask; he sensed that he owed James an apology, but for what exactly, he didn't yet know.

"Remember the smell?" James asked. "The vanilla and strawberry? When you drove into the city, going down the highway?"

Patrick smiled. "Yeah. Dad always drove with the windows down. I loved that."

"When did you find out it was a Jack Daniel's distillery? I was older. Fifteen, I think. I'd already started drinking then." He blinked very slowly, as if fighting sleep. "Figures such a smell would come from them. It's like they were waiting for me."

They sat quietly for a long time, staring out through the windshield.

Finally, Patrick said, "I'll come visit. I'll be back in a week. First day I can."

James nodded and opened the car door. Patrick got out, came around the front, and stood with his hands in his pockets while his brother pulled the duffel bag from the backseat. They stood awkwardly, looking beyond each other's shoulders and staring into the thick surrounding trees.

"I'm scared," James said softly. "Can you believe that?"

"You're gonna be fine here. You'll see."

James set his bag down, and gave his brother a hug. Patrick stiffened; he couldn't remember the last time his brother had shown him affection. Slowly, he relaxed his shoulders, and squeezed back.

"You tell him 'Bye' for me, okay?" James said.

"I'll do that."

Released, Patrick stepped back, and James scooped up his bag, his eyes set on the front door of the rehab clinic, and strode forward. His brother reached the door, opened it, and walked inside, letting it swing closed behind him, never once turning around to look back. Patrick stood still, studying the surrounding woods, struggling to find his feelings. Then he climbed into his car and drove back to the hospital.

"They're still doing tests," his father said. This was his third day in the cardiac ward. "Christ knows what they're looking for."

Patrick wondered if all the tests and information had brought his father an untrustworthy knowledge, like a luckless gambler with an inside scoop. The union card games, weekend five-card stud that always sent his father home broke, and then the robberies, were just a series of uncatchable wins his father had to chase.

"Last night," his father said, "there was this program on about Cincinnati in the twentieth century. They talked about how it laid the groundwork for the industrialization of the thirties and forties, then about this great revitalization plan they had in the seventies. Fucking idiots. You get all the coloreds moving into the city, and what are you going to do? There isn't much a city can do when all the jobs move away."

"They have new plans for downtown now. Redevelopment, new condos and lofts, tax incentives for businesses. Taken all together, it should work."

"But no one wants to spend time there. You can't go anywhere and smoke. Everybody goes to Kentucky now. Why go to a bar if I can't smoke?" He cracked his knuckles.

"Most people don't smoke now. Lots of cities are luring people back. It happens everywhere. It can still happen here."

His father shrugged. As if a switch was thrown, the color drained from his cheeks, and his eyes glazed over, heavy eyelids bouncing open and closed, then refocused behind Patrick. His father stared at the dresser, its top absent of flowers, balloons, or

163

get-well cards. There was simply no one in his father's life that would send such things.

The heart monitor gave a shrill beep. Patrick stood and walked to the window, and looked down into the shadows in front of the hospital. He held the image of James striding toward the rehab clinic, and felt a wave of both pride and sadness; he knew, somehow, to keep James' illness to himself, to protect it from his father.

"I signed the forms," his father said. "The DNI and the DNR."

Patrick turned. Just for a moment, his father looked the same way James did outside the rehab facility. He pulled his hands against his stomach and laced his fingers together, then lowered his chin and stared at his knuckles as if he regretted every scar on his blocky hands. Above his father's head, the EKG monitor beeped, and the steady hum of his weak heart waved across the screen.

"I'll be back tomorrow," Patrick said. He headed for the door.

"Before you go," his father said. "Do you remember when you whipped that kid in high school? You were seventeen."

He looked over his shoulder, and waited.

"He gave you shit because you got a scholarship," his father continued. "And you kicked his ass. Then, you came home crying about getting suspended, afraid you would lose your scholarship." His father snorted. "Principal wasn't going to let that happen. You could have been a good fighter. Golden Gloves, for sure."

Patrick nodded. In his pocket, he wrapped his hand around his cell phone.

"When I'm dead," his father continued, "you give the money from the house to James. You don't need it, and I don't have much else to give. Then you cut that son of a bitch off. Otherwise, he'll be after money for the rest of your life."

"I'll see you tomorrow, Dad."

His father grimaced. He flopped his head against his pillow

and closed his eyes. "Sure. See you tomorrow."

The next afternoon Patrick went to the gym. His father's doctor scheduled additional tests, and Patrick decided he would visit in the evening. He drove to the gym, empty at midday, and borrowed a basketball from the front desk. Each dribble echoed loudly through the rafters, and Patrick found the solitude of dribbling soothing. He began circling from spot to spot on the court, lofting jump shots. It had been years since he shot a basketball, and the rhythm of the shot—the bending of the legs, leaping straight up from the floor, the cocking of the elbow and wrist, spreading the fingers, and then the easy follow-through—came back fast and natural. He shot baskets until he was breathing hard and pouring sweat. Then, in a rush of anger from somewhere deep within him, he snatched the ball and threw it as hard as he could against the backboard, the sound like an explosion, and the backboard shook long after the ball rolled to a stop at the opposite end of the court. In the locker room he showered, tugged on his clothes and once outside, he stood on the sidewalk staring into the hot, muggy July afternoon, unsure what to do or feel. For no particular reason, he decided to go to the train station.

On the western edge of the city limits, Union Terminal was once the main artery for the region's bus and train routes; now it housed three of the city's attractions: the Omnimax Theater, the Natural History & Science Museum, and the Cincinnati History Museum. Inside, a gigantic mosaic detailing the history of the city's blue-collar workers circled the large, half-domed ceiling. He had never been to the city museum; his knowledge of Cincinnati came from his father's stories. Curious, he bought a ticket, and walked past the souvenir stands to the entrance where a girl smacking gum wordlessly tore his ticket, and he walked through the double doors into an open atrium.

Inside, the walkway curved downstairs, leading visitors to a massive pictorial of Cincinnati's founding as a trading post, each room gliding through the past and into the present. But he never made it through the city's history. Instead, he stayed at the end of the tour, right where he entered, facing the gigantic model replica of Cincinnati.

It was the jewel of the museum: over seventy feet long, the replica highlighted each and every borough within city limits. The scaled model sprawled out in a curve, just like the city itself; to his right, against the far wall, a floor-to-ceiling window looked out onto the city, and Patrick could see all the real buildings and skyscrapers against the clear sky. In the replica, each portion of the city—Mount Auburn, Over the Rhine, Mount Pleasant—was represented in large sloping models, mimicking the rolling hills. The windows of miniature buildings lit up, and the city trolley raced through the districts, the electric whirl of its wheels crackling loud.

The city was laid out in a perfect grid; simple, dignified names such as Elm, Race, Vine, Walnut, and Main raced north from the river, creating right angles from Pete Rose Way to Second Street, all the way up to Fifteenth. Tiny models of people sprinkled the streets: vendors selling newspapers, businessman racing out of buildings to hail taxies, theatergoers entering the building in furs and minks. All of the city's landmarks—Fountain Square, The Scripps Center, the Isaac M. Wise Temple—were shrunken to an observable height, clear and exact in a way the city could never appear in the late-night realism of his living room. There, on Arlington Street, was the old WLW facility, the radio tower stretching high out of the rectangular building. Patrick pushed the speaker button. Then a man, in an eloquent, professional voice, began to speak clearly and cheerfully from the tiny speaker. The voice reminded Patrick of the announcers who introduce classical music. The voice said that this facility was where the Crosleys, owners of WLW, built assembly-line radios. From that one building, the entire city became connected, and the people, together, listened to big band music, baseball, and the news, the broadcast reaching from New York to Oklahoma City. Cincinnati, the voice said, was the center of the nation.

The Carew Tower was the tallest building in the city and, according to the voice, mandated in 1935 to always be the tallest. Patrick had been to the top once. An elevator took him to the forty-eighth floor where the elevator ended, and then he had to exit and walk up one more flight of stairs to reach the top floor. Patrick had always loved observing the city, feeling attached to it as if it was part of his body. Now, listening to the voice, he thought, in a businessman's manner, of the way this could stagnate growth, how there could be no new skyscrapers, no future construction. Beyond the edges of Cincinnati, the highways and entrance ramps and train yard lines became a series of easy curves, just like the Ohio River, constant in their change and movement. Patrick turned. He looked out through the window into Cincinnati, a city now in decay. There was no tragedy or lesson or meaning in this. Nothing came over him other than acceptance.

Batting a radio against his knee, a young man in a white shirt and black tie approached him. He told Patrick that the museum would close in ten minutes. The speaker voice stopped, and the lights over Vine Street dimmed, and then went out.

*

His father decided to have the operation. As soon as Patrick entered the room, his father blurted this out, and then considered the subject closed. He took a new interest in everything Patrick had done that day, and pressed him for details about the museum.

"They have this giant model of Cincinnati," Patrick said. "It's drawn to scale. The room's huge. They have all the old buildings, an electric train, and information on each neighborhood." He leaned forward in his chair. "They talked about the lifts. Remember telling me about those?"

"My grandfather used to ride the lifts. He had a friend die on the lift. Drunk, fell off. They had one in Mt. Auburn that ran to Western Avenue. I used to run up there when my father got off work." He frowned. "It was Western, right?"

"Sure," Patrick said. He didn't bother to tell his father it was actually Fifth Street. Western was on the other side of town. His father licked his cracked lips and stared down the length of the bed. "Tell me about the '75 Reds."

"Best team ever." His father sat upright. "No argument. I won't even hear it."

"Do you remember their starting lineup? Or their rotation?"

"Goddamn right I do. Just give me a second here."

"You used to talk about them all the time. You got mad at me when I said the '90 Reds went wire to wire and that made them better."

"Baseball." His father raised his eyebrows. "You and me didn't ever have much else, did we?"

Patrick shrugged. He watched his father, the way his fingers laced together on his stomach just like they always were when he listened to the Reds on the radio, rocking himself on the front porch with the push of one heel. He looked comfortable and aware, the best he had the entire week. He would remember how healthy his father appeared, again and again, when hours later a surgeon would stand before him and explain how complications happen with a high-risk patient. How people in surgery sometimes die right there on the operating table.

"C'mon," Patrick said. "Starting eight."

"Be patient. Bench behind the plate. Rose at third. Morgan at second. I think six of them scored a hundred runs that year. Seemed that way, at least." He said this gravely, as if he could see the sentence in an old book. "I tell you, Sparky had an easy time filling out the lineup. Perez at first. Concepcion at shortstop. Christ, he was amazing. You had hands like that."

"I don't think so."

"Maybe Larkin was better. I'm not sure. But I tell you, Concepcion made that play behind second base with ease, as if he was gliding to the ball. Damnedest thing."

"Barry Larkin was the best," Patrick said. "I mimicked my stance after him. Most of my buddies were Eric Davis fans. But I liked Larkin. His hands were so fast."

The loudspeaker said that it was time for visitors to go.

"I'll see you when you come out of the anesthetic," Patrick said.

When Patrick was at the door, his father called to him, "Foster, Geronimo, and Griffey. I knew I'd remember. Bench was the key. He held that squad together. You always need one guy to hold it together. Don't forget Bench."

When Patrick left the hospital, he walked down the long slanting driveway to the parking lot, and even in the dusk, he could see the steam rising from the macadam. From his vantage point, Cincinnati stretched before him in a wide, expansive vista of buildings under a bright, blue sky. His muscles burned with the pleasant exhaustion from basketball, his mind worn out from the museum.

He rolled his shoulders; around him, bright streetlights snapped on, casting a warm glow on the small, manicured gardens hugging the street. Patrick pulled his phone from his pocket. He wanted to leave a message for James. But to say what? There was, at this moment, no news. There was nothing to say. But this nothing was exactly what he wanted to tell his brother. There was a sense of possibility now, a future without burdens. Patrick wanted to tell his brother that he was there for him. He wanted to see James. He wanted James to see him, to stand by one of those large picture windows, holding a cup of black coffee, and picture this: his brother driving out of the city, the windows down and the smell of gingham grass and fresh apples racing in.

KEEP

I found my brother Kevin on our mother's front porch, sitting erect on the concrete steps like an expectant schoolboy waiting for the bus, his arms folded neatly in his lap and two mismatched suitcases behind him. Our mother's house was a small split-level in Blue Ash, a tiny lot close to the train tracks in an otherwise desirable neighborhood in Cincinnati. Kevin and I had grown up here, sharing one of two small bedrooms on the second floor, a room that had been his alone for his entire adult life. His expression remained unchanged when I put our mother's minivan in park and stepped onto the driveway.

"Is that all you're bringing?" I asked.

"No. There are boxes inside." He unfolded his lean body and stood tall. His disheveled black hair was flecked with gray and pushed back off his forehead as if he was standing in a storm. He wore a long-sleeved Detroit Tigers T-shirt that was so oversized the cuffs covered his hands. Inside were a dozen cardboard boxes of equal size, all taped shut and labeled with only the words "Up" or "Down" in black marker. Otherwise, the living room was hollowed out.

"Is this everything?" I asked.

"Yes, Henry. This is everything." For a moment, he stood unmoving, anchored in place, then he shuffled outside and picked up his suitcases.

My mother had owned the same furniture and the same

photographs and the same books for decades; every few years, she bought a new television, and once I started working, I was the one buying her a new set. She didn't want anything else; she read library books and sat in her chair, its indention formed perfectly to her body. The house was always cluttered, well-lit, and horribly sad. Over the last two weeks, I had sold everything I could and donated what I couldn't. We kept the photos and Kevin had a box of mementos that remained taped shut, but that was all. It only took fifteen minutes to load the van.

Since my mother's death, I had been driving her minivan, using the extra space to tote items away. But I'd also begun to drive it to work, leaving my Mercedes behind and the minivan's benches stored along the back wall of the garage, and when I drove it, I could feel the cabin's great emptiness behind me. Though my mother had owned this silver minivan for five years, the faint aroma of new-car smell lingered; the mileage was still under thirty thousand. She bought the minivan because it rode high up, and she felt safer on the road, safer walking to her car, safer able to see if anyone was hiding behind the driver's door, ready to abduct her. The only mourners at her funeral were me and my wife Gretchen.

Kevin was thirty-seven years old, and had lived his entire life—with the exceptions of the time he spent in mental hospitals—with our mother. Every day she made his bed and cooked his meals, and asked him to do small chores around the house. She had been shopping at Kroger, studying the price of breakfast cereal, when she collapsed from a massive heart attack. After hearing the news, Kevin wouldn't come out of his bedroom. I had listened outside his locked door, his tears coming as a series of deep-choked heaves, as if a great weight was repeatedly dropped on his chest.

It was an unseasonably cool August day; with the windows down, I drove us south, then east, neither of us speaking, and turned onto our street. Our winding road had no sidewalks, just long, immaculate lawns and hundred-year-old trees that lined the block like sentries.

"Which one is yours?" Kevin asked.

"You don't remember?"

"I haven't been to your house in years."

"This one," I said. "Right here."

We turned left into my driveway. Three massive red oaks shielded my home from the street, and passing beneath their shade always made me feel I was tunneling into a secret world. My lawn sloped slightly downward as if it was running away from our street, and in the small gulley below, my house was a small castle nestled in the woods, its dark walkways from the garage to the front door, and shadows falling from the dormers like lowered, suspicious eyelids. We parked near the front porch and the winding brick walkway surrounded by pretty flowers whose names I did not know. Above us were the windows of two empty bedrooms, their blinds open to make them appear warm and inviting from the outside in a way I knew they were not on the inside. These were once furnished for the additional children Gretchen and I never had, and their doors were always closed. Now one of those bedrooms would be occupied by my brother.

Gretchen waited for us by the large picture window of the living room, and when we entered through the front door, she greeted us at the threshold of the foyer. She stood with her arms folded across her chest and quietly said hello to Kevin, said she was glad to have him here. Tall for a woman, she still wore her dark blonde hair to her shoulders, and the crow's feet around her eyes made the blue of her irises penetrating. I have witnessed the way her sleek arms and muscled calves generated looks of envy and admiration. Even in capris and a cardigan, without jewelry or makeup, she was a striking, formidable presence; Kevin seemed to wither under her gaze, which flickered over him as if he were litter blowing down the street. She leveled her eyes at me and gave a tight smile.

I cleared my throat and called Catherine. We stood in the foyer and stared at each other like tired, sober strangers waiting on a platform for the night's last train out of the city. I thought vaguely of Catherine's birthday: she would turn fourteen in December.

She thumped down the stairs, her blonde ponytail bobbing against her shoulders, hopped to the bottom, and gave a weird playful bow to Kevin, then spread her arms wide and stood tall, pleased with whatever joke she was making. She wore her typical summer uniform of running shorts and a T-shirt from one of the soccer camps she attended. She was tall for thirteen, as willowy and stately as her mother. When no one spoke, Catherine smirked and raised her eyebrows at us. Finally she said, "Okay. Hey, Uncle Kevin. Want to see your new room?"

He nodded, and with a smile, she led him upstairs. She jogged up with quick, athletic bounds, as if she was running tires, and Kevin strained to keep up by taking the steps two at a time. Gretchen looked at me blankly, arms still folded, before she turned and walked away.

I started bringing in the boxes. The contents of each were written in Kevin's perfect handwriting: algorithms, textbooks, computer, printer, memorabilia. I left the "Down" boxes in the foyer and took the rest to his room, setting them outside his door. The room was sparsely occupied: a new twin-size bed, a desk, and a junky armoire Catherine and I had carried up from storage. The armoire was all that remained of the first bedroom set Gretchen and I bought as a newly married couple. Kevin sat on the bed with his hands tucked into his sleeves and folded neatly in his lap.

"I'd like to move the furniture around," he said.

"Sure. Where do you want things?"

"The desk here," he said, pressing a fist on the mattress. "I want it by the window. I don't care where anything else goes."

The view through the second-floor window was into the tall oaks on the front lawn, the five-pointed leaves waving like hands in the breeze. I slid the window open.

"Wireless?"

I said, "I'll give you the password. There are towels in the top drawer of the armoire. Bathroom is down the hall."

Kevin nodded and wrung his hands together. He bent to the floor and opened a backpack, pulling out two notebooks and two paperbacks with rounded edges and scooted back against the wall. He said he was just going to read for a little bit and I said that would be just fine and eased the door half-closed. Downstairs, Catherine waved, said she was riding her bike to her friend Madison's house and I told her to be home for dinner. From the same front window where Gretchen had observed Kevin and I arriving, I watched Catherine pedal up the driveway, her calves bulging as she pressed down on the pedals, the lean muscles of her arms flexed, her body pressing forward and out of the seat. Since the day she was born, there are moments in my life when I feel—with an intense, irrational panic so visceral I can't breathe—that I will never see Catherine again, that she will somehow disappear around the bend and never return. This fear was so strong that once, many years ago, I made an appointment to see a psychiatrist about my condition, but after three sessions, the doctor had assured me that the sadness I was feeling was normal rather than a mental illness. In the here and now of modern medicine, I wonder if this same psychiatrist today would prescribe some sort of medication, mix a chemical that would dull the synapses in my brain. I have tried to embrace this sadness at Catherine's departure as a good thing, a sign of my love for my daughter, that being a sentimental father is not the worst thing in the world. Still, it makes me feel weak and foolish and I have never spoken of it to anyone.

I turned. My house was still. The sun slipped behind clouds and once the outdoor light vanished, the entire first floor was shrouded in an unsettling shade of gray. I walked down the hallway to my study, a slim room nestled between the kitchen and garage, a surprisingly peaceful place with a good, clear view of my backyard. On the desk were three manila folders. Inside were a series of brochures and tax assessments of investment properties throughout the city. Besides the potential for diversity in our portfolio, Gretchen wanted me to find a multi-family building so that we could give Kevin his own place. She placed her objection to Kevin moving in with us as an intrusion on the structure of our lives, that his own apartment would be good for him, and a wise business investment for us. I refused, and said there was nothing to be discussed: Kevin would live with us. This conversation occurred within days of my mother's death, and I had spoken with the same level, quiet conviction Gretchen often used on others, and it had the effect I wanted of angering her and making clear that I would not change my mind. Since then, she and I had said no more than was necessary to each other, leaving our home a tense, sullen place that Catherine had made an increasing effort to avoid.

I picked up the folders, each tab marked neatly in my handwriting, and placed them in the desk filing cabinet. I turned on the radio, set it to a classic station, and sat down to listen to cello suites the rest of the afternoon, sitting unmoving by the window, watching the day darken. Distantly I heard Gretchen in the kitchen, and as I wondered where she had been all afternoon, the smell of mashed potatoes and pork chops filled the air. Sometime close to seven we all sat down for dinner, and I realized we hadn't heard any noise from Kevin all day.

"Did you call him?" Gretchen asked.

I said, "Of course I did."

"Did you go up there?"

I rose from the table, careful to keep my face expressionless.

The upstairs hallway was uncluttered and dark. No light came from the crack at the bottom of his door. I pressed my ear against it, heard nothing, then stood tall and knocked softly. "Kevin?"

There was no answer. I touched the doorknob, uncertain if I should turn it. I knocked and called his name again, remembering the time I had found him in high school. Back then it was our bedroom door, which was unlocked, and I had been the one to discover him after his failed suicide attempt, the one who consoled him while we waited for help to arrive.

I opened the door. He was asleep, but had moved the furniture without asking for my help; the armoire now stood between the door and the closet; the desk was under the window, the laptop closed and a neat stack of papers next to it; and the bed's headboard was pressed against the hallway wall. Kevin was curled in a tight ball, his face slack and calm, a pillow wrapped in his arms and a small puddle of drool on the sheets. All the boxes were broken down and resting in a neat pile at the foot of the bed, and I couldn't imagine how he had done all this without me hearing a single sound.

I closed the door gently and walked downstairs. My family had already started eating.

"He's asleep," I said. "He must be exhausted."

Without comment they both smiled tightly and then they picked up a conversation that had apparently begun when I was upstairs: Catherine started her freshman year next Wednesday, and they discussed her courses, how many were AP, what she knew about her teachers from the juniors and seniors on the soccer team. Speaking precisely and with textbook annunciation, Catherine sounded older, confident, and robotic. I contributed nothing. When we were done eating, Gretchen set her linen on the table and gathered the dishes in silence.

"May I watch television?" Catherine asked.

"Thirty minutes," Gretchen said. Catherine stood and went to the family room where she sat directly in front of the television, two floor pillows behind her head, her legs stretched out, feet flat against the base of the television stand. Gretchen and I gathered the dishes from the table and began to stack them on the island. She plugged the drain, turned on the water, and squirted in dish soap. From where we stood, we could see down the length of the kitchen all the way to the far end of the family room where our daughter lay.

"I hope the noise doesn't wake Kevin," I said.

"I'm sorry," Gretchen said. "I can't hear you with the sink

running."

"Kevin's asleep upstairs. I don't want to wake him." If she heard me she gave no indication. "Being in a new home has to be exhausting."

She continued to fill the sink with soapy water, clattering pots and pans into piles on the counter. I placed the large serving bowls down and neatly stacked our plates in front of me. Her back remained turned.

"It'll take time," I continued, "for him to get comfortable with you. With all of us. He's not used to having people around all the time."

"You sound like you're talking about a feral dog." She shut off the sink, and a final drop struck the soapy water. Steam rose, fogging the kitchen window.

"Kevin really needs us," I continued, "even if he hasn't said so to me. I know he does. And I know he really appreciates being here and living with us. Everything's going to be great. You know what he said to me today? He said he didn't remember which house was ours. Isn't that weird? How do you forget a house?"

"Why does she sit so close to the television?" Her face was in profile to me, staring out at Catherine, the dishtowel cocked against her hip like a sidearm. "Why do you let her do that?"

"I'm his older brother and there are times when I think about how I could have, should have, done more for him. Not that I didn't do what I could. I always did. But with Mom gone, I feel responsible."

A silence fell.

"Switch places with me, please," she asked.

I went to the sink and rolled up my sleeves. Our backs were to each other again. I heard her rummage below the island for Tupperware, and then the hissing pop of plastic as she opened each container.

"I never really knew your mother," she said.

"Mom was shy. She always liked you." I glanced at Gretchen, but her eyes were down, scooping and scraping the bowls for every last bit of food. "To tell you the truth, I think she was a little scared of you. She might have been embarrassed by how her house looked to you."

"You know I never cared about that."

She raised her enormous blue eyes and contemplated me in such a way that I could not understand her expression. I turned back to the sink and scrubbed the nearest frying pan.

She asked, "How often have we seen my brothers since our wedding? Once? Twice? I know Catherine doesn't have any memory of them. She told me that. My brothers have their own lives. They have their careers, their families, take vacations abroad, see new cultures. We all have our own lives to live. It's difficult to even imagine a person who doesn't have any ambition."

"Kevin has serious psychological issues."

"Don't we all." She snapped two lids shut; the refrigerator opened. "It just seems like a terrible influence on Catherine. All the other girls look up to her. I'd hate for her to lose focus."

Saying nothing at all seemed to be the only way I could respond. After the kitchen was clean, Gretchen announced she had a terrific headache and was going to bed. She walked past Catherine without commenting on how long she'd been watching television or how close she sat to it. After Gretchen was gone, I pulled out my laptop and sat down on the couch behind Catherine. She twisted onto her hip and looked up at me. I raised my eyebrows, waiting for her question, knowing that whatever was coming would be vaguely dangerous. Taking in my face, something rippled through her eyes and although she remained silent, we looked at each other for a long time. Then she rolled back off her hip and onto the floor pillows, and we ignored my wife's ultimatum and watched television for several hours, until finally Catherine stood, stretched, and said she was going to bed.

At some time after midnight, I crept upstairs. Our bedroom was pitch-black; we kept the room's thermostat ten degrees cooler than the rest of the house and thick, heavy curtains made the room impenetrable to light. Gretchen suffered from migraines that came in unannounced, debilitating waves that she had learned to manage with a mixture of strong prescription drugs and eight hours of sleep. In this darkness, I stood unmoving until the outline of her body appeared; then I listened for her breathing and waited to be sure she was asleep before slipping into the bathroom and pushing the door softly closed. On the countertop was an open prescription bottle of sumatriptan, a nasal spray, and a cold cream with its lid askew. I picked up the cream, vaguely aware of how expensive it was, the steel top surprisingly thin and fragile, and resealed it. I yanked my shirt over my head and used it to wipe my face, then turned on the faucet and stood bare-chested before the mirror and waited for the water to turn cold.

Gretchen was the youngest of three children. She grew up in Anderson and attended the Seven Hills School. Her parents were wealthy: he was an attorney, she was an interior decorator, and they spent most of their time away from home. Often by herself, Gretchen played alone, creating worlds and people in her mind with her dolls, with Legos, with her brothers' toys. She was the middle child; her two brothers both became attorneys like their father, and both left the Midwest as soon as they could. One is a Yale graduate who works in New York, the other a Stanford graduate who lives in Santa Barbara. We often spoke of them this way: lawyers identified solely by their prestigious university. After their parents died, they split the estate three ways, sold their parents' house, and the brothers have never returned to Cincinnati.

Gretchen and I met when I was getting my MBA and working for Proctor & Gamble. I liked to believe I was a different person then. When I was younger, I had presence when I entered a room; people were glad to see me and I spoke with ease and confidence, genuinely interested in the people I met. I truly believed I would run the company one day, be one of those CEO's on the cover of magazines with a *New York Times* bestselling book of my eight steps to business success. Back then, when we were naïve and optimistic, it seemed perfectly reasonable to me that I could rise through the company and be CEO one day. Proctor & Gamble was founded in Cincinnati, developed in Cincinnati, remained in Cincinnati: I saw the company and myself as being one and the same, a romantic dream in the worst sense of the phrase. At first, everything seemed fine: I was promoted at regular eighteen-month intervals and when the time became right, we had Catherine.

But her birth was difficult, and permanently damaged Gretchen's body. Her physician warned us that the stress from Catherine's birth had caused internal bleeding and scarring that would prevent additional children: fertilized eggs would no longer cling to the walls of Gretchen's uterus. But we were defiant. We pressed on. We stretched our finances and bought our current home in Indian Hill, an upstairs with four bedrooms and a downstairs centered around the massive kitchen that would be the hub of our lives. We believed in our plan: three children, just like her parents, only our children would grow up close, relying on one another, needing one another, and our family would be everything that Gretchen and I believed we deserved.

She miscarried five times before we finally gave up. The first was when Catherine was two, and shortly after, the migraines, which were infrequent in Gretchen's youth, became commonplace and intense: sometimes there would be an entire week of debilitating pain, headaches that pressed behind her eyes like industrial drills churning into her scalp; a pain that brought exhaustion and irritability and planted the first seeds of doubt as to who she was and what she could achieve with her life. She began to fold into herself. Our conversations became monotone recitations of our workdays. Each failure to conceive brought something else: anger, not just frustration; distrust rather than skepticism; and a sense that her world and the people in it must now become something wholly different.

Our marriage seemed frozen, and as we grew apart, I grew closer to Catherine, fostering our togetherness, and fostering an emotional separation from my wife, who became increasingly aloof until it seemed like Catherine and I lived on a different planet. At first, Gretchen didn't recognize that I encouraged this, that I let her push me away, her refusals to participate in our lives goading me to drive Catherine to sleepovers, soccer games, birthday parties. Gretchen was the one who begged off PTA meetings, who didn't want to take Catherine shopping, who refused to take part in our family. In time, however, she did become aware that I wanted this emotional separation from her; I wasn't just helping ease the burden of raising a daughter but also keeping Catherine away from her mother. This new awareness created a paranoia based on a certain amount of truth. Gretchen believed we thought she was cold, callous, distant, and she acted on this belief until it became true, her own vertiginous, self-fulfilling prophecy.

Her professional life, however, was a tremendous success. After we graduated college, she started as a branch manager for Fifth Third Bank, using her spare time to write action memos on their small branch model, identifying areas of expansion, pushing her service reps to ask customers about IRAs, home mortgages, and saving accounts for college. When she was promoted to corporate, she spent her weekends working on a comprehensive competitive analysis of national mortgage companies, demonstrating how Fifth Third could become not just a major player in the tristate area, but throughout the entire country. She evaluated new markets, made acquisition suggestions, and demanded precision of both thought and presentation from her marketing and management teams. She redesigned her sales force, streamlined costs, and bullied her way to vice president of wealth management, arguing that her knowledge of their business made her ideal to run this particular unit. And here she met face-to-face with wealth, people with net assets over ten million dollars, people who solve problems by signing checks. They wore tailored clothes with designer labels and shoes with immaculate stitching. Even the shoelaces seemed expensive. These wealthy men and women with expensive haircuts spoke with their hands and twirled their wrists so she could see the two-thousand-dollar watch, the gold bracelet, the immaculate cufflinks: these millionaires were gargantuan spenders, the revolving balances on their exclusive credit cards alone enough to make a poor man weep. Peel back their layers, however, and look beyond the accounts, the figures, the paperwork and the two-hundred-dollar ink pens, and Gretchen discovered lying beneath them all was fear. Fear of losing everything they worked for their entire lives. Fear that Gretchen would see through their confidence, their education, the numbers in their bank accounts. Her own fear—of the lack of children, of the decay of our marriage, of the distance between her and her only daughter—found itself to be an asset with the wealthy of the city, and there was satisfaction in being needed and respected and feared. Gretchen recognized that what drove them, drove the people she recognized as her own, was not family or business but the constant terror of how easily it could all fall apart.

As our daughter grew older, the interactions between my wife and daughter became a series of precise commands and matriarchal nods: Sit up straight, Catherine. Finish your chores, Catherine. Excellent grades, Catherine. Never too extreme in any direction. Never reveal anything that could show vulnerability, not even at—especially at—home. At times, she stated that Catherine appreciated these commands. Children needed orders, needed to recognize who was in charge at all times. As a child, Catherine was happy, laughing and playing, spilling drinks and sharing toys. Gretchen now felt a need to mold her, needed to tell her only daughter that this kindness, this hopefulness, would only lead to suffering. Catherine's smiles now were slighter, restrained, the expression of an adult with the certainty of a child, a smile given only to herself when things were done right. There was a quiet war being fought for our daughter, a war that I had only just begun to realize I had started many years ago.

I cupped my hands and drank, then splashed water on my face and the back of my neck. Our master bedroom was once one of our favorite places to be, a hideaway for my wife and I. It was a triangular room in the northeast corner of the house; surrounded by glass on two walls, the view was into the thick, dense forest surrounding the back of my property; in the Jacuzzi nestled in the outer corner, it was almost as if one was floating through the forest on a raft. Built into the walls were Bose speakers, the sound system hidden in the oversized walk-in closet where we kept our bathrobes, towels, and the wide range of soaps and moisturizers Gretchen loved. The counters were marble; the porcelain spotless, and small nods to Zen serenity—Chinese symbols, two bonsai trees, small, smooth stones, jars of creams and lotions on mirrored plates—decorated the room. Above, through the skylights, the stars shone brightly, and the entire room was lit by the natural gray of evening light.

I entered the two-person shower and pulled the door closed behind me. In the corner, from floor to ceiling on a series of stainless steel shelves, were bottles of shampoos, conditioners, and body lotions stacked all the way up, our razors resting at the top. What am I doing, I wondered. I said it aloud, softly, a whisper, and let the words hang before me as if they could manifest themselves in thin air, and I knew it was a question much larger than that evening and this strange sight: a forty-one-year-old man, barefoot and shirtless, in the gray moonlight of his home, asking himself questions he couldn't understand, standing alone, feeling the walls that he could not see beginning to squeeze him in.

Here is a list of the things Kevin has been diagnosed with in his life: dyslexia, depression, social anxiety disorder, schizophrenia, epilepsy, agoraphobia, obsessive compulsive disorder, attention deficit disorder, and separation anxiety. There are certainly others, but after a while, when nothing changes, they all blend together into a single mass of multi-syllabic words that mean nothing.

Kevin had been a Golden Gloves fighter, and when he was fifteen, he had quit in the middle of a fight he was winning, raced to the training room, stripped off his gloves, and walked into the January night wearing only his jock strap. When he was found, he rambled incoherently about the beauty of molecules, the way water's shape changes from liquid to solid, the wonder of the natural world. When winter passed, his wonder became an obsession: he dug into science and calculus books, earning honor roll grades, and our mother thought that was the end of it. On scholarship, he enrolled at Georgia Tech, and while he was there, his grades slipped even though he spent all his hours working in the labs. After his sophomore year, he moved back in with our mother, and while he would say he was interested in going back to school, he never did, spending his time watching television and reading library books in his bedroom, and about once a month, I'd drive to Mom's house and watch the Reds game with him, or if it was winter, college basketball. His twenties were marked with rages, disappearances, hysterical fits of crying and screaming that terrified my mother and brought the police to her door, put Kevin in hospitals. It took years of therapists and new drugs to find a medication that worked, and when he was thirty-two, we finally found a drug that soothed the demons in his head and allowed him to live with some semblance of peace. And Gretchen feared that if these demons ever returned, Kevin's rage would be turned on us rather than himself.

"I think she's wrong," Erica said. "She just doesn't understand him."

"Neither do I. I feel protective of him, not scared."

"Older brothers are like that."

We were naked on her bed. I was leaning against the bedpost, and she was against the headboard. With my thumb, I massaged the arc of her foot, kneading the muscle and sinew with absent concentration as if this was merely reflexive.

I said, "It would be better if Kevin left the house for a job."

"But he is working."

"For free. And he doesn't need to see anyone for that. With the Wi-Fi and cable in his room, he doesn't need to ever leave the house."

"Is it money?"

I waved my hand. "He gets disability checks from Social Security. He insisted on cutting me a check to subscribe to the MLB Network and Extra Innings. He doesn't need anything else." I stopped massaging her foot. "I don't mean to dump this on you."

"You aren't dumping on me. We're talking. That's what people do."

Erica and I had been together for three years. She was married twice, and seemed to have figured out some inherent fault in the concept of marriage—especially since she didn't want children—and has never pressured me to leave Gretchen. She said that I'm not ready to leave her. I knew this was true, though I did not know why this was true. Erica understood things about me that I did not no matter how long or hard I thought about them, and this was one of the many things I loved about her. Why she continued to love me, I didn't know.

"We should go to dinner again," I said.

"Can we?"

"Sure. We put a set of files on the table, don't drink too much, and don't touch in public, it would work."

"Rather elaborate, isn't it?"

"Definitely. But kind of fun, too. Like setting up a prank, or playing a part in a play."

Her chin turned toward the floor. "A part in a play," she repeated.

I stopped rubbing her foot and slid my hands around her ankles and stared the length of her lean, naked leg. The truth was that I never tired of it, that I loved the sneaking around, loved that there was a part of my life that remained my own and did not—could not—be shared with my wife and daughter. Erica continued to smile in a mysterious way: perhaps sadness, perhaps a secret. She looked up and tapped her wrist to indicate it was time to go. In silence we dressed quickly. We tried to see each other at least once a week, but sometimes, we would go three weeks without seeing each other. Often, I imagined this schedule was a matter of her convenience rather than mine, but I realized that this too was okay, that the way our relationship was flexible and strong was exactly why it worked.

We walked down to the garage, and dropped our briefcases in the trunks of our separate cars. Something must have crossed my face because Erica suddenly looked worried, and she came to me and took my face in her hands.

"It's going to be fine," she said. "Kevin has your phone number. You can always be home in fifteen minutes." She traced my chin with her finger, and lowered her eyes. "Have you two talked about your mother yet?"

"No. I haven't brought it up. No one has, really."

She stepped back and appraised me.

"You haven't talked about her either," she said.

"What's to say?"

She smiled sadly, my reticence something to be pitied, as if an adult in his forties couldn't possibly have anticipated his mother's death years ago and been long prepared for the emotions and responsibilities of her passing. She kissed me hard, and told me to call her next week. The garage door opened and she watched as I backed down her driveway, waiting for me to wave before I turned up the street and disappeared.

After work, I went to the gym to run and lift, preludes to the shower I needed to remove the lingering perfume of Erica from my body. As usual on the days I saw her, everything about my life was clear, like I was seeing the ocean for the first time. At home, however, this feeling vanished. My house was silent: the wooden floors and baseboards shined, the furniture looked untouched, as if no one dared sit there, and everywhere I turned I recalled the cost of every item, meeting with decorators and designers, ordering items that took months to locate, negotiate a price, deliver. Catherine's soccer bag was at the foot of the stairs; Gretchen wasn't home yet. The first floor was empty; distantly, I heard the hum of the washing machine. Upstairs, Kevin's open door threw the only light on the dark hallway, and I could tell his window was open from the warm scent of the outdoors trickling through the house.

On the floor, Kevin and Catherine sat cross-legged. The room hummed with the noise of the muted television, turned to a baseball game that neither was watching, and the afternoon light shone off the bare, white walls, making everything bright. She was hunched over her algebra homework, frowning, her fingers working a pencil like she was playing the trumpet. Gretchen often chastised her to sit up straight and do her homework at a table like an adult. Across from her, Kevin had a calculator and two blue binders open in front of him. I asked what he was working on.

"Next season's free agent outfielders." After he dropped out of school, he began to read the newspaper with fierce intensity, focusing on baseball box scores, which I found curious since he had always loved boxing and, as I recalled, never liked baseball. Whatever it was, though, it gave him something to do, and as he learned about the game, he started writing his thoughts into essays that resembled business plans in their format—bullets, boldface subject headings, pithy titles for each section—along with graphs, charts, and formulas. Anything he wrote would always be exactly twenty-five pages in length. When finished, he would send them unsolicited to the scouting departments of major league, minor league, and independent league teams. In time, his phone began to ring and the emails trickled in; someone evidently read Kevin's reports and discovered they had merit. Soon, he was assigned work. He never said who he regularly worked for, but our mother had told me that envelopes and package came from teams like the Colorado Rockies and the New York Mets. They loved his conclusions and his commission: he worked for free because he didn't want payments to affect his disability status, which would have, consequently, affected his disability checks. Instead, the clubs paid him in T-shirts and books mailed in large cardboard boxes that would be dropped on the front porch by UPS. Kevin found this tradeoff agreeable.

In front of him were several charts and a series of numbers

that looked, at a glance, like calculus equations. "That's baseball?"

"I'm charting defense."

I stood tall and placed my hands on my hips. I felt like an intruder in my own home.

"Bring you guys something?" I tried.

"I'm good," Kevin said. Catherine just shook her head.

"All right. I'll be downstairs." I stepped back into the dark hallway, feeling as if I had once again just been shut out of something important happening in my own home.

II

In the last three years, the Indian Hill Braves had become a powerhouse of women's high school soccer. The reason for this was the hiring of a new head coach, a four-year starter at Virginia who had tried out for the Olympic team and had strong ties to the Cincinnati community: she was a graduate of Cincinnati Country Day and her family's German heritage could be traced back through the city's history to the 1850s. Her husband was a trusts-and-estates attorney with Thompson and Hine, which allowed her the time to take a lax teaching job that allowed her to be head coach during the fall semester and run her own clinics in the spring.

Indian Hill improved immediately: the girls spent August doing two-a-days, mornings of explosive drills for their lateral quickness, closing speed, and footwork, and then the coach ran them to the point of exhaustion, all scheduled to begin at dawn; in the evenings, they worked through fundamentals of team defense, more footwork, more balance drills, finally ending the day with a scrimmage that concluded with the coach blowing the whistle, leading the girls to the trunk of her Mercedes SUV, opening up the back, and giving the girls Gatorade and words of love and encouragement for everything they gave and left on the field that day.

It was Thursday night and Catherine had raced home after school to complete her homework before her soccer game, an early season conference showdown for first place. Gretchen was still at work and Kevin hadn't looked up from the stack of binders on his desk when I asked if he would need anything while we were gone; he raised a hand and waved and for a moment I stared at the full water glass on his desk and wondered how many days it had been sitting there. I hurried down the stairs, a bit excited myself about Catherine's game, and I entered the garage just as Catherine threw her bag in the back of the minivan and slammed the trunk shut. She climbed into the passenger seat, feet flat on the floor and her back straight. I backed us out of the driveway and when I was in the street, my hand on the gear shift, we both turned our heads and looked at the house, as if we never expected to see it again. After we drove off our street, she tilted her chin, appraising me, and asked, "Are we rich?"

"Rich?"

"I mean, we live in Indian Hill."

"You have a pretty big game tonight. Shouldn't you be thinking about that instead?"

She shrugged and stared out through the windshield. At this age, her curiosity had turned inward, the precocious, adorable little girl now more reserved, yet awkward, as if inside her was a whirlwind of leaves that refused to reach the ground.

"We couldn't live anywhere else," I said. "Indian Hill is the best public school in the city, one of the best in the nation. We chose to live here for you. And we've put a lot of time into the house to make it look and feel the way we want. I thought you were happy at school. Do you want to transfer to CCDS?"

"No." She tugged on her earlobe, a habit of mine she'd picked up. "Jenny Dempsey said that her dad said we were rich. Really rich."

"And?"

"I just wanted to know if that was true."

"I'm not buying you a car. You're still a few years from a driver's license."

"Dad," she whined. "Come on."

We headed east on Kugler Mill Road. Since I could now carry all the girls to and from their games, I had become an eager attendee of not just some but all of Catherine's soccer games. I was not unaware, of course, that this kept me out of the house, away from Gretchen, away from Kevin. We came to an intersection and turned right down Given.

"Well?" she asked.

"Why do you want to know?"

"So we are?"

Our net-worth figure, a number I checked religiously every quarter, floated through my mind's eye like a passing cloud above a summer beach.

"People have the wrong impression of wealth," I said. "There are some people, like celebrities, who buy things like designer clothes and fancy jewelry. They earn a lot, spend a lot. They don't accumulate wealth. Wealthy people drive pickup trucks and shop at Sears. They aren't flashy."

"That type of wealthy doesn't live in Indian Hill."

This, I knew, was correct, and my chest expanded with pride. "What about the Fischers?"

"They're weird. Who wants to be like them?"

"Our neighbors are not weird. And this isn't about being like others."

"Then why are we in Grandma's minivan?"

"We're in the minivan to pick up your friends."

As if on cue, we arrived at the first house, and two girls in soccer uniforms stood and lifted their massive black soccer bags, still texting with their thumbs, and strolled to us. I popped the trunk, they threw their bags in, and the endless chatter of teenage girls began, a nonstop commentary on everything that continued uninterrupted for forty minutes as we swung by two more houses, picking up three more teammates, then continued south into Mariemont. The stadium lights illuminated the field, visible from the dark parking lot, and distantly I heard Catherine say "Thanks, Dad" among the chirps of "Thanks, Mr. O'Brien!" as they clambered out of the car, and with a click of a button I locked the minivan and stayed three steps behind the girls as we walked toward the field's entrance.

I sat down on the bleachers, the aluminum surprisingly warm through my pants. Around me sat parents I didn't recognize and teenagers—all bad haircuts, acne, and slouched shoulders—laughing and thumbing their phones. Pressing my palms together, I sat far removed from the other parents, high on the bleachers and close enough to the press box that I could hear the announcer, the father of one of the girls, light his cigarettes or clear his throat before announcing substitutions and goals. This was one of the only images I had as a young father that had actually become true: sitting by myself at my child's sporting events, proud and peaceful in the way only a parent can be.

When I was a boy, I used to wander away from the house, tramping through the backyards of our neighborhood, hopping fences and ducking behind trees, so I couldn't be spied on the sidewalks by my friends racing on their bikes or their parents zipping by in their cars. The Blue Ash Golf Course was several miles from our house, and I liked to sneak my way through backyards and creeks, make reckless dashes across suburban intersections, all the way pretending I was a valiant soldier escaping a German POW camp. Once I was off the suburban streets and into the woods around the fairways, my pace slowed, and when no one was on the hole I would walk through the fairways, always ignored by the older men who assumed I worked for the club, and I'd climb trees and sit with a pile of comic books stuffed into my book bag hanging from one of the branches, or walk along the man-made creek beds and hide under the walking bridges, watching the golfers' white legs and plaid shorts clomp overhead. When I was old enough to drive, I'd go get lost in the city, driving toward any part of town I did not recognize, my stereo turned high enough to drown out the thoughts in my head. Even when I was still a young man I seemed to find time to steal two or three hours to myself, parked in front of a newspaper in the corner of a diner or coffee shop, undisturbed by the demands of the day.

Now this is impossible. I reflexively pulled my Blackberry out and scanned through the six messages I had received in the last forty minutes alone; I leapt to *Politico*, *The Times*, checked the market, stuffed the device back into my pocket. The only solitude I would get would be here in the bleachers. I had learned that appearing slightly manic and demented watching your child play a sport only encouraged parents to act equally puerile, and that if you wished them to leave you alone, silence and a curled posture was most effective.

The JV game had just ended; Catherine scored twice, one on a breakaway and another on a rebound, and Indian Hill won easily, 6–1. Now was the varsity game. Catherine started on JV, but sat varsity. Usually, just being asked to sit with the seniors and juniors was enough of a compliment for a freshman, but my daughter, typical of her drive and intensity, seethed to start for the varsity squad. During the summer, Catherine had begun to brush her teeth standing on one foot—left in the morning, right in the evening—to strengthen her ankles and improve her balance.

At some point in the second half, she was inserted at forward. She was on the left side of the field and the team was mostly on defense and she had little to actively do. They were already down 2–0 at half, and Mariemont's lead was now pushed to four, a disappointing showing from Indian Hill, a team that I knew was much better than this. But after a series of volleys, stunts, and setups, Mariemont finally made a mistake, and turned the ball over. The midfielder cleared and Mariemont's backline, pushed up to midfield, fumbled the ball, and the Braves were on the attack. The ball skidded to a brunette girl, and seeing an opportunity to score, she raced forward, sprinting the ball downfield with controlled kicks, the three defenders backpedaling. She faked a pass right, stopped on a dime, and passed left to Catherine, the defense beginning to set up.

The ball careened, the pass a little rough, bouncing in

staccato bursts to my daughter. She cradled the ball with her left foot, and turned upfield, time to dribble once before the defender, barreling in from a perfect defensive angle, attempted to slide tackle Catherine.

After the accident, when I was standing alone in the hospital, this moment, this image, was what returned to my mind.

Catherine's eyes took it all in: the sliding attacker, the ball, the field, the goalie. The decision was fast, instinctual, unplanned, a reaction honed from hours of practice, repetition, drilling, the determination that she had shown even as a child, snapping together Legos or practicing her alphabet and penmanship until our dining room table was covered in paper. With her left foot, she planted, bending slightly at the waist. Her left knee shot up, and with her foot, she caught and lifted the ball. The defender was down, sliding, cleats up. The ball still against her instep, Catherine flicked it shoulder high and away from her body. Dirt and grass flew up. She sprang off her right foot. She leapt, tucking her knees, arms akimbo for balance, and the defender skidded beneath her, missing ball and ankle, missing everything. Catherine landed, and the crowd whooped with the heady awareness of witnessing something physically incredible. The goalie took one step back, then held her ground, cutting off as many angles as she could.

It didn't matter. In full stride, Catherine brought the ball right and rocketed a shot to the far post, beyond the goalie's outstretched but late hand, her body arching backwards in the hope of getting a finger on the ball, the shot catching the inside of the post as it spun into the net so the sounds were back to back: the leather exhalation of foot against the ball followed by the faint ping of aluminum when the ball ricocheted off the high post and came to a spinning rest at the bottom of the net.

The visiting Indian Hill crowd roared. Grins appeared on the faces of everyone who had remained sitting, a literal eyeopener, the expression of surprise and elation on their faces. Eyes turned toward me that I did not acknowledge. Catherine held her stoic expression until her teammates came around her with their palms raised, slaps on the back, and hugs, and only then did she give a teenage grin, childish joy finally released with a smile. But as soon as the ball was placed at midfield and the game was restarted, her face turned stony and controlled, even when they gave up two more goals, even when she turned the ball over, even when they lost.

After the game, the girls piled into the minivan. The cabin filled with the smell of grass and youthful sweat, and I thought about how the seats and floors had been so clean when Mom died, and pictured spending my Saturday morning vacuuming the carpets and wiping down the windows, attempting to recapture the scent of factory freshness that remained in the minivan for years after my mother first bought it, lingering in the air during those first weeks after her death, and recalling moments from my childhood—driving to baseball practice, trips to the library—and somehow I ended up driving the van without any awareness of where I was, surprised at the click of the sliding door popping open, hearing one of the girls climb out, finding myself unaware of how I drove here, how I drove anywhere.

We dropped the last of her teammates off well after dark. Mosquitoes circled the streetlights. Large stretches of the neighborhood were veiled in summer shadows, hiding imperfections. We drove with the windows down, the breeze matting Catherine's hair back against her skin. At a glance, she looked like her mother: the same curvature to her forehead and chin, the shape of her mouth, and it was only when she spoke and her face softened that I recognized her for who she truly was rather than some ghostly silhouette.

"Thanks for coming, Dad."

"You don't need to thank me."

"I know. But you're always there, you know?" She turned her head toward me. "Do you think Uncle Kevin would like to come to my games?"

"I'm sure he would. He's still adjusting, sweetheart. He never went out much when he was living with Grandma."

"Is he agoraphobic?"

"No, just shy. Baseball gives him purpose, something to do, and during the season, he's really focused on each night's action. He doesn't like to miss anything."

"But he might come?"

"I bet it would mean more to him if you asked rather than me."

She faced forward and drummed her nails on the armrest, a calculating gesture that I recognized as one of my own.

Catherine said, "I like being around him because he's so calm. When I'm with my friends, we always end up talking about stuff and I never get any work done. But when I'm alone, doing homework? Sometimes I feel like I'm missing out, that I shouldn't spend so much time on everything, you know? But Uncle Kevin, he's like that. He does the work because he likes the work, and I'm the same way. And, with his mental stuff, I don't want to mess up his routine."

"I'm sure he wouldn't think of it like that."

"Mom does."

I couldn't remember the last time Gretchen came to one of her soccer games. We drove beneath a canopy of trees and in the shadows, Catherine's expression was unseeable.

"Do you like playing soccer?" I asked. "Do you actually enjoy it?"

"Of course I do."

"You never smile," I continued. "I just can't always tell."

"Coach said that's a problem with women's sports. Women are supposed to be competitive and cute at the same time."

"I wasn't trying to be misogynistic."

She nodded, more to herself, it seemed, than me. "I know." Then, softer, she said, "Coach called it discipline. But I think it's like wearing a mask."

She tilted the seat backwards, then pulled her knees up and rolled onto her side, tugging her seatbelt with her like a blanket, and looked up at me. She seemed so young then, and when she gave me a sleepy, happy smile, I recognized my little girl and felt the way I did when I was a young father, how watching my daughter made my stomach plummet with happiness and dread at the power of unconditional love.

"Tired?" I asked.

"Exhausted." She closed her eyes. "The goal I scored? That was a good move, wasn't it, Dad?"

"You busted her ass."

She smiled, eyes still closed, and remained that way until we turned into our driveway. As if possessed, Catherine opened her eyes, faced forward, pulled her seat erect, and set her feet flat on the floor. All the windows of our house were black, and when the garage door rose, shining light on us from such a cavern, it felt as if we were travelers being devoured by some great sea monster, never to be heard from again.

The fall fundraiser for the Freedom Center was on a Saturday night in late September. My company, Proctor & Gamble, was one of several tristate businesses that was functioning as a major sponsor to raise money for this new museum—one of those causes that everyone is for without really caring why. Often, when attending these fundraisers—and Gretchen and I usually go to one per season—Milton Friedman's words creep into my mind. Even if I'm paraphrasing and misinterpreting badly (although I'm not entirely sure I am), his words are to the effect of this: a corporation's function is to earn money for its shareholders, nothing more and nothing less; therefore, any charitable giving, anything falling under the category of "corporate social responsibility," is only allowable if it creates profits for the corporation. Simply, CSR is permissible only when it is disingenuous.

Dressed in my tuxedo, cufflinks gleaming, I stood with my hands clasped behind me and observed Gretchen putting in her earrings. This was always the very last thing she did before we came down the stairs and headed out for the night; there was a reason behind it, a superstition or a ritual, I wasn't sure; she had told me why once before but because I'd forgotten something so crucial to her character I was too embarrassed to ask again. Standing in the frame of the bathroom where the soft lights and warm-colored stones gave the inviting spa-like feel we wanted, Gretchen was luminous, a secret smile on her face as she dipped her head to one side and slid the diamond earrings into her lobes, her makeup and hair lovely, her dark purple dress elegantly exposing her shoulders and neck.

"You look wonderful," I said.

"Thank you." And she turned and gave me a genuine smile, a flash of teeth and a spark of happiness in her eyes, and everything between us seemed just fine again.

But by the time we reached the bottom of the stairs, her eyes deadened: the sight of Kevin and Catherine at the kitchen table, both of them hunched over their work, the tabletop invisible beneath the stack of graph paper and textbooks and binders, all opened to various pages streaked with highlighters and pen marks. Catherine was old enough to take care of herself but Kevin's presence made me again think of her as a child, a girl still in need of protection from the world. Our descent didn't get either of them to raise their heads.

It was an unsettling surprise to see them downstairs rather than working up in his room. During the rare times he joined us for dinner, Kevin ate with his eyes down, picking his food up and raising it slowly to his tucked-down chin, as if afraid of breaking the silverware. He never finished the small portions on his plate. Gretchen stabbed at her food, glaring at him, killing any conversation with her one-word answers. I was always very calm, and it struck me that having Kevin sit silently next to me at dinner was a relief. He was always the last to get up; he would sit until we were all done, his hands folded in his lap as if he knew he caused this discomfort and must bear witness to its aftermath. Sitting here on the first floor seemed, to me, a small nod toward accepting his place in our home and embracing life with my family.

"We'll be back late tonight," I said. "There's plenty of food in the fridge, and feel free to call if you need anything." To Catherine, I said, "Don't stay up too late."

"I won't," she replied. Kevin waved without looking up.

I turned to get the keys. Gretchen's expression was stolid, and in the foyer, I plucked the keys to my Mercedes, then walked through the dining room, leading my wife. We were almost to the garage door when she turned back. Gretchen walked to the dining room, placed both hands on Catherine's shoulders, and gave her a kiss. She closed her eyes, resting her chin on the crown of her head. Catherine stiffened and stared into the mass of papers. We were a household that never showed such affection and I had no idea what it was that drove my wife to do this, why then, why here. What it could have possibly meant? Gretchen released her and walked back toward me, her eyes focused on some point below my chin. From the expression on Catherine's face—her eyes latched on mine, narrowed into a question, pleading with me for some sort of explanation—she too had no understanding of what had just transpired. Gretchen slid by me, careful to not brush a hand or shoulder against me, and walked into the garage.

In the car, Gretchen took my hand. Hers was surprisingly warm. After we exited the highway and cruised to a red light, I looked at her face, but she turned her chin toward the window and looked out on the city. Somehow, over all the years, our sadness had stripped away my ability to talk to my wife, and there was something absurd about this that I didn't know how to fight. Gently I turned my palm upward, curling her hand up and into the light shining through the windshield. She had a French manicure and both her wedding and engagement ring were freshly cleaned, the platinum spotless. The bones in her hand jutted out, as if her fair skin could no longer hold them in, and the thinness of her hands appeared skeletal. The light turned green, and we continued without speaking through the intersection and into Cincinnati.

The Freedom Center was a new museum built between the two ballparks on the bank of the Ohio River. Despite the luminaries that had arrived for its grand opening in 2003, the museum had floundered financially almost from the beginning. From its inception no one quite knew what the Freedom Center was or what it intended to be, and walking through the building, a three-story brick square of gleaming newness, whatever loose concept of freedom the museum generated had clearly become an afterthought to interactive screens, high-definition short films, and immaculate displays and artifacts of slavery that were nothing but clever reconstructions. Everything about the museum was a contradiction.

The driveway leading up to the museum was cobblestone, the low, uneven rumbling under the tires exciting, and Gretchen's demeanor steeled as we approached the valet. Outside in the cool night air, her composure returned, and I loved her then for her ability to play a public role and fearlessly navigate the world, and I thought of us again as a couple in that most lovely and intimate meaning of the word.

Once, when I was a young man and newly married and believed that the city owed me something, I could speak to people and make them feel, for those five minutes, that the sun shone its warmth on them, just them, and that once I moved away from our conversation, it was as if dark clouds had reentered the sky, and they would look after me, admiring. Somehow, adulthood had stripped this away, and in crowds, particularly at company events when we all have cocktails and music I vaguely recognize is playing too loud and in every direction you look there are bleached, shiny teeth gleaming from mouths wide open from laughter, I felt a vertiginous spiral, my organs descending through my body, hollowing me out, and if I took one step back, I'd fall away completely. And no one would notice or care. Among them all, fueled by alcohol and ambition, those parties made me want to slink back against the wall and slide to the floor like a punished child.

Inside, hundreds of the city's elite were greeted with flutes of champagne and hors d'oeuvres served on silver trays by young men in spotless white jackets. We crossed the room and lingered in circles for no more than five minutes, enough time for me to slap the backs of men I knew and shake the hands of men I didn't, enough time for Gretchen to get compliments and display her wit, enough time for us to radiantly smile before circling to another group of donors, parading ourselves around the room for all to see. Our hands often lingered on each other—her hand on my shoulder, my hand on her lower back—but this touch was so light and public we might not have touched at all, as if an invisible membrane prevented out bodies from really being close, and when we walked side by side, we held our drinks between us so we did not touch.

We had been there for almost forty-five minutes when I saw Erica. She was about twenty feet away in a circle of administrators from Christ Hospital. When she caught my eye, I realized that she had seen me much earlier, and had made an effort to stay away. Gretchen was speaking to an executive with Great American; I touched her elbow, said "Excuse me," and moved over to Erica's group.

She was radiant. She wore her brown hair up and a sleek cocktail dress that revealed her runner's curves. She both appeared to embrace her age—in her forties, like me—and escape it, a youthfulness to her eyes and smile despite the lines of adulthood around them both. She turned from the woman she was speaking to, introduced us, and I immediately forgot the other woman's name, but she was corralled by her husband, leaving Erica and I effectively alone in the circle.

"How long ago did you spot me?" I asked.

"Almost thirty minutes. I've been weaving behind you the whole time."

"You look fantastic."

"So do you."

I shifted my weight backwards so I wasn't leaning in; turning slightly, my face in profile to Gretchen, so I was not looking at or evading her; my eyes fluttered above and beyond Erica as if searching for someone more important to talk to, and flattened my mouth. I always assumed Gretchen's eyes were on me.

"You're quite the actor," Erica said.

"Thank you." I raised my eyebrows as a man's face turned in my direction, as if saying *I'll be there in a moment*. "I'm sorry. I didn't know you'd be here."

"Well, I didn't know you'd be here either. But we both still had to be, right?"

"That's true."

Her gaze was too intense, and my throat went dry, heartbeat echoing in my ears; I wanted to hold her then perhaps more than I ever had before. Unable to think of anything to say, I sipped from the flute, and concentrated hard on the carbonation gurgling down my throat.

"She's lovely," Erica said. "I mean, I always knew she would be, but I hadn't really thought much of it."

"I'm really sorry."

"Don't be." She gazed over my shoulder; she too was playing a role in case Gretchen observed us. "She was an abstraction before and now she's real, and I'll tell you, Henry, I'm jealous. I didn't think I was capable of that anymore, but I am. Shake my hand and go back to her. Call me tomorrow. Okay?"

Champagne flute held high near her cheek, she extended her right hand, and I took it delicately, sliding my fingers into hers, then her palm, and she did the same, almost as if we were stealing a long, secret kiss. We squeezed and held hands for just a moment too long and said "It was great to meet you" and "You, too," and when she let go, she lowered her face away from Gretchen's view, her lips trembling. Erica placed her hand against her chest to calm her breathing, and walked away as casually as she could and joined another group, and I swung around, turning my face toward Gretchen without trying to see her, and butted into a conversation two men were having about college basketball. I stayed here for a while, then moved to another, then another, and when people started shuffling off to the ballroom for dinner, I had lost track of both women.

Inside, the ballroom was immaculately lit: the soft lighting throughout the room was refracted through the glassware at each table, as if everything was sprinkled with fine diamonds. At the far end of the room was the long row for distinguished guests, the lectern's veneer polished and the plaque on its front announcing our location was buffed and shiny. My mind blanked on who was the night's featured speaker. Not that it really mattered. As long as we made an appropriate donation with our tickets, and the auction went smoothly, and everyone mingled and felt as if enough business cards were exchanged and hands shaken, and there was enough wine and liquor to go around, tonight's fundraiser would be considered a success.

"There you are," Gretchen said. She stood inside the entranceway, and slipped her hand into mine. Her palm was warm and slick. "I lost you there for a moment. C'mon, don't make me sit alone."

"Having a good time?"

"Actually, yes. We've been to so many of these and I know they can get dull, but something is different tonight." We wove around a table, searching for table 34. "I feel very relaxed for the first time in a while."

"We haven't been out much lately, have we?"

She squeezed my hand; her mood was too good to consider the question deeply. "No, I guess not. Have you seen Stephen?" She was referring to a managing partner at Fidelity's branch in Cincinnati. "I thought he and Rachel would be here tonight."

"No, but I haven't been looking either. Give him a call."

"I am not using my cell phone here. We'll spot him. Just keep your eyes open."

The people at our table were a mixture of our interests and strangers. Gretchen sat on my left; on her other side was Bruce Adams, another vice president at Proctor & Gamble, and his wife. To my right was Janet Stern and her husband Tom—a colleague of Gretchen's and the vice president of risk and compliance. There were two other couples who seemed to know each other but not us; I forgot what they did, but we all seemed to be vice presidents of something. A waiter came by and brought us another round of drinks even though all of us already had wine and champagne glasses, and our voices grew louder, fueled by alcohol and a relaxation into the night's atmosphere. We doused our salads in dressing, instructed the waiter on whether we wanted chicken or salmon, and chatted amicably about sports and home renovations in a pleasant, nonconfrontational way.

Tom had thick gray hair that was perfectly parted, and the large build of an ex-football player. On his right hand, he wore his class ring and the smallest finger was bent outwards at an impossible angle: he had mangled it in a lineman's face mask when he was in college and it no longer worked properly. I wondered how he typed his emails. His wife Janet had, like Gretchen, immaculate Norwegian hair and skin, and an expression of regular delight at the world. The Sterns were a decade or two older than us, and appeared to be a fine couple. Tom and Gretchen were gossiping about a colleague's poor work, and the mood was light, their colleague's repeated mistakes humorous rather than exasperating. Janet and I had little to contribute but we were both smiling and nodding and laughing at the right times, and when she finally spoke, I realized I had only been vaguely listening.

"We've had such a problem with Tom's brother," Janet said.

"He's one crazy son of a bitch," Tom agreed. He shook his head, laughing, and finished his drink.

"Brother?" I echoed.

"My brother." He settled back into his chair and looked skyward, a storyteller easing into his delivery. "He lives in Savannah. I haven't seen him in years. He has one of those beards without the mustache and always wears a hat. He's a bit of a dandy that way. Anyway, he studied art and architecture in college and he moved down there and got involved in historical preservation and small museums and such. I guess he's kind of a big deal down there."

A waiter placed another drink down, and Tom absently picked it up without comment and sipped. His eyes were still focused on some distant point over our heads.

"So our father died," he continued, "and his estate was in a bit of flux. The old man kept his eye on the tax laws, watched too much CNBC, and he started talking to all these different advisors and setting up these weird trusts for his grandchildren, and some things got finished and other things didn't. Just a mess. Anyway, to make a long story short, my brother is fucking up the process. Basically, he's claiming that one of the trusts was set up for historical preservation in Savannah, and it's total horseshit."

Janet whispered, "It's been very hard on Tom."

"I don't know why," Tom continued, "my father was supporting this. We hadn't seen my brother in years. My father went down there once in a while, but my brother never came back up. Not once."

"Families are hard," I said.

"Goddamn right. I mean, can you believe the position he's putting me in? I'm trying to follow the old man's wishes. I don't need the money. It doesn't make any difference to me. But he can't screw around with my father's legacy."

"I have a brother." Under the table, Gretchen's hand slid over my forearm. She squeezed hard: *be quiet.*

Tom said, "There's just no appreciation for what I have to do. None. All the lawyers, the trust, the tax laws? I deal with that. And my brother just keeps saying that the foundation was promised this support, over and over again, as if repeating that is going to make it any more true."

"Have you spoken to him?"

He waved my question away as if it was a fly circling his head.

"That's what attorneys are for."

"I'm sure it will be fine," Gretchen said.

"Just horrendous," Janet murmured.

The room seemed to shrink, my sight disoriented, until my

frame of vision was filled by just the Sterns: their bodies seemed too large, and no matter how much I blinked or what direction I twisted my neck nothing appeared in front of me other than this man and his indignation. Gretchen dug her nails into my arm; when I turned toward her she was smiling politely at the Sterns and their troubles.

"You see," Tom said, "this is not about money. It's about the principle. About what my father wanted and what he had established in his will and the trusts that I know he set up years ago when he was of a sound state of mind. It's just unbelievable to me, simply unbelievable, how my brother could be so stubborn."

Pulling against my wife's nails, twisting in my seat, I craned my neck around the room, searching for Erica. Above their necks pinched tight from their bowties, the faces of men all seemed red and bloated from alcohol and laughter, eyes closed, jaws open in soundless laughs so that I could see the wet scarlet roofs of their mouths. Where was she?

Tom continued speaking and when I turned back in his direction, I could no longer hear him: there was a buzzing around me, like a swarm of bees surrounded my head. His mouth flapped like a fish's and I lowered my eyes to my plate. Shuffling noises were made at the head table, a finger tapped the microphone, throat clearing, and a merry "Good evening" silenced the crowd. The buzzing continued, and I jammed my knuckles into my ear and twisted.

"I need to go home," I whispered to Gretchen.

"We're not going anywhere."

"Please."

The speaker made some sort of joke. While everyone laughed politely, Gretchen slid her hand onto my leg. "Do not do this to me, Henry."

"How can he be like that?"

She removed her hand and clapped along with everyone else. I lifted my head as if an invisible wire tugged upward on my chest and robotically I applauded, a grin on my face, and my sudden transformation startled me. It felt like a game then: could I pretend to have no real emotion? I beamed, feeling Gretchen's icy stare melt as she observed me playing along. Folding my hands in my lap, an obedient altar boy, I concentrated on stoning my face, a gargoyle observing the sinners from above. My stomach gurgled and I can't remember speaking again during the final two hours of the event.

We drove home in silence, Gretchen's hands again in her lap and her face turned toward the window. Once inside the garage, the idling sounds of the engine reverberating, my hand on the gear shift, anticipating something I could not articulate, Gretchen exited the car without comment. I shut off the engine and listened to her heels on the concrete. She entered the house without turning around. I removed the keys from the ignition and held them in my palm, studying them as if I had no idea how they had arrived there.

When I entered, the only light on was over the kitchen sink, illuminating the stainless steel and its lack of clutter. From my pockets I removed my wallet and the business cards I had accumulated during the evening and set them on the granite countertop, picturing tomorrow morning and how Gretchen would softly scold me to put those things in my office where they belonged. I opened the fridge, looked inside for a beer I did not want, then closed the door again, and stared at the stainless steel appliance and the outline of my head hazily mirrored in its surface.

I turned off the light and waited for my eyes to adjust to the darkness around my home. Outside, on the patio, sunk back far into one of our recliners, was Kevin.

This was not an unusual sight. Since he moved in, Kevin had taken to rising in the middle of the night and moving around the house like a ghost. I don't know if he suffered from insomnia or simply slept all morning. When he first moved in, his movements during the night woke me, and turned on my side, I tried to still my breathing and listen as he crept down the stairs, through the foyer, into the kitchen, and out onto the back patio. He learned where to step to avoid making the floors creak, how to move around our furniture even in the dark, and only with tremendous effort could I hear him and each of his footfalls. By Labor Day, I too was rising in the night, walking through my black bedroom and following Kevin downstairs to stand far back in the family room to watch him sit outside for hours.

Kevin would take a blanket from the family room and slip through the French doors and walk to the edge of our patio. He would shift his weight from foot to foot, and with time, settle into a lawn chair, leaning back deep into the plastic. From where I stood, far back in the dark threshold where I was capable of ducking out of sight if he suddenly looked up, I tried to imagine what ran through my brother's mind. When he finally dropped into one of the deck chairs, he sat for hours, and I too would stand, never tiring, watching as if his thoughts would appear in clear bubbles above his head, revealing some deep mystery. I don't know why I stood there watching him, how his insomnia became mine, or why I never spoke to him. Maybe I believed he was waiting me out, some sort of staring contest between brothers. I really have no idea. But every morning, long after I gave up and went to sleep, I would find the blanket neatly folded, the corners of the fabric perfectly aligned and placed back in the top shelf of our hall closet.

Now I made sure I was loud: I clicked the patio door when I turned the knob, and my shoes clacked on the brick as I stepped outside. I pulled the door shut and cleared my throat before stepping away from the house, and I circled Kevin slowly, as if appraising a sculpture. With my hands in my pockets, smiling and attempting to be casual, I asked if I could join him.

"Sure." His voice was clear and sonorous. He kept his eyes on the tree line, unsurprised by my presence, as if he had been waiting for this moment for weeks.

I sat in the lounger and propped my feet up. I batted my hands on the arm of the chair as if I was a child, and waited for Kevin to say something. He didn't. He watched the world with the same glazed expression as a person watching television for hours. I folded my hands against my stomach and quieted. Late at night, the world is quite loud if you listen. The chirp of crickets, calls of birds, hums of air conditioners throughout the neighborhood, distant cars on the road creeping toward home, the shudder of electricity coursing through these houses. Everything was active and seeable to me if I just could stay still.

Finally, Kevin asked, "How was your evening?"

"Long. What are you doing out here?"

"Sitting. Thinking. I don't know."

"About what?"

"I'm taking the meds."

"That wasn't what I was asking."

He considered this quietly for a few minutes. Then he said, "Sometimes, I'm thinking about baseball. The formulas I'm working on, trying to see what I haven't figured out yet. Nothing in particular. I have these great gaps in my memory. There are whole years I can't seem to remember at all. But if I sit here and focus on it, focus on a year, a season, things begin to come back to me. Snippets. Sometimes coherent things, but mostly not. I haven't been sleeping well. I didn't realize how soothing the train was. You didn't hear it much during the day, but at night, lots of trains went by Mom's house and it sorta helped me sleep."

I laced my fingers together. "How's Catherine?"

Kevin frowned. "Fine, I guess. Why?"

"You two spend a lot of time together. She does all her homework in your room now."

"We usually don't talk."

"Nothing? Not about boys or school?"

"No, not really. She sometimes asks for help with her math." He lowered his eyes, then looked back into the night. "She asked about you and Gretchen once."

"What do you mean? Asked what?"

"She's perceptive, you know. She knows you two aren't happy."

"I'm not unhappy."

"Sometimes," Kevin said, "you come home happy. You look relaxed."

He glanced at me, and I met his eyes. One side of his mouth curled, a shrug of the face. He seemed okay with this.

"Her name's Erica," I said. There was a great opening in my chest, like the tide being pulled back into the ocean, leaving the beach bare and clear.

"I figured something like that."

"She was at the fundraiser tonight."

Kevin rolled onto his side, facing me. "Jesus, Henry. What did you do?"

"Nothing. Crossed the room and said hello, acted like she was just another person, and that was it."

"Does Gretchen know?"

Incredible as it may seem, until my brother asked, the question hadn't even occurred to me, and this blind spot to my life was a strange revelation.

"I don't think so," I said. "But honestly? If she did, I don't think she would say anything."

Kevin rolled onto his back and looked down the length of the chair. The blanket was tangled around his legs, and he unwrapped his arms from the fleece and crossed them across his chest.

"That's really horrible," he said softly.

"You don't know what Gretchen's like."

"No. I really don't."

He gazed up at the stars then with the expression of a man who understood just enough about the sky above him to accept that his knowledge of astronomy was nothing compared to the vast complexity of the universe.

"All week," he finally said, "I was thinking about fighting. I can't remember why I liked to box, if that was Mom's idea or mine. I remember, though, I was pretty good. When you break someone's nose, there's this sound. It's really clear, even with all the noise of the fight around you. There's nothing like it. There's this crunch, kinda loud and muted at the same time. Maybe it's louder because you feel it right there on the end of your arm. Like my knuckles amplified it. Cartilage and bone cracking under your fist."

"She doesn't hate you." At the edge of his mouth, his lips raised slightly as if my words were a bitter taste he had to politely force down his throat. He didn't bother to refute my lie. Kevin's shoulders were almost to his ears; hunched like this, he almost seemed like a turtle, and I remembered Catherine's science textbook from grade school, and how a snapping turtle's head was actually incredibly fast and could bite a man's finger clean off.

"The horrible thing," he continued, stretching out his legs from under the blanket, "is how much I enjoyed it. Hurting other people. I hated that about myself."

"I'm afraid to disappoint people."

"I know." He tilted his chin downward and closed his eyes. "Sometimes I fall asleep out here. But I always wake up before dawn."

"I'm going to sit here a while longer."

Kevin stood, triggering the safety light in the backyard. From behind me, the light cast out like an accusation and he raised a hand to shield his eyes, leaving his face shadowed. To his back, I said I needed to get up early and that I should head inside, too. He said nothing. And I found I was still sitting there when the safety lights darkened again, my hands steepled in front of my face, waiting out the long and unquiet night for a revelation that never came.

III

I woke to my neighbor Paul Fischer staring down at me, a bemused expression on his face and a cigarette between his lips. He pointed at me with his cup of coffee.

"Goddamn, Henry. You okay?"

I pressed my hands into the lounger, and scooted myself upward. Though I was still wearing shoes, my feet were cold, and my bowtie remained knotted around my neck. Above, the sky was purple, bringing the world into light slowly, like healing from a wound, and the morning dew sparkled on my lawn. Throat dry, I smacked my lips and ran my tongue around my teeth. I looked up at my bedroom window, half-expecting Gretchen to be standing there and staring down at me with disdain, but the drapes were closed and I realized that if she had woken up during the night and noticed me missing, she had not bothered to get up and find me.

Paul followed my gaze. "She kick you out?"

"No, I just feel asleep. I was talking with my brother and he went to bed and, well . . ." I shrugged.

"Gotta lay off the booze."

"I wasn't drinking."

With his coffee cup, he pointed at my tuxedo. "No one wears one of those unless he's drinking."

I swung my feet to the concrete and rested my elbows on my knees, blinked away the morning grogginess, and then smiled at how ridiculous this was: a man in a tuxedo sleeping in his own backyard. I imagined Paul stepping outside for his morning cigarette—his wife didn't permit him to smoke in the house anymore, a thing he conceded with a strange mixture of annoyance and pride—cupping his hands, squinting his eyes as he thumbed his lighter, and then, with an animal awareness he did not know he had, raising his head, somehow perceiving something was wrong, and looking across his yard to see a middle-aged man stretched out and not moving on a patio lounger. He probably muttered something like "Jesus, Henry," lit his cigarette, and took a few amused puffs before walking over and verifying I was alive.

"What time is it?" I asked.

"Almost six. What time did you come out here?"

"I don't remember."

"How you feeling?"

"Stiff. I guess these things aren't made for sleeping."

"I wouldn't know. You want some breakfast? Why don't I make some breakfast for us?"

When I stood, every muscle from my neck to my knees tightened, constricting around my bones. I loosened my bowtie, letting the fabric dangle on both sides of my neck.

"What are you making?" I asked.

"Frosted Flakes. Hell, Henry, whatever you want." He started toward his house. "Breakfast food I can make, and anything that involves grilling. I know you're hungry." As if on cue, my stomach growled and I followed Paul across my lawn, the morning dew wetting my shoes, the deep rich green of our lawns pleasing to my eyes, and even resting my hand on the wooden gate between our homes—a decorative fence that I still found ridiculous—there was a sad pleasure in recognizing all of it as my home.

Paul Fischer has been my neighbor for seven years. As a teenager, he was a three-sport athlete at Elder, all-city in football, wrestling, and baseball. He worked construction for his father in the summers, and after graduation, he decided to hell with college and centered his life on construction projects during the day and bodybuilding at night. A love of cigarettes and cheap beer—he always insisted beer tasted better out of an aluminum can—prevented him from ever having much success in bodybuilding, and he soon carried his strength like the man he was, an ex-athlete conserving energy he would never need. In time, he took over his father's business, and then expanded it into Indiana and Kentucky until it became one of the most successful privately owned companies in Cincinnati. Like me when I was a young father, he was here in Indian Hill because of the public schools. His was another of those secret worlds of the wealthy, one of pickup trucks and Land's End catalogues rather than BMW's and Cartier; more than once he asked me why I owned the things I did and I could never give him a satisfactory answer.

At his back door, he held up a finger, took the final drags of his cigarette, then stubbed it out in an ashtray on the window ledge. When I first entered his house years ago, tempted by an offer of a cold beer, I was pleased to discover the layout was greatly dissimilar from my own. Now, the newest housing developments—often far north of the city, beyond Mason, each decade pushing closer and closer to Middletown, almost thirty miles from Cincinnati's proper northern city limits—were cut from the same design, and I was unnerved by the sterile uniformity of these new houses dominated by a three-car garage, all the while aware that when Indian Hill was first incorporated, the homes in my neighborhood were probably viewed the same way.

Inside, Paul motioned to a chair, and once I was seated, gave me a cup of coffee. His dog, Huggins, a collie mutt, wagged his tail and sniffed my knees.

"I'm thinking a little bit of everything," he said. "Bacon, eggs, pancakes, you name it. Wake up the missus with the good aroma."

"How late does she sleep?"

"Depends. The kids are at her sister's for the weekend—nephew's birthday—so we have the house to ourselves. I've always been an early-riser. When we were younger, she could sleep all day, but I guess kids change your internal clock, you know?"

He placed two frying pans on the stove and tossed a pat of butter in each The coffee was a good, rich, dark roast and before each gulp, I held the cup to my nose, savoring the smell.

"Catherine doesn't really sleep in. I mean a little, but not much."

"How old is she now?"

"Thirteen. One of the youngest in her class."

"Yup, about that age I started driving my parents batshit."

I couldn't picture Catherine that way. I pictured her sitting upright at her desk, college applications to the left, textbooks to the right, all of it neatly piled and accurately labeled.

"Well, so far, she's great," I said. "Still a straight-A student. Plays varsity as a freshman." I pushed my coffee handle in a circle. "Gretchen says the other girls admire her."

"That just means they hate her fucking guts because they wish they were her." Paul cracked eggs into a bowl, his hands holding three at a time. "She actually said 'admire'? That's funny."

"Okay, maybe Gretchen is a little off with that one."

"You're being generous, Henry." He cracked more eggs and dropped them into the pan, which sizzled loud and pleasant. "Boys are different. I can see it in my girls already and they're just in the second grade. Boys compete in things where they keep score. Winners without any resentment. Girls don't. And they're always being judged. Always. They don't get left alone like boys do."

I turned the handle back toward me and held up the mug: it was black with a Cincinnati Bearcats logo on the side, the cartoon character's paw reaching out fiercely.

"Can they make the tournament this year?"

"UC?" He shook his head. "Let me tell you something, Henry." He then proceeded to tell me many somethings about Bearcats basketball. Paul Fischer was the kind of man who spoke of his University of Cincinnati education with the kind of awe and devotion that makes university presidents weep. After he gave up bodybuilding, he enrolled in classes at UC, and what he learned in school set the groundwork for him to improve and expand his construction business, and consequently, he believed all his success was due to UC's business school. He thought my luxury goods were a waste, and perhaps he was right, but in his basement was a complex home-entertainment experience centered around a massive projection screen that was created solely for the pleasure of University of Cincinnati sports. With Pentecostal intensity, Paul dissected the basketball team—its strong interior defense, poor shooting, inability to find a point guard, the schedule (which he knew by heart)—waving his spatula in the air, jabbing to emphasize a point, all while making breakfast, a combination of pancakes, eggs, bacon, sausage, hash browns and coffee, dropped onto the table without me stirring from my chair. As I scooped food onto my plate, he leaned against the side of the kitchen island, still discussing the Bearcats and how they need to go to a high-post offense and use their bigs passing ability, and a look of satisfaction crossed his face because of the way I started devouring his food.

"They don't serve you much at those fundraisers, do they?"

"It's always chicken or salmon, and you never feel full."

"Why do those things anyway? Why not just write a check? Meals and all that have to be expensive."

"People won't donate without the wining and dining."

"And what does that say about us?" He cocked his head, then turned and looked down the hallway. He took two steps toward the door and held up his hand.

A woman said, "Oh, did you make me breakfast?"

"Henry's here." He put both his hands on the doorframe as if he were holding it in place.

"Henry's here? Right now?"

"See for yourself."

His wife Susan ducked her head, and only her head, around the corner and under his arm. Her eyes grew wide.

"Hey, Henry!"

"Morning, Susan."

"I'll be right back. Great tux, Henry!" She padded down the hallway and only when her feet hit the stairs did Paul look away from her and back at me.

"What was she wearing?" I asked.

"Nothing."

"Nothing?"

"Told you, Henry, kids aren't here this weekend." He sipped his coffee. "It's been a good time."

Susan returned wearing an oversized robe and pajama pants. She was a small woman who looked even smaller next to her husband, and had dark hair that had begun to gray. She sat opposite me at the far end of the table, and I asked her about her job and her children, and she was off, talking between bites of food, and Paul and I listened quietly, saying nothing more than the occasional conversational inquiry that would keep her narrative running, both of us pleased to be in her company. There was a gust of wind, and I realized then that the windows were open, and that it would be a cool day, and that I was sitting with friends who loved each other and were relaxed in each other's presence. The newspaper was scattered on the island and there were dishes in the sink; the fridge was covered in magnets and children's drawings and photos; fingerprints were on the walls and pencil marks crept up the doorframe, indicating the heights of their children. There was something in this house that was unfamiliar to me, a lingering tranquility that I was sadly aware had not existed in my home for a very long time.

After breakfast, I crossed back to my yard and entered my house through the unlocked patio doors. Although everything was in the same place, the house seemed changed from the night before, and I picked up all I had emptied from my pockets last night, still untouched on the island, and walked upstairs. No one seemed to have stirred: both Catherine and Kevin's doors were still closed. Left, down the dark hallway to my wing of the upper floor, the bedroom door was cracked, and when I entered, I discovered the covers thrown back and Gretchen nowhere to be found. I frowned at my mental calendar of Saturdays: Was she at yoga? Work? A jog? It didn't really matter, and the quiet acknowledgement of this saddened me. I stripped off my clothes and climbed into bed and despite the coffee I drank, fell quickly into a hard sleep.

Kevin only attempted suicide once. This was during the summer between my junior and senior years of college, and I was home for one month, a period of time that I resented, and spent most of the days asleep and nights in bars down in Clifton, listening to mediocre bands and drinking light beer, eager for my senior year to start, head back to Ohio State and be as far away from my mother and brother as I possibly could. During that summer, I had spent eight weeks in England researching Keynes and Galbraith for my economics professor, an excuse to spend time in English pubs, a foreign country, as far away from Ohio as I could possibly imagine.

Despite my best attempts at appearing spontaneous and free, I have always been a man of order and direction. I liked deadlines and lists of things to do, and even during the rare times I was out all night, I did the same thing: I rolled off a friend's couch or out of a woman's bed in the early afternoon, ate the same meal of three pancakes and two eggs and a side of sausage at the same Clifton café, and drove north to my mother's house, arriving somewhere around four-thirty, well before she came home from work. Kevin knew this.

So when I came in that afternoon, perhaps the only surprise was that I entered through the front door rather than the kitchen. I had parked the car in front of the garage, then walked down the driveway to fetch the mail, why, I don't remember. But when I came through the front door, grocery fliers and junk mail in hand, there was an unnatural stillness in the house, as if a heavy but invisible fog clung to the room. I tossed the mail on the nearest chair and placed my hands on my hips.

"Hello?" I called. "Is anyone here?"

I walked through the house as if anticipating an attack, and in the kitchen, I searched for some sign of disorder. What I saw instead was a neat, clean kitchen, and on the newly uncluttered freezer door, a Garfield magnet held a folded piece of paper that read "Henry and Mom."

I took the note down and read slowly. I read it again, because it didn't make sense. Then, I raised my chin and eyed the ceiling. Above me, there was a tremendous crash, almost an explosion, and I dropped the note and raced upstairs.

I leapt up the stairs two at a time. All three doors were open except the bedroom that Kevin and I shared. My heartbeat pounded, echoing in my ears. I pushed the door open, and surprised at what I saw, stood cemented in the doorway.

Above, where a ceiling fan had once been, was a gaping hole, bits of wood planks shaped like decaying teeth surrounded by a hovering plume of dust. Three thick dangling wires led to the floor, still connected to the ceiling fan, now askew on the floor, one blade bent and broken like a fractured leg. My desk chair was on its side. And between the fan and the chair was Kevin, his legs spread in front of him, his head and shoulders covered in plaster and dust, a noose of thin rope around his neck, his chin tilted downward, his eyes wet with tears that had not yet fallen.

"Jesus," I said. "Kevin?"

"I'm really sorry about the fan," he whispered. "I thought it was strong enough."

"Strong enough for what?"

He tried to raise his hands from the floor, but his elbows remained locked on his thighs, like his arms were somehow held down by invisible chains. Now the tears came and he started sobbing, his entire body shaking.

"I'm sorry," he choked. "I'm sorry. I'm really sorry."

I took one step into the room. His neck had raw, red marks from the rope, and I noticed for the first time a long, deep gash along his temple; blood ran down his cheek and jaw, spilling onto his shirt, splattering drops on the floor.

"You're bleeding," I said. "Your head is bleeding."

He cried harder, and I couldn't help thinking of him as pathetic and weak. Without taking my eyes off him, I picked up the cordless from my desk, and called 911. They asked me to stay on the line and I did, reciting for them the facts of the last ten minutes, pressing the phone against my ear, and I sat down cross-legged in front of my brother and looked at his forehead. I asked the dispatcher if she could hear my brother crying, and she answered with a neutral affirmation and told me that help was on the way, and that they were contacting my mother. At some point I must have hung up.

Kevin stopped crying. He sniffled, watching the mixture of blood, dust, and plaster on the floor in front of him. We didn't speak. My clothes smelled like stale beer and cigarettes, and mixed with the plaster and dust, it was a stifling odor of waste and decay. I was close enough to him to see that he had shaved this morning, and I watched his expression as he puzzled through what went wrong and why he did it. We were strangely calm. When I heard a vehicle pull into our driveway, I reached out, and thumbed a rivulet of blood from his eyebrow. My hand moved gently against his skin, palming his head softly, the blood thick and gelatinous. He neither resisted nor encouraged my touch, but let me wipe his face, let me do what little I could as I hoped that this small gesture would somehow preserve his dignity.

He spent thirty days in a mental hospital, on suicide watch the whole time, though he never seemed to have any interest again after his failed hanging. I never asked him about that day, but I always believed it was somehow an accusation. For what, I do not know. But it was there, a shaming: he knew I would be home first. He knew I would find him. And I have always believed that as Kevin's brother, I had somehow failed him.

When I awoke, my tuxedo wrinkled in a pile on the floor, this same feeling of failing came over me. And like it had nearly twenty years ago, I couldn't place the source of this feeling, the actual cause of this shame. Hints of sunlight trickled out from behind the heavy curtains but I couldn't begin to guess what time it actually was, and when I placed my feet on the floor, I found that I didn't care. From the dresser I pulled out a pair of jeans and a white T-shirt, dressed, and walked down the hallway. I passed the stairs, then the hall bathroom, Kevin's room on my right and Catherine's room on the left and opened the last, closed door.

This was one of our four bedrooms, a room that once was supposed to be a place for Catherine's baby brother or sister. It was a spacious room with a single bed hidden by a dust cover and a dresser with empty drawers. A thin layer of dust covered everything, a gray mist, and I wondered when a person had last entered this room; we had given instructions to our housecleaners that they were never to open this door. I pulled back the walk-in closet door: not a single hanger was on the rack, not one box of old, unlabeled photographs was on a shelf. The emptiness of this large room was almost impossible. At the window, I looked down on my yard and imagined three children, my children, playing together, a game of tag or cops and robbers, arguing about who was what, and how miserable these thoughts were.

"What are you doing?"

I turned. Gretchen stood with her arms folded across her chest. I couldn't tell from her clothes were she had been or if she had even been out of the house.

"Just looking around," I said.

"You shouldn't be in here."

"What time is it?"

"Why are you in this room?"

"I had a bad dream."

Her tight lips softened ever so slightly and she came to me and wrapped her hand around my elbow. "Dreams are just dreams. Let's go downstairs."

She led me out, closing the door with a forceful click, and brought me back down into the kitchen. The clock said it was three in the afternoon. The newspaper was in front of me, then a cup of coffee, and when I looked up Gretchen was watching me, and she nodded at the paper as if to say *Go on now, it's all right* and I lowered my head and started reading again, for how long I'm not sure, but when I looked up again she was gone. I wiped my palm across my face and blinked. Gretchen wasn't here, and when I called her name, there was no answer.

I crossed the kitchen and entered my office. My cell phone was on the desk; when I unlocked it, I discovered my hands were sweaty, and my throat was very dry. I sent a message to Erica and asked her to meet me at my mother's house in a few hours. In the shower, turned to the hottest temperature I could tolerate, I scrubbed my skin until it was pink and sore, then leaned back against the tile and focused on my breathing. Dressed and eager to escape, I left my house without calling out to anyone who I knew wouldn't answer me. Gretchen's car was missing from the garage, which I noted without emotion, and I headed west to my mother's house.

Erica waited for me in her car, pulled up to the front of the garage. I parked behind her and shut off the engine. When I exited the Mercedes, she didn't move, and I came around to the driver's-side door, and she smiled up at me. The window was down, the classical station playing Schubert.

"I'm sorry I'm late," I said.

"I thought I'd been stood up." She turned off the radio and got out. "What are we doing here?"

"I just wanted to show it to you."

"But why?"

In answer, I opened her car door and took her hand to help her out. I led her up the steps and we entered the kitchen through the back porch, the way I always entered this house as a boy. The kitchen was small even without the kitchen table and three chairs pressed beneath the large window and its view of the backyard. This was the place where the three of us had sat and had breakfast my entire childhood and without furniture, the kitchen seemed incomplete for my memories, as if there was a missing puzzle piece that could somehow still be discovered to complete the image. A scent of bleach and lemon-scented cleaner hovered; I walked to the sink and pushed open the window that looked out onto the driveway. Everything—the floor, the cabinets, the sink— was spotless and sterile. I opened the fridge and stared at the baking soda sitting on the middle shelf, the cool air drifting onto my feet.

"Are you worried someone is going to break in?"

I pointed at the seat close to the back door. "That was my seat. By the door, always ready to go. Mom sat in the middle so she could get up and grab things for us, and Kevin sat there, in the corner. The fridge used to have all these magnets holding up photos and coupons and newspaper clippings. You couldn't even see the door. I hated it. I hated being here."

Erica took my hand.

"This is the dining room," I said, leading her through the doorway. "We didn't use it much. There was a china cabinet against the back corner, and a serving table to your left. Papers always covered everything. Magazines, envelopes, I don't know what, just lots of stuff. I never paid much attention to it. Over there was a birdcage. Mom had birds for a while when we were younger. Even when they weren't singing or chirping, they seemed to make a lot of noise. The house seemed very still once they all died."

"She always had them?"

I nodded. "Until the last year or so. It's like she knew the heart attack was coming." We stood at the edge of the room. I had ordered the carpet removed; it had food and pet stains that would never come out, and the rank smell of mildew and neglect.

"I began to miss it," I said, as if talking only to myself, "sometime after Catherine was born. Home is always home, like it or not, and I wanted to be here again. Kevin and I used to watch baseball down in the basement. I'd tell Gretchen where I was going, come to talk to my mom for a few minutes, then head downstairs with Kevin. No one bothered us and we didn't talk much. Just three hours watching the game and then I'd head home. I was really happy then."

We stood in the front room. The house faced east; along the north wall was a fireplace that we never used; south, a small landing lit by a stained-glass window and then the stairs to the second floor. After removing the carpeting, I had discovered that the wood floors were dark brown and in good shape; I ordered them refinished, and the house shined with new polish, and for a moment, it didn't seem like such a foreboding place. I pictured living here. I pictured living here with Erica, and living in a house shadowed in memories. A great sadness overcame me when I thought of my Indian Hill home across town and the way my voice went unanswered, rooms filled with things like catalog photos, all the warmth and comfort of it predesigned for people that didn't actually exist. Erica placed a hand on my arm. Our footsteps echoed as we crossed the room and I said I'd show her the upstairs, the small bedrooms, the bathroom where I found Kevin. But on the landing, she grasped my elbow and took my face with both hands and kissed me.

We made love fast and hard on the stairs; she straddled me, we left our shirts on, our sweat coming through the fabric, damp beneath our palms. The stairs pressed into my lower back and her knees banged against the wood: the discomfort somehow made the sex more erotic. When we were finished she closed her eyes and pressed her forehead against mine, her breathing low and harsh, and pulled me tight against her back. We rolled to the landing, still intertwined, and lay on our sides.

"I've never had sex in this house," I said.

"Me either."

Together we laughed softly, running fingers and palms over the other's face. She tucked her head beneath my chin.

"I love you," I said.

She said nothing. But her body shifted ever closer to mine, her lips against my neck, her breath releasing a soft gasp of relief.

The night of the accident, Gretchen was in Columbus for a conference on charitable donations and minimizing taxable income, and I was in a late-night production meeting. Proctor & Gamble was rolling out a new type of Tide detergent: small packets of soap in easy-to-use plastic packets that dissolved in the wash. My cell phone was off. I didn't notice the missed calls until the phone in the conference room, from beneath a stack of binders, rang.

Catherine came home from school. She had a few hours before her soccer game, and had homework to do, and the floor of Kevin's room had become the best place to study. She got ninety minutes of work in, and then went down the hallway to change into her uniform. She sat in the front room, her ankles crossed, her soccer bag at her feet, looking out the front window, waiting for her ride. It never came. Her phone buzzed with a text. Her ride, another soccer player named Julia Ogden, had gone home sick and forgot to tell her. Catherine now realized she was already ten minutes late, and started calling all her friends. No one answered, of course: they were already at the field, warming up, their phones tucked away in their soccer bags. She called me once, then again, then again.

Catherine was furious. She stood up and slammed her foot down. She stood tall, like a taut string had pulled her upright, and with her cheeks flushed, she looked like her mother: willowy, beautiful, and angry. Then she ducked her head and slouched her shoulders like a teenager and started furiously sending out texts. With no answers coming, she lost control, and started to cry. She called me for the fourth time.

Kevin came softly down the steps. He asked what was wrong.

"I'm gonna miss the game! Julia didn't tell me she was sick! I'm going to miss the game. Uncle Kevin, I can't miss the game! I can't! I just can't!"

Her crying choked her until she couldn't breathe. She started shaking her hands, her feet cemented to the ground, and her words came out unintelligible. Kevin stood closer, trying to understand what she was saying.

He turned. There, along the wall by the front door, were the spare keys to my mother's van. They must have been an awful temptation. They must have caught the sunlight and shone, refracting the light the way a type of wind chime can, its melody calling to you, giving you the sounds and sights of a world better than the one you live in. And Kevin must have seen those keys and knew my wife thought of him as shiftless and dangerous, and knew I thought of him as weak and defenseless, and that by driving his niece to her soccer game, he could show his family that he was capable of being a good uncle, and that he wasn't a burden, that he wasn't an albatross for us to carry for the rest of our lives. Because I can't think of any other reason Kevin, who hadn't driven a car in over fifteen years, would have taken the van keys, shushed Catherine, and ferried her out to the garage.

Kevin was nervous. He turned the ignition, and thought that the car seemed too loud, too powerful. Catherine, calming down, flipped through the radio stations, switching off the AM my mother preferred to find something peppy and loud to get her ready for the game. I received a text from her then: "Everything's fine, hope you can make the second half. Luv you." Kevin should have told her to turn the radio off, that he needed to concentrate, but he didn't. Instead, he adjusted the rearview and side mirrors, tilting the mirrors again and again, trying to eliminate the blind spots he knew the car possessed. Long streaks of sweat poured down his cold ribcage. He searched for memories of driver's ed, and only remembered that he should look in the mirror frequently. He mashed on the break, put the van in reverse, and eased the car down the driveway.

He drove with both hands on the wheel, his knuckles white and his palms slick, each vibration of the van's shocks jolting his spine. He squeezed his shoulder blades together and in response they seemed to tighten even further. He drove down the empty street with the windows up and came to a complete stop at the first stop sign, and then the second, praying that no other cars would be on the road. And they weren't: not one car, not one jogger, not one kid racing down a mammoth front lawn in pursuit of a soccer ball about to roll into the street. The subdivision was deserted. Kevin jammed the van to another complete stop at the intersection of Loveland Madiera. This road had a speed limit of thirty-five, which meant cars regularly zipped by at fifty. The buzzing sound of metal, tremendous and fast, made the van tremble.

They sat at the intersection, waiting. Finally, Kevin asked, "Which way?"

She pursed her lips. "You don't know?"

Maybe this is the first time Catherine became aware that something was wrong. In her sudden anger at missing her soccer game, perhaps she didn't fully grasp that Kevin, despite his size and age, was not a normal adult. Didn't she know that already? Isn't that why she did her homework in his room, on the floor, her uncle familiar yet strange, his innocent adulthood peculiar and charming? Was she scared to ask him to turn around, take them home? Would that have been worse? Instead, she gazed out into the street and said, "Turn right. And then at Camargo you turn left, then a right on Drake. The school will be on the right."

Kevin nodded and flipped on his right blinker. The instructions were a relief: the only left turn was at an intersection with a traffic light and turn lane. After making the turn, if he stayed in the right lane, going slow, he would get Catherine to the game safely.

He waited until no cars heading east on Loveland Madiera were visible, and then he steered right, accelerating choppily, trying fiercely to look up the road rather than at the yellow line dividing the macadam and the steady blur of cars racing north past his window, the whip and roar of their air space so loud Kevin thought it could shatter the windows. He began to make a choked, whirling sound in his throat, and tears pressed against the backs of his eyes. His hands trembled on the steering wheel, rocking the car ever so slightly back and forth in the left lane.

"Uncle Kevin?"

"Almost there," he choked. He took his foot of the gas and let the car coast to the intersection, passing the Wendy's and the BP, hypnotized by the stoplight dangling high above the street. The light was green, but he had missed the turn signal. Distantly, he recalled the rule of clearing the intersection. He crept forward over the crosswalk and into the intersection. Cars lined up behind him, and they too pressed forward, hoping to, at the yellow light, make the left to cross Camargo and turn onto Drake.

The sun appeared, and the light turned the van into an oven. Sweat trickled down from his temples, and he swallowed, his throat parched and dry. He leaned forward, trying to will traffic to clear away, vanish.

"You don't have to drive me," Catherine said, her voice panicked again, aware of the danger she was in. She leaned forward so her uncle could see her. "Honest, you don't."

"Almost there, almost there," he said, repeating this like a chant, stealing glances at the street, the light, back to the street. The light turned yellow. She leaned back into her seat. He remembered the rule: clear the intersection. The car behind him sat on the horn, furiously bleating.

The light turned red. He didn't turn. The car behind him hit the horn again, and this time, he could hear the driver, a man screaming, cursing *Go goddammit go!* And without looking up, Kevin began to turn.

It was a maroon four-door sedan, a family car. It was driven by a man on his way home from work, his briefcase tucked behind the driver's seat, and his Blackberry in his left hand. He wanted to make it home because, like many of us, after a long day at work, all we want to do is go home and strip off our work clothes and settle into something comfortable. He had run red lights before. Who hasn't? But this time, running the red light, at a little over forty-five miles per hour, this man plowed his car into my mother's van, putting his grill directly between the front-quarter panel and the passenger-side door, directly into Catherine. She never saw it. She would only remember the sound of the impact, a tremendous crunching of metal, and then so many shards of glass, all over the dash, the floor, her body, and just before she became aware of the pain, how still and silent the world was after a crash.

At the hospital, I parked outside the emergency room and stumbled out of my car. Despite the adrenaline and panic of that first phone call from the hospital telling me about Catherine's accident, all the muscles in my legs seemed to turn to liquid, and after I closed the door, I rested my hot and sticky arms on the roof. My breath came out painful and wheezy, as if I suffered from asthma. Framed by the bright walkways outside the hospital, the dark windows, climbing high into the skyline, their long rectangular shapes like coffins, the blackness encroaching on it all, I thought of my mother. My mother, wheeled out of the back of an emergency van, already dead, already a body on a stretcher whose organs needed to be harvested, just a slab of meat for people I did not know. Then, finally, I grieved her, tears running down my face, and I walked away from my car, swinging my arms, my steps kinetic and choppy, like a creature trying not to drown in the sea. My fists churned through the air, slapping at nothing, gasping out *I'm sorry* as if the words could somehow save me. I cried until my throat ached, and I leaned against my car and pressed my face into my hands.

Exhausted from crying, I stood up straight and pushed my hair back, and straightened my tie. My hand against my stomach, I inhaled deeply ten times before walking into the hospital and its cool, antiseptic air. A great calm overcame me. I asked for directions to my daughter and the nurse at the triage desk pointed me down the hallway. I found my wife standing with her arms folded across her chest. Gretchen ignored me and continued to direct all her questions to the doctor. When she was done speaking to him, I followed her back to the waiting room where she stayed far enough away from me so that we could not touch. Her expression was one of controlled anger, as if the embarrassment of berating me in public wasn't worth the satisfaction of showing me her fury.

The van was totaled. Given the damage to both cars, it's amazing to me that no one was seriously hurt. The other driver was unscathed, just a little whiplash. Kevin had bruising along his face and ribs but was otherwise fine.

Catherine, though, had a broken ankle, ending her soccer season. There was no permanent damage to her femur or knees, and aside from a small gash across her forearm, she was unscathed and remarkably lucky. She seemed, despite the cast, in good spirits. The doctors assured her she would recover and be out of the cast in no time, and she took it all with a stiff upper lip and wondered aloud who would be the first person to sign her cast.

Kevin rode with me and in a low monotone, explained what happened. He kept his eyes down the entire time, his shoulders rolled forward and his chin dipped as if he was bracing to be punished. I said nothing. We parked in the garage and though I turned off the ignition, I made no move to exit the car.

"I'm sorry," he said. "I just wanted to help her."

"I know."

"It was a stupid, stupid thing to do."

My mind leapt to the folder of real estate brochures Gretchen gave me. I knew exactly where they were in my office, and I thought, with startling clarity, of a two-family in Clifton, in the city, across town, far from me.

"I know," I repeated. "Why don't you get some sleep. We can talk in the morning."

He closed his eyes and frowned down at his hands folded in his lap. He nodded. I got out of the car and he slid by me, head still down, and took the stairs slowly. The lights remained off, and our home possessed an electric stillness.

I still couldn't decide if I was angry with him. As with most decisions in my life, I believed that this emotion needed careful calculation and that I alone needed to maintain control over all this anger. The inside of my house felt still and funereal, as if no one had been inside for years and years, and I stood by the living room window and waited just as Gretchen had waited so many weeks ago for me to arrive with my brother in tow, and then the headlights broke through the trees and her car rolled down our driveway, stopping outside the garage. She said something to Catherine, who nodded and opened her door.

She slid her legs out of the car and placed her crutches on the concrete, leaning her weight forward, the tops of the crutches pressing into her armpits, and rose. She turned her head down the length of the driveway, and her expression was one of hope and watchfulness, as if she wanted someone to see her do this. But there was no one on our street, and for a moment, a look of disappointment crossed her face; just as quickly, it vanished, her mother's stoicism returned, and Catherine began to hobble her way to the front door. Gretchen remained unmoving behind the wheel.

I held the front door open and Catherine looked up at me and grinned. She made little grunting sounds as she made her way into the house.

"Air conditioning feels nice," she said. "Mom wouldn't turn it on in the car."

I closed the front door. "Is that comfortable?" I asked.

"Not really. I'm just not sure where to go." She smiled brightly, and then a thought crossed her mind and the smile vanished. "Mom's still sitting in the car. She's acting weird, Dad. I thought she was going to start screaming at me."

"She's just a little scared. We all were."

"It's my fault."

"It's no one's fault."

"Yes, it is. I didn't wait. I didn't think. I'm really sorry."

"Sweetheart, you aren't to blame."

"Mom blames you."

I crossed my arms. Catherine looked back at me, unblinking.

"No she doesn't," I lied.

"She didn't talk to you at the hospital at all. You know that look she gives you when you do something she disapproves of? I bet she's looked at you that way all night. She always looks at you like that. Always. She blames you, Dad. She hates Uncle Kevin. And I hate her."

I closed my eyes and pinched the bridge of my nose. Too tired to argue and unable to lie, I hoped for some miraculous event to occur: Gretchen to walk through the front door and embrace us both and tell us how much she loved us, no matter what. I knew this would never happen. I placed my hands on my hips, and waited for Catherine to go upstairs. She stood silently on her three appendages, waiting for me to upbraid her for saying she hated her mother, but the effort was too great, and her words, however petulant and myopic I might have wanted to believe they were, happened to be true. We stared at each other for what felt like a long time, and finally she turned and faced the staircase.

She placed the crutches on the first step, but she couldn't raise her left arm high enough, and the crutch rattled against the stairs and slid to the floor. For the first time all night, Catherine seemed defeated. Her shoulders slumped and she dropped her chin, trembling. I wrapped her in my arms; she turned into my chest and sobbed silently, my shirt soon wet with her tears, and I made gentle hushing sounds into her hair, just like when she was a little girl.

Sniffing, she said, "I can't."

I nodded. She wrapped her arms around my neck, and I scooped her up, taking the stairs one at a time. She seemed so light then; how small women's bodies are, how delicate. This fear for my daughter's happiness would last the rest of my life, and right then I had never wanted this responsibility more. At the top of the stairs, I somehow knew to keep carrying her, and went down the hall to her bedroom and placed her in her bed, and when her head touched the pillow, she closed her eyes. I tried to pull away, but she clutched my hand.

"Would you just sit here?" she asked.

"Sure," I said. She smiled and in a few short minutes, her grip slackened. Though I knew she was in a deep sleep, I waited, watching Catherine breathe. I sat there, very still, until the room darkened. I lifted her hand gently to her side and pulled her blanket up to her neck. When I stood, my whole body ached, as if I was the one who had been in the collision.

It was very late. Downstairs, the house was dark, and the picture frames down the hallway seemed to be nothing but canvases of blackness. I walked downstairs, and all our furniture appeared to be a series of large silhouettes and odd shapes. At the front window, I peered outside; the car was empty, and I wondered how long Gretchen had been sitting out there, and what she had been thinking. Perhaps if I had done something decades earlier about my mother, about my brother, about my marriage, all of this could have been prevented. This accident revealed something insidious about my family, a culmination of unspoken thoughts and emotions wrapped up in one horrible car accident that forced me to realize how awful I'd let my life become.

A floorboard creaked. Gretchen stood in the kitchen. Her arms were folded across her chest, and her expression was hidden in the shadows.

"I want him out," she said.

"Gretchen, it was an accident."

"I don't care. I don't want him in this house. He could have killed Catherine. Don't you understand that? What if he turned a second sooner and that car hit the door head-on?"

"But it didn't."

"Unbelievable." Her voice was even and low. "Henry, what's wrong with you?"

"Nothing's wrong with me. It was an accident. He was trying to help."

I stepped closer, and a smile, an angry smile full of sharp incisors, spread across her face. I knew then that she knew about Erica.

"Henry, either he goes or I go."

"He can't live on his own. Where is he supposed to go?"

"I don't care."

"He needs us!"

"No, you need him! You need to lord over him like you do everyone else!"

"Are we still talking about Kevin?"

"We're talking about all of it!"

We both heard the sound. We had moved closer to each other, jabbing the air with pointed fingers, accusations slung like arrows. But that sound stilled our voices and made us turn. We realized then that the patio door was open. As my eyes adjusted, I saw that Kevin was sitting in one of the lawn chairs, wrapped as always with a blanket around his shoulders.

I took a step toward the patio, my movement rubbery, and I realized I hadn't slept in almost twenty-four hours, and I crossed the living room slowly, as if my feet were too heavy to walk. At the screen door, I looked back at my wife. Her expression was one of contempt and disgust and I wondered when I had last told her that I loved her with any conviction. I opened the screen door and stepped outside.

The chill in the air surprised me. How had I not felt this cold? Perhaps Kevin had walked by as we argued, and the door hadn't been open long. This seemed unlikely. Now, standing in the autumn night, I could feel the season changing, and even in the dark, could see the colors of the dead oak leaves on the trees, the hints of red and yellow obscured in the darkness. It was both peaceful and terrifying. I walked up to Kevin and stood behind him.

How did he see the world? I always pictured my brother in action: the young boxer dancing around the ring; the obsessed man scribbling equations into a notebook; the frightened uncle trying desperately to please his sister-in-law by driving Catherine to a soccer game. But it was these times, in stillness and thought, when my brother was most unknowable to me.

I said his name quietly. He didn't respond. When I looked down at him, his eyes were wide, as if held open by tiny wires, and his cheeks were tense, his jaw clenched tight.

I turned. In the living room, my wife's silhouette stood tall and defiant, staring out at us. Through the screen door, the entire room seemed closed off. I raised my chin and looked to the second floor. I knew Catherine was not at the window. Still, in my heart, she might as well have been, looking down at me, wondering what her father would do.

Knees groaning, I bent down and faced my brother. I put my hand on his arm, and his skin was clammy. Looking back, I think of this moment, and of how I knew what I could abandon, what I could leave behind. I knew what I was ready for, and recognized what it was Erica said I could not do.

"Kevin," I said again. His chin turned ever so perceptively in my direction.

I said, "I'll never leave you." All the tension ran out of his face, and I could feel the tremor in his arm as I wrapped my hand around his elbow. His blood pulsed beneath his skin, and I thought: this is my brother. This is our blood. Catherine would understand, and she would stay, and the three of us—me, my brother, and my daughter—would remain this way, always.

Acknowledgements

I am grateful to the editors of the following publications in which these stories first appeared: "Projection," *Crab Orchard Review*; "A Fully Imagined World," *Boulevard*; "Sparring Vladimir Putin," *Red Cedar Review*; "Exit 17 Does Not Exist," *REAL: Regarding Arts & Letters*; "A Surgeon's Story," *South Dakota Review*; and "Union Terminal," *New South*.

A huge thank you to Erin McKnight and Queen's Ferry Press for bringing this book into the world. The book's epigraph is from Joyce Carol Oates's essay "They All Just Went Away," which first appeared in *The New Yorker*, and is reprinted with permission from the author.

I'm deeply grateful for the generosity of my patient writing teachers over the years: Mary L. Tabor, Stephanie Grant, Melanie Rae Thon, Bill Roorbach, Lee K. Abbott, Mary Troy, Rick Skwiot, Phyllis Moore, and John Dalton. Big thanks to all of my classmates in the creative writing workshops at the Ohio State University and the University of Missouri-St. Louis, especially Valerie Cumming, Sara Ross, Becky Pastor, Marie Goyette, Reggie Poché, Joanne Drew, Bridget Healy, Dylan Smith, Seth Raab, Anne Earney, Jason Rizos, and Ryan Stone.

Thank you to everyone at *The Missouri Review*, especially Speer Morgan, Dedra Earl, Evelyn Somers, and Kris Somerville; same goes to the wonderful friends, interns, and editors at *River Styx*: Kara Moyer, Jessica Rogen, Katie Moulton, Ben Moeller-Gaa, Amy Debrecht, Julia Gordon-Bremer, Lisa Ampleman, Carol Niederlander, and, of course, Richard Newman, for being a mentor, friend, and everything else.

Thank you to the friends who have made my life what it is: Dave Becker, Joel Bozman, Stacey Brown, Rob Foreman, Deb Garwood, Nancy Gleason, Sarah Jones, Michael Lin, Grace Lillard, Nell McCabe, Marc McKee, Pat McManus, Andy McManus, Claire McQuerry, Nick Pretnar, and Fred Venturini.

Special thanks to Adrian Matejka and Eve Jones: the things I'd write about each of you would embarrass us (especially you), so I'll keep it simple: you mean more to me than I can possibly express here, so let's agree to just wink, nod, and smile at this paragraph. We know, and that's what matters.

Thanks to my entire family for their love and support, especially my mother, Kathy; my sister, Robyn; and my cousin, Justin. Most of all, Jessica Harvath, for her love, her patience, her humor, and for showing me in every way what it means to truly be a part of another person's life.

Photo courtesy of August Kryger

Michael Nye was born and raised in Cincinnati, Ohio. A graduate of the MFA program at the University of Missouri-St. Louis, his stories have appeared in *Boulevard*, *Crab Orchard Review*, *New South*, *Sou'wester*, *South Dakota Review*, and many others. He is the managing editor of *The Missouri Review*. Visit him online at mpnye.com.